DEATH ON ARRIVAL

Alfred Hitchcock, Editor

A DELL BOOK

Published by
Dell Publishing Co., Inc.
1 Dag Hammarskjold Plaza
New York, New York 10017

ACKNOWLEDGMENTS

GENTLE BLUEBEARD by Richard Deming. Copyright © 1965 by H. S. D. Publications, Inc. Reprinted by permission of the author and the author's agents, Scott Meredith Literary Agency, Inc.

COUSIN KELLY by Fletcher Flora. Copyright © 1967 by H. S. D. Publications, Inc. Reprinted by permission of the Estate of Fletcher Flora and the agents for the Estate, Scott Meredith Literary Agency, Inc.

FAT JOW AND THE RELUCTANT WITNESS by Robert Alan Blair. Copyright © 1968 by H. S. D. Publications, Inc. Reprinted by permission of the author and the author's agents, Scott Meredith Literary Agency, Inc.

THE LONG WAY DOWN by Edward D. Hoch. Copyright © 1965 by H. S. D. Publications, Inc. Reprinted by permission of the author.

THE FLY SWATTER by Frank Sisk. Copyright © 1975 by H. S. D. Publications, Inc. Reprinted by permission of the author and the author's agents, Scott Meredith Literary Agency, Inc.

DOUBLE ZERO by Robert Colby. Copyright © 1975 by H. S. D. Publications, Inc. Reprinted by permission of the author and the author's agents, Scott Meredith Literary Agency, Inc.

YOU AND THE MUSIC by John Lutz. Copyright © 1975 by H. S. D. Publications, Inc. Reprinted by permission of the author and the author's agents, Scott Meredith Literary Agency, Inc.

THE IMPOSSIBLE FOOTPRINT by William Brittain. Copyright © 1974 by H. S. D. Publications, Inc. Reprinted by permission of the author and the author's agents, Scott Meredith Literary Agency, Inc.

FIRST PRINCIPLES by Donald Honig. Copyright © 1975 by H. S. D. Publications, Inc. Reprinted by permission of the author and the author's agents, Raines and Raines.

THE SIXTH MRS. PENDRAKE by C. B. Gilford. Copyright © 1968 by H. S. D. Publications, Inc. Reprinted by permission of the author and the author's agents, Scott Meredith Literary Agency, Inc.

A LITTLE KNOWLEDGE by Arthur Porges. Copyright © 1962 by H. S. D. Publications, Inc. Reprinted by permission of the author and the author's agents, Scott Meredith Literary Agency, Inc.

ROPE ENOUGH by Dick Ellis. Copyright © 1967 by H. S. D. Publications, Inc. Reprinted by permission of the author and the author's agents, Scott Meredith Literary Agency, Inc.

THE TOKEN by Hall Ellson. Copyright © 1968 by H. S. D. Publications, Inc. Reprinted by permission of the author and the author's agents, Scott Meredith Literary Agency, Inc.

SHERIFF PEAVY'S FULL MOON CAPER by Richard Hardwick. Copyright © 1963 by H. S. D. Publications, Inc. Reprinted by permission of the Estate of Richard Hardwick and the agents for the Estate, Scott Meredith Literary Agency, Inc.

Copyright © 1979 by Davis Publications, Inc.

All rights reserved. No part of this book may be reproduced or transmitted in any form or by any means, electronic or mechanical, including photocopying, recording, or by any information storage and retrieval system, without the written permission of the Publisher, except where permitted by law.

Dell ® TM 681510, Dell Publishing Co., Inc.

ISBN: 0-440-11839-5

Printed in the United States of America
First printing—September 1979

CONTENTS

INTRODUCTION *by Alfred Hitchcock*	9
GENTLE BLUEBEARD *by Richard Deming*	13
COUSIN KELLY *by Fletcher Flora*	33
FAT JOW AND THE RELUCTANT WITNESS *by Robert Alan Blair*	48
THE LONG WAY DOWN (novelette) *by Edward D. Hoch*	72
THE FLY SWATTER *by Frank Sisk*	97
DOUBLE ZERO *by Robert Colby*	114
YOU AND THE MUSIC *by John Lutz*	135
THE IMPOSSIBLE FOOTPRINT *by William Brittain*	142
FIRST PRINCIPLES *by Donald Honig*	159
THE SIXTH MRS. PENDRAKE *by C. B. Gilford*	174

A LITTLE KNOWLEDGE *by Arthur Porges*   192

ROPE ENOUGH *by Dick Ellis*   206

THE TOKEN *by Hal Ellson*   213

SHERIFF PEAVY'S FULL MOON CAPER
(novelette) *by Richard Hardwick*   220

Your traveling companions include:

—Arthur Pendrake, who has just been acquitted of murdering the fifth Mrs. Pendrake. Why is wealthy Fern Spencer so eager to become *The Sixth Mrs. Pendrake*?

—Teresa Standish, who is eight. Her dearest friend is Cousin Kelly. Why does everyone insist that Kelly died years ago in *Cousin Kelly*?

—Arlene Mosher, who is in the hospital. Her symptoms suggest she's been poisoned. Sergeant Harris wonders about her pharmacist husband. Could the prescription have been murder in *Gentle Bluebeard*?

Send all the postcards you want, but don't bother to mention a return date. That's never part of the itinerary when Hitchcock plans for...

DEATH ON ARRIVAL

THE BEST FROM
ALFRED HITCHCOCK'S MYSTERY MAGAZINE #38

INTRODUCTION

We have an addition to the family. Its name is *Dracaena deremensis*. No, it is not some species of dinosaur that has crawled up out of the primordial ooze and taken up residence under our kitchen table. Nor is it a new strain of dandruff. It is a plant, a specimen of flora with the general appearance of a green geyser that has been frozen in mid-eruption.

We had to think twice before becoming foster parents to another plant. Our first experience was traumatic. On that occasion, we took in an English ivy, and it repaid our kindness with deviltry. No sooner was it in the house, than it began growing at a rate that was phenomenal. Before long, it was everywhere, creeping into everything. We had ivy in the refrigerator (lapping up the cream), ivy in the bread box (nibbling the icing and almonds off the Danish), and ivy in our dreams (tripping us up when we were fleeing the bogeyman). We finally did what had to be done—we drove it out into the country and replanted it by the side of the road.

It was with wariness, thus, that we returned to the

florist for a second plant, specifying that we wanted nothing more to do with English ivy. The florist, hoping for a more compatible match between plant and guardian this time, gave us a form to fill out. Some of the questions were rather puzzling (Do you have friends? Are you sometimes scolded by complete strangers?). We answered them, nonetheless, and based on this scientific determination of our need, the *Dracaena deremensis* was handed over to us.

We placed it on the patio, as far away from the fridge, the bread box and our beds as possible. And, at first, all went rather well. The *Dracaena deremensis* showed no signs of having the glandular problem that had caused the ivy to outgrow its welcome. In fact, it appeared to remain the same size, day after day and week after week, a most happy development (or nondevelopment) after our experience with its predecessor.

Then a friend, Hoskins, dropped by one day.

"How old?" he asked, eyeing the *Dracaena deremensis*.

"Days, weeks," I replied.

"Something's stunting its growth," he said. "Getting too much sun, I suspect. You want to move it into the house. Put it in a south-facing window. Otherwise it's going to be a dwarf. You don't want that."

He was right, we didn't want *that*. The possibilities for guilt feelings on our part if the *Dracaena deremensis* failed to reach its full height were terrifying. So, we moved the plant into the house and placed it in a south-facing window.

Shortly thereafter, we were visited by another friend, Palfrey.

"I don't like the look of that *Dracaena deremensis*," he said, concerned. "It's too pale. How often do you water it?"

"When it begins gasping and clutching at its throat," I replied.

"That's not the problem, then. Hah!" he said, suddenly brightening. "You've got it in a south-facing window. It's not getting enough sun. Try it in an east-facing window. Or, better yet, put it out on the patio."

We couldn't have Palfrey gossiping in the neighborhood about a pale *Dracaena deremensis* in the Hitchcock house, implying something sinister. So, we put the plant back on the patio.

Friends appeared almost daily after that. Each one expressed shock at the state of the plant's health and proposed a cure-all. As a consequence, the *Dracaena deremensis* spent time under a mosquito netting in a north-facing window, under a sunlamp in the sauna, and in the company of a dehumidifier in the root cellar. The only counsel we turned down flat was that we send it on holiday to St. Tropez over Christmas.

The final straw was the appearance of the complete stranger at our door.

"I understand there's a *Dracaena deremensis* in this house that's being overwatered, underwatered, oversunned, undersunned, and kept chained in the root cellar with a savage dehumidifier!" he said. "There are laws against that, you know!"

Stunned, I asked him where he had got such a scandalous story.

"From a well-informed ivy I met along the road," he told me.

I'm afraid the savage dehumidifier in my nature took over. I closed the door rather forcefully in the complete stranger's face.

The following day I returned to the florist's once more, taking the *Dracaena deremensis* with me. I asked to exchange it for a plant with a stronger constitution.

"Why, that's nearly the hardiest plant there is," he responded. "That's why I gave it to you—after reading the answers on your form. Being the sort who has friends and is sometimes scolded by complete strangers, I knew you would be getting a great deal of bad advice on raising your plant. The *Dracaena deremensis* can survive all that."

The Drac is back on the patio once again. When friends stop by with advice on bringing it up, we give the friends our full attention and the counsel our total disregard. And, as for the unsigned poison-pen letters we've begun getting on the stationery with the telltale scent of ivy, we've turned that matter over to the police.

Other matters that could very well deserve the attention of the police are the goings-on in the stories that follow. I can guarantee that you will meet some old friends, the spinners of these tales. And I wouldn't be surprised if you came upon a stranger or two, each one more mysterious and more devilish than the last.

—ALFRED HITCHCOCK

The road (of marriage) reputedly "lies long and straight and dusty to the grave," and little relief attends him who attempts to curtail the route.

GENTLE BLUEBEARD
by Richard Deming

The lieutenant was the only one in the squad room when I came back from lunch. He was just hanging up the phone.

"I've got an oddball one for you, Sod," he said. "Run over to the Exchange Building and see a neurologist named Dr. Herbert Muntz."

"About what?" I asked.

"He has a patient at St. Luke's he thinks may be a poisoning case. Only he doesn't think anybody tried to kill her."

"You mean a suicide attempt?"

The lieutenant shook his head. "He's satisfied the stuff wasn't self-administered. He thinks somebody fed it to her. But if it's what he thinks it is, it isn't strong enough to kill, only enough to make the patient sick."

"Why would anybody do that?" I inquired.

"That's why you're going to see Dr. Muntz," he told me. "To find out."

The doctor's office was on the third floor of the Exchange Building. Several patients sat in a plush waiting room. There was a pretty redhead in a white uniform behind a counter.

I showed the redhead my badge and said, "Sergeant Sod Harris of Homicide. Dr. Muntz asked for a cop to stop by."

"Oh, yes, sir," she said. "He's with a patient, but he left word to send you right in. You may wait in his office."

She came from behind the counter and opened one of two doors leading off the waiting room. We went down a hall past a couple of closed doors to the doctor's private office. As no one was in it, I assumed the doctor was in one of the other cubicles with his patient.

The receptionist indicated a red leather chair before the desk and left me there.

It was about ten minutes before the doctor appeared. He was a lean, wiry man of about fifty with an air of bouncing energy about him.

When I stood up, he gave me a vigorous handshake. "Sorry to keep you waiting, Sergeant. Sit down."

I resumed my seat and he sank behind his desk. "This is a most peculiar case, Sergeant. I'm almost certain it's a case of deliberate poisoning. But if the drug used is what I think, it's a poor choice for murder, because it's hardly likely to cause death."

"That's what the lieutenant told me," I said. "Who's the patient?"

"A Mrs. Arlene Mosher. She was referred to me a couple of weeks ago by an oculist she'd gone to because she was having trouble with her vision. The oculist couldn't find any organic cause for her trouble, so he sent her along to me. By the time she got to me, she had also begun to experience difficulty swallowing and had developed a shuffling gait."

"These symptoms suggested some kind of poisoning?"

"Oh, no. Poisoning didn't even occur to me. My first throught was either the onset of multiple sclerosis or a brain tumor, though it could have been any number of other conditions. Contrary to popular conception, neurological diseases seldom have such clearcut symptoms that they can be immediately diagnosed. It usually takes a long series of tests to arrive at a final diagnosis by a process of elimination. I had her hospitalized and began running tests."

"That's when you discovered she'd been poisoned?"

He shook his head. "Don't put words in my mouth, Sergeant. I only strongly suspect poisoning. I couldn't possibly prove it."

"Well, on what do you base your suspicion?"

"Again, symptoms. The patient's physical symptoms increasingly indicated a brain tumor. She suffered from insomnia, had odd tremors, clouded sensorium, drooling and rolling back of the eyes—all classic symptoms of a tumor. However, her blood tests began to show a peculiar thing. First there was agranulocytosis, which is a depression of the number of white corpuscles, then aplastic anemia, which is a similar depression of red corpuscles. This, along with the other symptoms, led me to the incredible suspicion that she quite possibly could be suffering from regular and continuing overdoses of proclorperazine, easily obtained."

"What's that?"

"The generic name of a quite common tranquilizer which, under various brand names, may be purchased without prescription in any drugstore."

I looked at him in astonishment. "You mean you can buy stuff that'll do all that to a person?"

"Oh, it's hardly a dangerous drug. As a matter of

fact, it's quite useful. It isn't nearly as dangerous as aspirin, for instance, which kills hundreds of people a year through overdoses. Many common drugs which are regarded as safe to dispense without prescription can induce dangerous symptoms if taken irresponsibly. And of course there are clear warnings on the tranquilizer bottles that if symptoms develop, they should immediately be stopped."

After absorbing this, I said, "You asked her if she'd been taking this stuff?"

"Naturally. She said she had never even heard of it. I took some steps to test my suspicion. I forbade her anything except hospital food, such as candy or fruit from outside, barred visitors during mealtime, and administered benztropine, which is an antidote for proclorperazine. Within twenty-four hours she began to improve, and within forty-eight was as good as new. She could go home now, if I thought it safe to let her."

I regarded him thoughtfully. "When you say you suspected regular and continuing overdoses of this stuff, do you mean even after she entered the hospital?"

"Oh, yes. Right up to the time I laid down the new rules."

"You suspect anyone in particular?"

"Well, her husband was always there during the evening meal. The tranquilizer could have been dropped into her tea. He also brought her fruit and candy a time or two. When I laid down my security rules, I confiscated the last of this and had it analyzed. The results were negative, so if he was dosing her, it must have been during mealtime."

"I see," I said. "But why would he do it, if he knew it wouldn't kill her? It seems all he got out of it was a doctor and hospital bill."

"It's possible he didn't know it wouldn't kill her," the doctor said. "I know nothing about Mr. Mosher except that he's a garage mechanic, but in that occupation it's unlikely he would know much about drugs. Perhaps he thought it would kill her."

"Mmm. I suppose there's no way now to establish that the stuff was actually administered. I mean like testing blood samples, lab tests."

He shook his head. "There's no longer any in her system, if there ever was. And it's only a strong suspicion that proclorperazine caused her symptoms in the first place, not a definite fact."

I rose to my feet. "Well, thanks a lot, Doctor. What room is Mrs. Mosher in at St. Luke's?"

"Three twenty-three. What do you intend to do?"

"Just nose around a bit."

His expression became slightly worried. "You won't confront the husband and tell him I've accused him of anything, will you? Since I can't prove it, I'm not in a very good position to fight a suit for defamation of character."

"I'll be discreet," I assured him. "I won't get you into any trouble."

Afternoon visiting hours, which started at two, were on when I arrived at the hospital. Three twenty-three turned out to be a private room, and no one was visiting the patient.

For some reason, maybe because you don't expect men to attempt the murder of young and pretty wives, I had expected to find Mrs. Arlene Mosher a middle-aged drab. But she wasn't more than twenty-two, and was quite pretty in a slightly too thin sort of way. She had honey blonde hair which framed a baby-doll face, and big blue eyes. There wasn't a bit of sparkle in her, though. Maybe it was because she had been ill, although I got the impression she just naturally had a dead personality.

She wasn't in bed. She was seated by the window in a robe and slippers. When I came in, she gave me an inquiring look.

"I'm Sergeant Sod Harris of the police, Mrs. Mosher," I said. "You don't look very sick."

"I'm not, but they won't let me go home. What do the police want with me?"

"Just routine. Possible drug poisonings are always reported to the police, and we have to follow up. We got a report that you may have had too many tranquilizers."

"That's ridiculous," she said. "I've never taken a tranquilizer in my life. I told Dr. Muntz that."

"Uh-huh. What do you think was wrong with you?"

"I haven't the faintest idea. And I don't believe the doctor has either. Whatever it was, it seems to be gone."

There were a couple of other chairs in the room, so I took one. Glancing around, I said, "Isn't a private room here kind of expensive?"

"We have Blue Cross and Blue Shield. It pays most of the bill. Harry wanted me to have the best, with no expense spared."

"Harry's your husband?"

She nodded. "We couldn't afford it without hospitalization, of course. With all these lab tests, my bill is running into more than fifty dollars a day. If we had to pay for it ourselves, I'd be in the charity ward. Harry's only a mechanic at the Sutter Repair Garage."

"That big garage on Gravois?" I asked.

She nodded again.

"I need a little car work. Is he any good?"

"Oh, he's a very good mechanic. It's funny, because

he hates being one. I mean having to work at it. He always loved working on cars, but just as a hobby. He hates having to do it for a living. There's a little snob in my husband."

Before I could comment on this, a pretty young brunette of about the same age as the patient stopped in the doorway. She was wearing a blue spring coat and a premature Easter hat with flowers. Easter was still two weeks off.

"Hello," she said to the blonde Arlene. "You look all recovered."

"I am," the patient said. "Come on in."

I rose as the woman entered the room. Arlene Mosher introduced her as Mrs. Carole Wagner, adding the information that Carole's husband had been best man at her and Harry's wedding, and Harry had been best man at Walter and Carole's.

"You were all just recently married?" I asked.

"Oh, no. Walter and Carole were only married this past June, but Harry and I have been married three years. Walter and Harry were fraternity brothers in college."

So Harry was a college man, I thought, wondering why he had to work as a garage mechanic if he had a college education. I decided to ask.

"Can't Harry get a better job than garage mechanic if he's a college man?"

"He only had two years at Washington U.," Carole said before Arlene could answer. "He quit to get married."

Something in her tone suggested a slight resentment that her husband's friend hadn't finished school. I decided it might be interesting to talk to Carole alone.

The brunette took a chair and I resumed my seat. Carole said, "Arlene introduced you as Sergeant Harris. Are you a policeman?"

"Yes, ma'am."

"You're visiting as a friend, I assume, not in your official capacity."

Arlene said, "He's here on business. That dumb Dr. Muntz reported that I'd had an overdose of tranquilizers. Can you imagine?"

"That you might have had," I corrected. "He was only going by the symptoms. Since you say you've never used them, it looks as though he guessed wrong."

Carole asked curiously, "Whatever made Dr. Muntz think that, Arlene?"

"I don't believe he has any idea what was wrong with me," Arlene said. "But you know how doctors are. When they can't diagnose a case, they make a wild guess."

"Don't malign doctors," Carole said. "Walter's business depends on them."

"What business is that?" I inquired.

"He's a pharmacist."

I sat back and let the women talk then. If they wondered why I remained, when presumably my business was finished, they were both too polite to show it. For about fifteen minutes they prattled on about mutual acquaintances, then Carole rose to leave.

I got up too. "I guess I'll run along too, Mrs. Mosher. Sorry to have bothered you about nothing."

"That's all right," she said. "I don't have many visitors afternoons, and time drags. Harry's always here evenings, but he works until five, then has his dinner."

It was a few more moments before we got out of the room, because Carole had to ask when Arlene was going home and, when Arlene said she didn't know, to speculate on how Harry was getting along at home alone. But finally the brunette and I were walking toward the elevator together.

I asked, "What was Harry studying at Washington U.?"

"The same as my husband. Pharmacy."

That was interesting, I thought. With two years of pharmacy behind him, Harry Mosher would almost certainly have picked some poison more effective than proclorperazine if he had meant to kill his wife. It began to look as though Dr. Herbert Muntz was way out in left field. Perhaps Arlene Mosher's opinion of him was right, and the neurologist had made a wild guess simply because he couldn't diagnose the case.

I decided to mark the record "No evidence of criminous action" when I got back to headquarters, then forget about it.

We stopped before the elevator and I punched the down button. Just to make conversation, I asked, "How old is Harry Mosher?"

"The same as my husband. Twenty-three."

"So he quit school to get married at twenty, huh?"

"Yes. It was too bad. Walter and I were smart enough to wait until he completed his education. Now Walter has a fine position with the Owl Chain, and in a few years will probably manage his own store. Poor Harry will probably be a garage mechanic all his life."

Again I caught the faint note of resentment. I said, "You think Harry made a mistake, eh?"

"Well, it was so unnecessary. They could have waited. Of course, Harry probably wouldn't have married Arlene if they had. She wasn't in school with us. She worked somewhere as a waitress. I think Harry was just playing around with her and never really was serious."

The elevator door opened and we stepped on.

There was a uniformed nurse on the elevator, so our conversation lapsed until we reached the main floor.

As we left the elevator and headed side by side toward the main door, I said, "Then why did Harry marry her?"

"She told him she was pregnant," Carole said casually. "By the time he discovered she wasn't, they were already married and he had dropped out of school."

The case suddenly became wide open again. Here was a motive for murder if I'd ever heard of one. Almost a justifiable motive.

"Didn't that make him a little sore?" I asked.

"Well, she claimed it was an honest mistake. He must have believed her, because they seem to get along all right."

We reached the main door and I held it open for her. As we went down the steps to the sidewalk, I asked, "Was she ever pregnant? I mean, do they have any children?"

"No. Arlene had a miscarriage when they had been married about a year, the time she fell down the stairs and broke her leg."

By now we had reached the sidewalk, and both of us paused.

I said, "This isn't her first time in the hospital then."

She emitted a little laugh. "Arlene? She spends half her time there. This is her fourth trip to the hospital in two years."

"Oh? What was wrong with her aside from a broken leg and this last mysterious illness?"

"Once she had food poisoning, and once some stomach pains which were never diagnosed. The doctor suspected ulcers, but after a couple of weeks of tests and X rays, they decided nothing at all was wrong. I'm beginning to suspect all her illnesses, aside from her broken leg and miscarriage, were psychosomatic."

I asked, "Were all her hospitalizations here?"

"Just the last two. The first couple were at Barnes. Why?"

"Just making conversation." I touched my hat brim. "Nice to have met you, Mrs. Wagner."

"The same to you, Sergeant."

We moved in opposite directions toward our respective cars.

I was driving a department car. I took it back to headquarters and got my own car from the lot. The automatic choke had been sticking for some time, and I kept meaning to get it adjusted. This seemed like a good time to do it.

It was past four P.M. when I drove in the service entrance of Sutter's Repair Garage. A coveralled man of about fifty came over to see what I wanted.

"My automatic choke's sticking," I said. "If he's not busy, I'd prefer Harry Mosher to work on it. He was recommended to me."

"Sure," he said. "He's on a job, but he can stop for a simple thing like that, if that's all it is." He directed me to drive into a vacant slot against the far wall, then walked away.

After a wait of a few minutes, a tall, good-looking young man with curling blond hair came over. He too wore coveralls. Examining me curiously, he said, "I understand you asked for me personally."

"Uh-huh. I happen to know your wife, and she said you're a good mechanic. My name's Sod Harris."

He pursed his lips. "I don't recall Arlene ever mentioning you. My hands are greasy, so I won't offer to shake hands. What's wrong with the car?"

"The automatic choke sticks."

He lifted the hood and it took him less than five minutes to get the choke working properly. After wiping his hands on a rag and making out a charge ticket, he asked, "How long have you known my wife?"

"Just since today. I visited her at the hospital. It was a routine call. I'm a cop."

His face smoothed of all expression. "Oh?"

"I'm not here as a cop," I said. "I needed the choke fixed and your wife recommended you."

"I see. Why were you making a routine call on her?"

"We always check out reported cases of possible poisoning. You knew the doctor suspected an overdose of tranquilizer, didn't you?"

"He mentioned it. But it couldn't have been that. Arlene doesn't take tranquilizers."

"Yes, she told me. She's been hospitalized several times since you were married, hasn't she?"

His eyes narrowed slightly. "Are you making some kind of investigation? Just what is this?"

"I've already made my investigation," I told him. "Right now I'm just making conversation."

For a few moments he studied me thoughtfully. Finally he said, "Yes, she's been hospitalized before. You can pay the bill at the cashier's." He turned his back and walked away.

I wasn't particularly disappointed at getting so little from Harry Mosher. All I had really wanted was a chance to size up the youth. I long ago learned that murderers don't look any different than anyone else, but you can get an impression of character and personality just by talking to a suspect. Despite his coolness to me, Harry Mosher seemed like an average, clean-cut young man who was probably highly regarded by his neighbors and his employer.

That didn't mean he was above killing his wife, because even preachers have been known to do that. But I hoped he wasn't a Bluebeard, because he impressed me as a nice kid.

It was nearing five when I drove away from the garage. There didn't seem to be enough urgency in the case to work overtime. I drove back to headquarters and logged out.

The next morning I was back at St. Luke's by nine o'clock. Only this time I visited the registrar instead of Mrs. Mosher. I learned that Arlene Mosher's previous admission, six months before, had been under the care of a gastrointestinal specialist, Dr. Norman Gateworth.

Gateworth happened to be in the hospital at the time, so I had him paged. We met in the lobby. He was a plump, benevolent looking man of about sixty.

After identifying myself and shaking hands, I said, "Do you recall a patient named Mrs. Arlene Mosher whom you had in here about six months back?"

He had to tug thoughtfully at an earlobe before he could sort her out from all his other patients, but finally he nodded. "A suspected ulcer case, referred to me by her family physician. We ran tests and took X rays for about two weeks without finding a thing wrong with her. She had been complaining of an acute burning sensation in the region of her stomach, but the symptom disappeared while she was here. It probably was merely a mild gastritis. That sometimes is cured by the barium meal we give patients when we run a G.I. series."

"Could it possibly have been a poisoning attempt?"

His eyebrows hiked upward. "I suppose it could have been. Any number of drugs could induce similar symptoms. But she wasn't that sick. She was never in the slightest danger of dying."

As it hardly seemed likely that a man with Harry Mosher's knowledge of drugs would twice pick poisons that wouldn't work, it looked as though my investigation were coming to a dead end. I thanked Dr. Gateworth and left the hospital.

I still wasn't quite ready to give up, though. My wife accuses me of a stubborn streak, and she's probably right. I'm not a particularly brilliant cop, so I have to make up for my lack of genius by being unusually thorough. Even though it looked like my investigation was headed nowhere, I decided to carry it on to the bitter end.

At Barnes Hospital I learned that both Arlene Mosher's admissions had been under the care of a general practitioner named Dr. Arnold Wing, presumably the same family physician who had referred her to Gateworth. She had spent six weeks in the hospital at the time she broke a leg and miscarried, and two weeks the time she was admitted for food poisoning.

Dr. Arnold Wing had an office on South Grand. I phoned him for an appointment and dropped in to see him after lunch.

Dr. Wing was a thin, stoop-shouldered, elderly man, apparently without a heavy practice, for no patients were waiting when I arrived. His office and examination room were combined in one big room, and we talked in there.

I asked about the food poisoning first.

"That was about a year and a half ago," he said. "There was nothing unusual about the case, except that we never were able to trace her condition to any particular food she had eaten."

"Had she eaten anything her husband hadn't?"

After thinking he said. "No, I don't believe she had. I recall that they hadn't been out for dinner anywhere, so it must have been something she prepared herself. Her husband experienced no symptoms, but that doesn't mean much. It's quite possible she merely ate from an improperly washed plate or with an improperly washed fork. Probably more so-called food poisoning cases result from unsanitary utensils than from tainted food."

"Could it have been a deliberate poisoning?" I asked.

He looked startled. "Why do you ask that?"

"Well, except for her miscarriage and broken leg, her illnesses all seem pretty vague. This present one, for instance. She went into St. Luke's with a suspected brain tumor, but now all symptoms have disappeared. The neurologist treating her suspects an overdose of proclorperazine."

Dr. Wing frowned. "I didn't know she was hospitalized. They must have changed doctors."

"She was referred to the neurologist by her oculist," I said. "She probably bypassed you because her first trouble was with her vision. Anyway, I'm checking back on her previous illnesses to see if they possibly could have stemmed from drugs."

In a slow voice he said, "Any of numerous drugs can cause an upset stomach, of course. However, she couldn't have been given anything very dangerous, because she wasn't sick enough. She was never listed as critical."

Again I felt as though I were wasting my time. It was inconceivable that a pharmacy student would three times choose ineffective poisons if he had murder in mind.

Then my interest perked up when he added in the same slow voice, "However, the time she fell down the stairs, I momentarily suspected a murder attempt."

"Why?"

"She insisted she had tripped over something at the top of the stairs. Her husband just as strongly insisted nothing had been there to trip over. But there was a cut on one shin such as might have been made by a tightly stretched wire. The only thing is that if it was a murder attempt, her husband must have changed his mind after she fell."

"Why do you say that?"

"He was home when it happened. Harry Mosher isn't an unintelligent young man, so if he did rig a wire for his wife to trip over, he must have realized the fall was unlikely to kill her. A tumble downstairs isn't likely to be fatal to a young, healthy woman. My reasoning at the time was that if he had planned murder, he would have finished her off after she fell, hoping no one would suspect the fall hadn't killed her. Since he didn't, I came to the conclusion my imagination was working overtime. What he actually did was immediately call an ambulance. He had applied an emergency splint by the time it arrived. His actions after the fall were hardly compatible with his having arranged it."

"No," I agreed. "If he has been trying to kill her, he isn't a very efficient murderer." I thanked the doctor for his time and left.

Even a stubborn cop can't keep beating his head against the wall over a case when there are no further leads to investigate. When I got back to headquarters, I wrote up the case record, concluded it "No evidence of criminous action," and put it on the lieutenant's desk. I wasn't really satisfied, though. I kept brooding about it, and finally phoned Dr. Muntz.

"I've checked back over Mrs. Mosher's previous hospitalizations," I told him. "I didn't unearth any evidence of foul play, but there were enough slightly odd circumstances in each case to leave me slightly uneasy about the whole thing. There's certainly nothing definite enough for us to take action on down here, though."

"Well, my mind's easier for having called you in, anyway," he said. "I'm letting Mrs. Mosher go home today, so let's hope my suspicion was unfounded. Mr. Mosher just phoned me, incidentally."

"Oh? About what?"

"To ask me to send him my bill in quadruplicate."

"Quadruplicate? What for?"

"I suppose he carries more than one health insurance policy. I often get asked for bills in duplicate, but this is the first time anyone ever wanted four."

Bingo! It fell into place so neatly, I wondered why I hadn't figured it out from the beginning.

"This may seem like an odd question, Doctor, but I have a reason for it. Do you mind telling me how much your bill is going to be?"

In a tone of mild surprise he said, "It is a rather odd question. But if it's important, I charge ten dollars a day for hospital calls. Mrs. Mosher was hospitalized a total of fifteen days, so my bill will be a hundred and fifty dollars."

"Thanks," I said. "If there are any further developments, I'll let you know."

I hung up and phoned the registrar at St. Luke's. Part of the information hospitals enter on admission cards is designed to let them know how the patient intends to pay his bill. It includes such things as what health insurance is carried and the name of the responsible person's bank. I got both items of information from the registrar, and also the amount of Mrs. Mosher's bill both for this period of hospitalization and for her previous time at St. Luke's.

Then I phoned Barnes Hospital and the two other doctors, aside from Muntz, who had treated her.

The banks were already closed for the day, so I had to wait until morning to complete my investigation. At nine A.M. I was closeted with the president of the bank where the Moshers had their accounts.

Bankers are stuffy about disclosing their depositors' affairs, even to the police, without a court order. However, they'll usually cooperate if you make it an off-the-record inquiry with a guarantee that you won't use the information you get as courtroom evidence without first going through the proper legal procedure to get it legally. I came away knowing the Mosher's exact financial condition.

Harry Mosher would be at work in the daytime, I assumed, so I waited until that evening to call on them. They had a small, two-story house on Jefferson, within walking distance of the garage where he worked.

Arlene answered the door. She seemed surprised to see me, but she invited me in politely enough. Her husband was seated in the front room drinking a can of beer. He rose to offer me a rather frigid handshake and asked without much enthusiasm if I would like a beer.

"No thanks," I said. "I just dropped by to discuss your wife's various hospitalizations for a few minutes."

I seated myself on a sofa opposite his chair. Arlene had taken another chair. She gazed at me expectantly.

"I've been checking up on the cost of Mrs. Mosher's illnesses during the past couple of years," I said. "It certainly costs to get sick these days. Doctor and hospital bills together have come to five thousand, eight hundred and thirty dollars."

"Most of that was covered by our Blue Cross and Blue Shield," Arlene said quickly, with a glance at her husband to see if the figure had shocked him.

"All but approximately twenty-seven hundred dollars," I agreed. "And since Harry's employer pays his insurance premiums, that's been your total medical expense. Except for the five hundred a year Harry pays out of his own pocket for your other three health policies."

She gazed at me puzzledly. "What other policies?"

"I didn't think you knew about those," I said. "They've paid off on your illnesses too. A total of seven thousand, four hundred and twenty-seven dollars, plus an additional five hundred and some dollars which will be coming in as soon as your husband submits claims for this last illness. Except for the thousand dollars he's paid out in premiums during the past two years, it's all in a savings account under his own name, presumably as a fund to finish his education when he finally finishes with you."

She looked at her husband with her jaw drooping. "What's he talking about, Harry?"

"I'll explain it bluntly," I said. "Your husband resented being trapped into a marriage he didn't want and being forced to abandon his chosen career for one he doesn't like. So he decided to use you as a means of accumulating enough money to go back to school. What his plans are when he decides he has enough of a bank account, I don't know. Maybe he merely means to leave you. Maybe he plans a final illness which will be terminal. You'll have to ask him."

Her face registered horror. "Harry! Is he telling the truth?"

Her husband glared at me belligerently. "Try to prove it, Sergeant."

"I doubt very much that I could," I admitted. "I'd hate to try to convince a jury that you deliberately caused your wife's illnesses, because there isn't a bit of actual evidence. And without proving that, we could never establish fraud. There's nothing fraudulent *per se* about carrying extra hospitalization. Many people carry enough to make a profit from their illnesses. I'm not planning to arrest you."

"Then why the devil are you bothering us?"

"Just to clear the air. In the event you do plan a terminal illness for your wife, I'd suggest you abandon the idea. I rather suspect she won't be around long enough for you to slip her more pills or rig any more accidents anyway."

He looked at her and saw what I meant. Her eyes were blazing at him with horrified indignation.

I got to my feet. "I'll leave you to work out your own solution, and it had better be nonviolent. If either of you ends up dead, I *will* prove what happened in court."

Arlene was on her way up the stairs, probably to start packing, when I let myself out the door.

When "dreadful innocence" emanates truth, can "dreadful reasonableness" deny?

COUSIN KELLY
by Fletcher Flora

She had an intimate little liturgy which she repeated every morning when she wakened, as if it were somehow essential, by the repetition, to orient herself anew to an ancient and confusing world in which, otherwise, she might easily become lost: *I am Teresa Standish. I am eight years old, and I live at the Eastland Arms in Apartment 515. Today I am going to* . . .

From there on the liturgy varied, of course, according to what she had planned yesterday to do today. She did not include the tedious details of what had been planned for her, or what, in the nature of things as they were, she would do simply because it had been ordained that she must. She included only the item or items on the day's agenda which offered the promise of being exceptional and exciting and of saving the day from the burden of expectations that did not. Sometimes the promise was fulfilled and sometimes it wasn't, for life is loaded with disappointments, but on Saturdays and Sundays it was *always* fulfilled, and Saturdays and Sundays were, therefore, the very best days of the week.

When she awakened in the morning of those days, the liturgy was invariably completed: *Today I am going to see Cousin Kelly.*

This particular day to which she wakened was Saturday, and between it and the preceding Sunday there had been six long days of broken promises, of hope and expectations unfulfilled. After repeating the liturgy, which was like an incantation to the shining sun that spilled its golden light through her window and across her bed, she lay quietly for a while in the warm and secure assurance of what the day surely held, and then she got up and began to dress.

Because it was the beginning of a bright and golden day, she put on a pale yellow jumper with a crisp white blouse. She would meet Cousin Kelly, she decided, in the park across the boulevard from the apartment building. Last Sunday had been a gray and sunless day, expiring interminably to the tearful sound of persistent rain, and Cousin Kelly had come to the apartment, right up to her room where she now was, and they had listened to some music on her phonograph and had talked about what had happened during the week and had played a long and delightful game of Monopoly, which she had won. It had been a good day, that part of it in the afternoon when Cousin Kelly was here, but it had not been as good by half as this one would be on the bright green grass of the park under the warm sun. They would sit on a bench and walk along the path under the trees and laugh with delight at their distorted reflections in the pool of clear water around the fountain. Cousin Kelly was actually old, over twenty, but he didn't look or act old, and he was more more fun to be with than anyone else in all the world.

It was odd that Mother didn't like him. After all,

he was really Mother's cousin, the son of her father's sister. Of course, lots of people didn't necessarily like their cousins, because there was no law saying you had to or anything, but Teresa couldn't understand why anyone wouldn't like Cousin Kelly, cousin or not. But Mother didn't. Neither did Father. Teresa could tell from the way their eyes went blank whenever she, Teresa, happened to mention seeing Cousin Kelly, and from the way, immediately after the mentioning, they deliberately tried to change the subject. Cousin Kelly knew, too. He knew, but he never talked about it. Maybe something had happened once in the family. Maybe something dreadful had happened to change everything from the way everything had been, and to make enemies of people who should have been friends.

Teresa didn't care. At first she had, but not any longer. Whatever the trouble, she liked Cousin Kelly better than anyone else. She *loved* Cousin Kelly. She wished and wished that he could come to live with them in the apartment. She loved him far more, to tell the truth, than she loved Mother and Father. In fact, she didn't love Mother and Father at all, although she didn't, on the contrary, hate them, either. She was merely indifferent to them. In the beginning it had made her feel guilty and unhappy, the secret knowledge of her indifference, but now it was just something that she lived with every day and hardly ever thought about.

Dressed in her pale yellow jumper and white blouse, she went out of the room and onto a gallery that ran along the wall above the deep pit of the living room. She descended the stairs at one end of the gallery and turned back from there through a dining room to the kitchen, where Hannah was. Hannah came in every day from nine to six to cook and clean. Sometimes, when Mother and Father entertained, she stayed later. She was fat and jolly and ages old, and Teresa liked her.

"Good morning, missy," Hannah said. "You're mighty prettied up this morning, I must say."

"This afternoon," said Teresa, "I'm going to the park to meet a friend."

"That's nice. Meanwhile, what would you like for breakfast?"

"A poached egg, please, with two strips of bacon. And one slice of toast."

"Simple enough. You just sit down there and keep Hannah company while she's fixing it."

Teresa sat at the kitchen table and watched while Hannah broke the egg in the funny little poaching pan and put two strips of bacon on the grill. The bacon began to sizzle, and the water began to boil in the little pan under the cup the egg was in. Teresa liked to sit in the kitchen and watch Hannah cook her breakfast. Hannah always said it kept her company, and it was true, although they talked very little while Hannah worked, or not at all. That was one of the nice things about Hannah. You could sit with her and say nothing and still feel comfortably that you were keeping company. It was different with Mother. When you sat with Mother and said nothing for a long time, you always felt uneasily that something should be said, and after a while you tried to say it, and it always came out wrong and awkward, and then you wished you hadn't tried.

Teresa ate her egg and bacon and toast at the kitchen table, and then, leaving Hannah to her work, went back into the living room and wondered how she could spend the time, which was almost forever, until it was afternoon. She thought about going down in the elevator and outside to talk to the doorman and stroll up and down the sidewalk, but she didn't want to do that because there was the day out there, warm and golden and waiting, and she wanted to enter it for the first time, fresh and exciting with nothing worn off, when she went out to meet Cousin Kelly. So, saving the day for a special hour, she looked at magazines in the living room until it was after eleven and she could go up to see Mother, who was now probably awake.

Sure enough, she was. Mother was sitting up in bed, braced against the headboard, and in one hand was a saucer, and in the other, momentarily stopped halfway between the saucer and her mouth, was a cup of coffee, which had been served by Hannah and from which Mother had just taken a sip. A second bed near Mother's was rumpled and empty. This bed was Father's, of course, and it was apparent that Father had risen early and gone away somewhere, probably downtown to his office. Father did not usually go to his office on Saturdays, but once in a while he went when he had an appointment that promised to be profitable, and you could always tell by Father's humor when he got home if things had gone well or not. If things had gone well, he was expansive and tolerant. If things had gone ill, he was cross and critical and could hardly wait for five o'clock, when he allowed himself his first cocktail of the day.

Mother's cup rattled in her saucer, and she spoke to Teresa with a cheerfulness that was forced and bright and artificial. Mother, in fact, looked as if she needed a cocktail already, although it was not yet noon; or perhaps she only needed a little longer to recover from those she had had the night before. The flesh was smudged beneath her eyes, and her face, cleaned of makeup, looked drawn and tired and older than it was.

"Good morning, darling," Mother said. "Have you been up long?"

"Oh, yes," Teresa said. "It's almost noon."

"That late? Did Hannah give you your breakfast?"

"Yes. I had an egg and two strips of bacon."

Mother reacted as if the words were painful to her. Her mouth turned down, becoming for a moment really ugly, and she set her cup and saucer carefully aside on the table between her bed and Father's.

"What have you been doing?"

"Nothing much. I looked at some magazines." Teresa hesitated, feeling within her the sudden singing exhilaration of her anticipation. "This afternoon I would like to go across to the park. May I, please?"

"I think it would be all right if you are careful crossing the boulevard. Why do you want to go to the park?"

"I'm going to meet Cousin Kelly there."

There it was again, that strange blankness in Mother's eyes, the curious, cold hardening of her face.

"I hope you are not going to be difficult, Teresa," Mother said.

The remark seemed so irrational, so utterly unrelated to anything that had been said or to any intention that Teresa had, that it was quite hopeless to try to respond to it. Teresa in her hopelessness was silent, and after a moment Mother's shoulders moved slightly in a gesture that was not big enough to be a shrug.

"Well, you have a nice time in the park, darling, and be sure you have your lunch before you go."

This was clearly a dismissal, and Teresa, relieved, went downstairs and out to the kitchen to keep Hannah company. At one o'clock Hannah gave her lunch: tomato soup and crackers spread with soft cheese and a green salad and milk. After she had eaten her lunch, it was almost one-thirty, and Teresa returned to the living room and sat down on the edge of a chair and deliberately waited and waited while her anticipation of the afternoon grew and grew and became so intense that it could no longer be borne, and then, at last, she left the apartment and went downstairs and out into the golden, sunbathed street. At the curb she paused and looked left for traffic, and then she ran across to a medial strip that divided the boulevard, there pausing again and this time looking right. Safely all the way across, she entered the park, passing between stone pillars, and followed a concrete walk as far as a green wooden bench within sight of the fountain, which tossed into the air a glittering shower that fell, the upward force of the fountain spent, back into the surrounding pool with a sound of summer rain. Sitting there on the bench, watching the fountain, she waited.

Waiting, she tried to remember where and when she had first seen Cousin Kelly, and she couldn't. As hard as she tried, she couldn't for the life of her. He had just suddenly come into her life, that was all, and her life, which had been lonely, was filled thereafter with love requited and promises kept. It did not matter where and when he had come. It only mattered that he had come somewhere and sometime, and that he was, having approached quietly in the midst of her pondering, there at this instant.

He stood a step away on the concrete walk and smiled down at her. His hair was thick and pale blond; he never wore a hat, winter or summer, and the sunlight touched the hair and turned it to silver.

His eyes were blue, brimming with grave and secret laughter, and below one of the eyes, running down at an angle across his cheek, was the lingering trace of an old scar.

"Hello, Tess," he said.

He was the only one who called her that. Hannah called her missy or Teresa, and Mother called her Teresa or darling, and Father called her Teresa or child, but Cousin Kelly always called her by the warm diminutive, and it was something special between them, another secret shared. Rising, she held out a hand, and he took it and kept it in his.

"Hello, Cousin Kelly. I've been waiting for you."

"Am I late?"

"Oh, no. I was early."

"I'm flattered. Shall we walk over to the fountain?"

"I'd like that. And then perhaps we can walk under the trees."

So they went over to the fountain and laughed at their distorted reflections in the pool, and Cousin Kelly told her about the foolish Grecian boy who had fallen in love with himself when looking at his reflection in another pool long ago. She had heard the story before, but it seemed new and much more exciting the way Cousin Kelly told it. Afterward they began walking on the grass beneath the trees, trying to identify each tree by the size and shape of its leaves, and they held hands all the while. There was only one tiny blemish on the nearly perfect afternoon.

That was when they met Mrs. Carter. Mrs. Carter lived in the apartment building on the fourth floor, and she was walking her poodle in the park on a leash. Teresa and Cousin Kelly had come across the grass, and Mrs. Carter was strolling along the walk, pausing now and again to let the poodle sniff at things and do his duty, and they all just happened to reach a certain point from different directions at the same time. Teresa spoke politely to Mrs. Carter, who pulled up the poodle and stopped to exchange a few words with Teresa, and this was all right except that Mrs. Carter paid absolutely no attention to Cousin Kelly, although he was standing there holding Teresa by the hand all the while. For all the recognition Mrs. Carter gave him, Cousin Kelly might as well have been somewhere else, and Teresa thought it was very rude of Mrs. Carter. Afterward she told Cousin Kelly how rude she thought Mrs. Carter had been, but Cousin Kelly only laughed and said it didn't matter, and actually, considering all the rest of the wonderful afternoon, it didn't.

Eventually they came back to the bench from which they had started. They sat down together to rest and talk, and Teresa was beginning to feel sad because it was getting late, almost five o'clock, and soon she would have to leave.

"Will I see you tomorrow?" Teresa asked.

"If you wish."

"Where shall I meet you?"

"If it's another nice day, we can meet here. Otherwise, wait for me in your room, like last Sunday, and I'll slip up."

It had gotten a little cooler, and the shadows of everything lay longer to the east on the grass, and Teresa's sense of sadness was growing stronger.

"It's so long from Sunday to Saturday," she said.

"Yes," he said, "it is."

"I wish you could come and live with me all the time."

"Do you, Tess? So do I."

"Why don't Mother and Father like you?"

"It's an old story, but never mind. You could make them like me if you tried."

"How could I?"

He reached into a pocket of his jacket and brought out a sealed white envelope with something it. His voice was light, and the grave laughter was in his eyes.

"By putting some of this in something they drink," he said.

"What is it?"

"It's a love potion."

"You mean like in fairy stories?"

"Yes."

"I thought that was only make-believe."

"Oh, no. There is more truth than you imagine in fairy stories. When your mother and father drink something with some of this powder in it, they will immediately like me, just as you do, and then they will ask me to come and stay with you all the time."

"Do you really think so?"

"Try it and see."

He extended the envelope, and she took it and put it in the pocket of her yellow jumper.

"I will," she said.

Then it was time to go. Father would surely be home from the office, and Mother would be getting cross and anxious, and pretty soon, if Teresa didn't hurry, would be sending Hannah across the boulevard to fetch her. Parting from Cousin Kelly was not so hard on Saturdays as it was on Sundays, anyhow, because the time between parting and meeting was so much shorter. So, saying good-bye, she hurried off down the walk toward the stone gate. Once she stopped and turned and waved, and Cousin Kelly, waiting and watching by the bench, waved back, then turned and went away himself in the opposite direction.

In the apartment, Mother and Father were sitting together in the living room. It was immediately apparent to Teresa from Father's expression that his day had not gone well, and the atmosphere in the living room was oppressive, but there was, fortunately, imminent hope of relief, for it was time for cocktails. Teresa said hello politely to Father, who grunted, and Mother looked as she invariably did when she was about to be moderately severe about something.

"Where have you been all this time, Teresa?" Mother asked.

"I told you where I was going, Mother. I went to the park. You gave me permission."

"I didn't give you permission to stay indefinitely."

"I'm sorry. It was such a nice afternoon, and I was with Cousin Kelly."

Father looked up angrily and slapped the arm of his chair with the flat of his hand.

"Cousin Kelly again! However did the child get started on this thing? When did she ever even hear of Kelly?"

Mother must have heard Father's outburst, but she gave no sign of it. Her expression had changed suddenly to the cold and stony one which warned that she had at last had all of something that she could stand, and had determined to resolve a problem, no matter how unpleasant the resolving might be. Her voice, as if in compensation, was softly fraught with dreadful reasonableness.

"You did not see Cousin Kelly," she said. "You did not see Cousin Kelly this afternoon or any other afternoon, because Cousin Kelly is dead. He was dead and buried, Teresa, before you were born."

Teresa heard the words, of course, but they had no higher meaning. They did not prick her intelligence or elicit an emotional reaction. How could Cousin Kelly be dead when she had just parted from him in the park?

"I saw him this afternoon," she said, "and I'll see him again tomorrow. I see him every Saturday and Sunday."

"The child has a morbid imagination, that's all," Father said. "She needs professional attention. Tell me, Teresa, what does Cousin Kelly look like? Describe him for me."

"He is about as tall as you," Teresa said, "but much thinner. He has very light hair that looks silver in the sun, and he has blue eyes that laugh. On one cheek he has a scar that sometimes you can hardly see."

Father looked stunned for a moment, and Mother caught her breath with a sharp gasp.

"She's seen a picture somewhere," Father said. "She's surely seen a picture."

"This must stop!" Mother's voice still held that dreadful reasonableness, her face the expression of grim decision. "Listen to me, Teresa. Cousin Kelly is dead. He is dead because I killed him. It was an accident, a tragic accident, and it happened years ago. We had gone on an outing in the country, Kelly and I and our parents. We had gone to a place high on a bluff above a river. Kelly and I had quarreled. I was furious with him. I wanted to be alone, and I walked away from the others to the edge of the bluff, but Kelly followed. He came up beside me and took me by the arm and started to say something. I turned and jerked my arm free. I don't know what happened exactly. I must have pushed him without thinking or meaning to." Mother's voice was silent, the horror of that remote moment invoked again by the telling, and then it went on quietly and quickly, as if to be done as soon as could be. "He was standing at the edge of the bluff, and he fell over. He was killed. He was dead when my father and my uncle reached him. They always blamed me, my aunt and uncle—Kelly's mother and father. They still do. They thought I pushed him deliberately in a fit of anger. But it was an accident. That's all it was, Teresa. It was a terrible accident, and Cousin Kelly is dead."

Teresa turned and walked away to the far end of the living room. Turning again, she looked back at Mother and Father.

"Cousin Kelly is alive," she said, "and he is coming soon to live with us here."

She went on into the dining room, passing from view. Ahead of her, beyond the louvered swinging door to the kitchen, she heard Hannah at work. She pushed through the door and saw that Hannah had deserted her cleaning paraphernalia long enough to prepare cocktails. The silver shaker was on a tray on the cabinet, and beside the shaker were two fragile, long-stemmed glasses. Hannah looked hurried and harassed. It was after five, and she was obviously anxious to be away by six.

"Let me take the tray, Hannah," Teresa said.

"I'm sure I'd be grateful to you for saving me the steps," Hannah said. "Mind you don't spill it, missy. Watch where you're going."

Teresa took the tray and pushed back through the louvered door into the dining room. In the pocket of her yellow jumper, the love potion felt as heavy as gold dust.

It was all over, everything done that needed doing, and everyone gone who had been there except a worn and rather seedy little man and Teresa and Hannah. The man spoke with gentle weariness in a tone of futility.

"Now, Teresa," he said, "tell me again exactly where you got the pois—the 'love potion.'"

"Cousin Kelly gave it to me. We were in the park."

"Why did Cousin Kelly give it to you?"

"It was supposed to make Mother and Father love him. Then he could come and live with us here."

"Your mother and father didn't love Cousin Kelly?"

"No." She paused, a shadow passing across her eyes, as if she were struck for a moment by a presentiment of wonder. "Mother said that Cousin Kelly was dead."

"I know."

"She said he died years ago. He fell off a cliff. But he wasn't. Dead, I mean. I was in the park with him this afternoon."

"And you met your neighbor there? What is her name?"

"Mrs. Carter. She was rude to Cousin Kelly. He was standing right there, holding my hand, and she ignored him."

"Are you sure she saw him?"

"How could she have helped? He was standing right *there*."

"Mrs. Carter told me that you were alone when she saw you. There was no one with you at all."

"I don't understand it." Again the shadow passed over her eyes. "He was holding my hand, and later he gave me the love potion."

"All right." The little policeman stirred uneasily. He was feeling, for some reason, a chill in his bones. "Last Sunday it rained. You couldn't go to the park, and so Cousin Kelly visited you here. Isn't that what you told me?"

"Yes. He came right up to my room. He was there all afternoon."

"Poor little dear." Hannah reached an arm toward Teresa as if to brush from the child the gathering shadows of evil. "She has been alone too much. She lives in fantasy."

"You are certain that no one came last Sunday?"

"There was no one here but the family and me. No one. The hall door is kept locked on the inside. No one could have entered without being admitted."

"Do you think that Mrs. Carter would deliberately lie about not seeing Cousin Kelly in the park?"

"No."

"Do you think your mother would have lied about his being dead?"

"No."

"Do you think Hannah would have lied about his not being here last Sunday?"

"No."

"There you are, then." Leaning forward, he spoke slowly with a kind of dreadful reasonableness, and every tired syllable was an echo of his dread and a measure of his futility. "Listen to me, Teresa. You must tell me exactly where you got the love potion. It's very important."

And she met his dreadful reasonableness, as he had known she would, with dreadful innocence.

"Cousin Kelly gave it to me. In the park. He was *there*."

The yield from "a fair night's work" may exceed one's hopes while meeting his fears.

FAT JOW AND THE RELUCANT WITNESS
by Robert Alan Blair

Fat Jow stepped outside his herb shop door to look up and down the steep street, but saw nothing unusual in the late-afternoon Chinatown traffic. He locked the door, drew the Closed shade, turned back to the worried young man at the wall telephone behind the counter. As the regular whirring of the ring repeated and repeated, Low Kan's agitation increased. He had just arrived in a cab, but he was breathing heavily.

"She ought to be home!" Low Kan muttered, and broke the connection to dial his number again.

"Perhaps the apartment manager?" said Fat Jow.

Low Kan tried another number, with success. "Mrs. Collins?" he fairly shouted. "I can't raise Sallie . . . No, I'm okay." His head snapped back as though dodging a blow. "When? . . . Did you ever see him before? . . . No, don't call the police—yet. We don't know anything for sure. Thanks." Slowly he hung up, looked at Fat Jow, his face haunted. "They've got Sallie. Somebody came and said I'd been hurt, and she went off with him."

He strode toward the door, but Fat Jow stood in his way. "Wait. Give your next move some thought. You dashed in here as one running away. What will you do now?"

Low Kan said helplessly, "I—I don't know."

"Why not the police?"

"They'd just make things worse, by putting me in protective custody. If I want to keep Sallie alive, I can't go near them."

"Alive? Do you not dramatize?"

Low Kan mastered the unsteadiness of his voice. "Didn't you ever hear of Cliff Sarazin?"

"Oh," said Fat Jow, hushed. Sarazin was nominally and flamboyantly an attorney, but a prominent figure in many circles, exerting indirect control over interlocking activities, with access to important people and their assets. There were rumors, whose confirmation Sarazin was able to prevent, that some of his connections went underground. "How are you involved with him?"

"One guess—he's an officer in Low Electronics."

"But yours is a modest firm. Why does he trouble himself?"

"Modest in front. In the back room he's raking in several thousand a day with an electronic horsebook. And he doesn't want me to blow it sky-high."

Fat Jow blinked. "You will help me understand." He gestured toward the rear stairs to the shop loft, which was both office and retreat. "Over tea you will better compose your thoughts, and so begin at the beginning."

"Tea? Now?"

"You were about to blunder frantically into peril. Which is better?"

Low Kan preceded Fat Jow up the stairs.

At the old teakwood table beside the loft rail, they

shared tea without conversation, while Fat Jow allowed his guest to choose his time to speak. Call no man friend until one may relax in his silent presence. He had known Low Kan better as a child, gathered with his playmates around a park bench to hear Uncle Jow, the storyteller of St. Mary's Square. As Charles Low, his was a rising name in electronics technology, and his small plant on Howard Street produced communications and computer components.

Low Kan folded his hands about the little porcelain tea bowl, studied the tracery of leaves. "You may remember when I designed that electronic brain to compute parimutuel odds at one of the racetracks?"

"We who knew you were most proud," said Fat Jow.

"The publicity reached Cliff Sarazin, and he came to see me. He called me the young wizard, and I was flattered. He had a deal to bring business my way. Before I knew it, he was my partner, and I was under contract to install a larger model of the brain in my back room for him. Bit by bit, I knew what he'd sucked me into. He dropped hints of what might happen to my key men and their families if I got stubborn. Ask First Son, sometime. He knows the setup."

Fat Jow became alarmed. "First Son has been threatened?" The son of his predecessor Moon Kai was as dear to him as if his own. Fat Jow had received the herb shop from his hands, as reward for his part in bringing to justice the killer of Moon Kai.

"Cliff's not that crude. He made sure we learned what had happened to some others: the yacht-club manager who blew up at sea with his cabin cruiser; the accountant who drove off a sea cliff; the bookie who 'committed suicide' in his closed garage." He looked up. "I've even thought of suicide myself. Or disappearing with Sallie, to a new life somewhere. But he'd follow. He'd follow."

"Is Sarazin more of a menace now than he was before?"

Low Kan laid upon the table a document. "A subpoena to testify before the state crime commission next week. Cliff has spies all through the plant. It wasn't an hour after I got this that he phoned. Special conference; he was sending his car for me. I know that car. We put the radio equipment in it. A cute backseat, with glass all around, that locks and seals airtight from a switch on the dash. And a tube from the exhaust manifold. I bolted, didn't even dare get my car out of the parking lot, but ran down Howard till I spotted a cab. You were the first one I thought of." He stood up, leaned heavily upon the loft rail, looked down into the shop. "I'm about ready to go to Cliff, if he'll let Sallie go."

Fat Jow stroked his chin. "No. Sallie's safety—and yours—rest upon his not knowing where you are, so he cannot communicate his terms. No matter what you do, he is not likely to release her without persuasion. We must devise a method of pulling the fangs of Mr. Sarazin."

"You don't know him," moaned Low Kan. "He hires toughs to do his heavy work, so he won't get his hands dirty. Cliff is clean."

"You have already suggested two latent weaknesses in his various strengths: gadgetry and delegated responsibility. His very dependence upon trivia makes him the more vulnerable when they are absent—or turned against him." Fat Jow pushed back his chair, moved to his great rolltop desk, stretched up to grasp the chain suspending the single bulb which was the loft's only illumination. An entire ceiling panel tilted down from a black hatchway, revealing on its upper surface a built-in ladder. "The small room above saw much use during the tong wars. One who had completed an assassination would wait there, while the members of the offended tong sought him. Tonight, after dark, First Son will drive you to the Delta, where I have friends."

Low Kan said, "I won't leave town till Sallie's safe."

Fat Jow placed an understanding hand upon his shoulder. "I could expect no less of you. But will you not trust me?"

"Crawling away to hide. Some hero."

"Against such a one as Sarazin, heroics are wasted. He requires different tactics. Go up now, and come down only when you know the shop is empty, or when you hear my voice addressing you directly. He undoubtedly knows of our acquaintance, and we must be prepared for him."

Low Kan climbed into the blackness, and Fat Jow raised the counterbalanced panel into place. Its decorative molding covered the seams, restoring uniformity to the discolored ceiling.

He settled himself at the desk; the silence was broken only by the ticking of the old wall clock, and by the detached murmur of the city outside.

At 4:50 he telephoned Low Electronics, spoke only the name of First Son, without identifying himself. When First Son answered, Fat Jow said rapidly, "If you are not otherwise engaged this evening, please come to the house."

First Son reflected no surprise, although such invitations were infrequent. "Nothing planned, old man. I'll drop by."

Fat Jow hung up at once. "Low Kan," he called, rising.

From above, "Yes?"

"My usual closing time approaches, and I shall not vary my routine. Listen for me later tonight—and if you have cause, telephone."

"Check. You're not forgetting Sallie?"

"I'm not forgetting Sallie. One thing at a time." He snapped off the light and descended the stairs.

As he puffed up the steep grade across Nob Hill, the booming of foghorns dominated the rumble of traffic. The afternoon had turned leaden and dank, with a heavy fog sliding over the hills from the sea, dissolving the tops of taller buildings.

Past Van Ness, he noticed a large black car cruising slowly toward him. It picked up speed, swung around the corner into Van Ness. The driver was watching him, the single passenger speaking into a hand microphone. The knot of uneasiness expanding within him, Fat Jow hurried his steps.

Adah Baxter, his landlady, black gown and high coiffure reminiscent of the departed century of the Baxter mansion itself, met him in the cavernous foyer. "Did you see that car?" she demanded. "This is the third time it's been by here this afternoon."

He crossed the parquet floor to the door of his apartment. "Perhaps, an unmarked police car," he said, unlocking the door. He turned. "Do you have any lawbreakers among your tenants?"

"Not live ones," she said quietly. A select group of former tenants reposed beneath the cellar floor, victims of their own avarice, and of a singular tea brewed by Adah Baxter. "You can't tell me that's a police car. Those two were faces you'd see on a post-office bulletin. Are you in some kind of trouble? If you are, I ought to know. I'll do anything I can to help. You know that."

"Thank you," he said without enthusiasm. The

thought of help from Adah Baxter was somewhat unnerving. Only affection, and the knowledge that this living relic of old San Francisco had few years left, allowed him to preserve her secret in conscience. "Be watchful—and go to the police, if it appears necessary." He bowed, closed the door.

He was pulling on his lounging robe of lined silk, for his customary evening interlude with his *Chinese World* newspaper, when his telephone rang. He was prepared to hear Low Kan, hoarse with repressed excitement: "They've been here . . . just left. They went all through the place. Two of them."

"As I thought, they are alert to my participation, and we must revise plans. However, their attention is now diverted from the herb shop."

"They may come to you. I could hear a few things they said."

"The possibility has crossed my mind. They have been watching the house."

"I can't get you into this any deeper, Uncle Jow. Maybe if I went to Cliff . . ."

"Remain where you are," ordered Fat Jow. "No noble gesture of sacrifice will benefit Sallie, in any way." He hung up.

The doorbell interrupted his reading. On his way to the door, he glanced out the window, saw in the dusk and thickening fog that the black car had stopped before the house. As he crossed the foyer, Adah Baxter's apartment door on the other side opened a crack. She was being watchful.

One of the two men under the dim, yellow porch light was the driver seen earlier, and the other was Clifford Sarazin, deliberately conspicuous in bowler, tweed jacket, cravat, checked waistcoat, watch chain slung across.

Fat Jow heard Adah Baxter's door click shut behind him. He wished she had a telephone in her apartment.

Sarazin removed his bowler and proffered his card. "Good evening, sir. I've been wanting to meet you. My associate, Mr. Haskins." And in an undertone: "Your hat, George."

George took off his hat. "Hi-ya."

Fat Jow bowed. "How do I merit your attention?"

"I have a business proposition that may interest you. May we come in?"

Curiosity mingling with apprehension, Fat Jow ushered them into his apartment. George posted himself near the door, but Sarazin accepted Fat Jow's invitation to sit on the sofa. He crossed his legs, carefully plucked his trouser creases out of harm's way, and looked about him at the former ballroom, at the mirrored walls and crystal chandelier. "Every time the wrecking crew moves into one of these charming old places, a little goes out of San Francisco. I can envy you, living here." From an inner pocket he took a small spiral notebook, flipped several pages, said without looking up, "You might say I've had my eye on you ever since the Lindner affair."

Leo Lindner, serving a life sentence for the murder of Moon Kai, had peddled protection to Chinatown merchants engaged in extralegal but strongly traditional gambling. Coldly and with resignation, Fat Jow said, "Mr. Lindner was a growing threat which had to be removed. I met it as best I could."

Sarazin put the notebook away. "Don't get me wrong. I'm not settling Leo's debts. He was just a small operator. You met the threat admirably. I can respect that. What motivates you? Certainly not money?"

"The personal reward of a task accomplished well. That is all."

"You and I have much in common." Sarazin pursed his lips, weighing a decision. "I'm prepared to make an opening for you, sir."

Fat Jow said without emphasis, "A grave is an opening."

Sarazin smiled appreciatively. "I was speaking professionally. I've needed a Chinatown representative for a long time. You'll enjoy the association."

Fat Jow drew a deep breath. "I tire of this cat-and-mouse game. It is no choice that you offer."

"Whatever are you talking about?" The smile was fainter.

"You would not have come personally, unless you were confident of obtaining what you wished—and unless your survival were at stake."

Sarazin made no immediate reply, and the smile had quite gone. He stretched lazily. "I've just told you what I came for."

"You have not."

"Suppose you tell me, then."

"We possess a mutual skill in dodging an issue."

The smile came back. "I do like the way your mind works! It'll be a pleasure doing business with you."

"Doing business implies a commodity to be bargained for."

"Well now! I can afford to be more explicit. I'm worried. My partner has disappeared, and I'm afraid something may have happened to him. Since he's known to you, we thought you might help us."

"A trifling detail: this missing person is Chinese?"

Sarazin snapped his fingers. "Didn't I say? I'm that upset over this. You do know Charles Low?"

"I have known Low Kan for many years."

"Did you see him today?"

Fat Jow said without hesitation, "He had tea with

me today, then we went our separate ways, and he did not confide his plans to me."

Sarazin partially closed his eyes. "What did you talk about?"

"When the acquaintance exceeds twenty years, there are many topics for discussion. But you wander from the subject—a commodity purveyed has a purchase price."

"Then you have your price?" mocked Sarazin.

"An insignificant price," said Fat Jow casually; "the whereabouts of Sallie Low."

Sarazin made his face a mask. "They have a pleasant apartment on Pacific Heights. Marvelous view of the Gate and the Marin hills."

"She is not there."

A polite arch of the brows. "Well . . . women go shopping, now and then."

Fat Jow placed his fingertips together before his lips. "It would seem that neither of us has the merchandise desired by the other."

A moment's irritation, then Sarazin resumed his easy affability. "Need I remind you, you're not in a bargaining position." He looked aside at George. "I thought you required finesse which my associates lack, but it may be running its course. Don't pain me by calling for more direct means. A man of your ability—"

A light tap at the door, and George said quickly, "Should I get it?"

Sarazin asked Fat Jow, "Are you expecting callers?"

Mentally berating First Son for coming early, Fat Jow said, "A young friend occasionally visits for the evening."

Sarazin nodded. "The young man whom you called at the plant. An odd coincidence that he drives a car and you don't, and that you invite him for the evening on the same day Charles drops from sight. Go let him in. He knows our car, so he can join the party."

As Fat Jow crossed reluctantly toward the door, George stepped close against the wall next to the knob, his right hand hovering ready above his lapel. "And don't try to tip him off. I'll be right here."

But it was Adah Baxter who confronted him, with a tea cart bearing an exquisite service of fragile, hand-painted china, which he had seen only behind glass in her parlor—never used. "I saw you had guests," she said brightly, "and I thought you gentlemen might like some hot tea. It's such a raw night out."

He went numb, eyes on the little flowered globe of the teapot. From somewhere far from his voice: "We are very busy, Miss Baxter. Perhaps later, if there is something you must do . . ." While his mind cried, get the police!

Sarazin was beside him, pulling the door wide. "Nonsense! Is that any way to accept hospitality? A spot of tea would go very well, Madam, and it was thoughtful of you to make the effort for complete strangers. Do come in."

Not trusting himself to meet the eyes of Adah Baxter, Fat Jow dazedly returned to his rocker.

She wheeled the cart to the center of the room, poured first for George, then for Sarazin, prattling about the weather and the cost of living.

"Beautiful china," said Sarazin, raising the translucent cup. "Imported?"

"Oh yes," she replied, pleased. "My grandfather brought many things back from Asia. He was a clipper captain, you know."

"The name of Jedediah Baxter isn't unknown to me," said Sarazin. "I'm a bit of a student of local history."

"Aren't you nice!" she beamed, peering closely into his face. "Have we met?"

"Have we?" he parried delicately as he sipped his tea. "Don't you remember?"

"Can't say I do, sonny," she said blankly, turning away to serve Fat Jow last. "I've met lots of people in my time, but I haven't paid much attention to them, the past thirty-forty years. My eyes and memory aren't so good anymore." She did not look at Fat Jow, and conveyed no message by her manner. She returned the teapot to the cart, bustled to the door with a swish of skirts. "I'll leave it here, if you should want more. Now I know you men have things to talk over, so I won't stay."

Sarazin gave a slight wave of dismissal, as much for George as for Adah Baxter. "Thank you, dear lady. I should like the opportunity of chatting with you at leisure, sometime."

After she had gone, George listened with his ear to the panel. "You must be slipping, Chief. I don't think she knows you at all."

"It's just as well," said Sarazin; "I'd hate to involve her in our problems here. Drink up, George. Don't look so sour. I know tea isn't your speed, but you never can tell—you might like it." He looked at Fat Jow, who still held cup and saucer with both hands at the level of his chin, contemplating the tea. "Something wrong?" asked Sarazin.

Fat Jow knew he could not delay drinking longer without arousing Sarazin's suspicion against Adah Baxter. "We Orientals prefer making a ceremony of tea," he said, wafting the cup beneath his nostrils. "The perfume is half the delight."

She had made no distinction between Fat Jow and his visitors; the tea had issued from the same container into three clean cups. He closed his eyes and took his first sip, for the fluid level must be seen to go down. He detected no added ingredients, but too vivid in memory were the cement patches in the cellar floor. His will would not permit him to swallow. While still he supported cup and saucer atop the angle formed by his forearms, he let the tea dribble from his mouth down his wrist and inside the voluminous sleeve of his robe. The discomfort of dampness was minor by comparison with others which came to mind.

He was thus able to dispose of three sips before lowering the cups. "Miss Baxter has a rare gift for tea," he said. "I am not ashamed to confess that mine cannot match it." He kept his eyes on Sarazin.

"I miss stimulating company and conversation," Sarazin said wistfully. "I should relax more. I'd like to spend a lot of time here. There's a mood about the place. If you'd give us half a chance, you and I could be great friends."

"Friendship must be mutual," said Fat Jow. "I do not take kindly to anyone who seeks to guide my steps or alter my values."

"Nor do I—nor do I. But you can understand that business pressures call for a little leaning on this one and that one. It's better to be the leaner than the leaned on."

Fat Jow let his voice sink into a low, hopefully sedative, monotone: "An unfortunate preponderance of small minds in positions of power dominates the world. Rather than aspire to greatness themselves, they demean or destroy what is not as small as they. The very essence of their being is smallness, and they are resentful of anything more."

Sarazin yawned, drained his teacup, set it aside. "Not so damn small, friend." His words were slurred, as though he were mildly drunk. "A lot of people—big people—jump when I press the button."

Fat Jow droned on. "You cannot equate power with greatness. Power is petty and transitory, but the effects of greatness are felt forever. The truly great men of history are those whose minds, not deeds, shine as beacons to the rest of a humanity struggling toward the civilized and rational state. The immortals elevate the art of reason to its proper stature. Therefore they live, wherever men hold discourse."

Sarazin had slid down in the sofa, legs extended before him. "You're being wasted, you know that? That two-bit, hole-in-the-wall shop. What're you getting out of life, anyway? You'll thank me for coming. Your style can take you right to the top—to the top, and no stops on the way."

George sauntered unsteadily forward with his empty cup, poured himself another. "It ain't gin," he said happily, "but it sure goes down easy." He dropped into a convenient chair.

Sarazin frowned; not angrily, but rather puzzled. He spoke with grave deliberation: "Say, does she spike her tea?"

Fat Jow clucked. "Such an old-fashioned individual?"

Sarazin nodded. "Course not. Course not." He giggled. "Ridiculous. Isn't it, George? George . . . ?" But George, second cup poised, was not answering. From a trancelike immobility he slowly relaxed, spilling the tea into his lap.

"There was something in that tea!" Sarazin lurched to his feet, swayed dizzily, put a hand to his eyes. "George, you idiot, wake up!" With grim concentration of will he plodded to George, fumbled inside his lapel, came around heavily with a .32 automatic wobbling in his hand. "Now," he gurgled deep in his throat, glancing down in fuzzy surprise as his uncoordinated fingers let the gun fall. He bent after it, and eased into a stupor on the rich carpet.

Fat Jow rescued the china from George's still fingers and replaced it on the tea cart. "Miss Baxter!" he called.

She came in at once. "Good," she said; "you didn't drink any. I had to leave that up to you. In any case, I was ready." She showed him a coil of sturdy rope. "This'll hold them till they come to. Now the police?"

"At the moment," said Fat Jow, kneeling to search Sarazin's pockets, "you and I are the transgressors, for our shameful treatment of these innocents."

Adah Baxter sniffed. "Innocents! I know who this is. He should've been behind bars twenty years ago."

"Many people know that, but as yet Mr. Sarazin has been able to manipulate the technicalities of law to his own advantage." He looked through Sarazin's notebook: names, addresses, license numbers, bank accounts. It would prove valuable reading for the authorities.

Sarazin was unarmed, but George carried, besides the shoulder-holster, an eight-inch clasp knife, brass knuckles, and a flexible, lead-filled blackjack. "This arsenal alone," observed Fat Jow, "will enable the police to hold this one. How long will they sleep?"

"I don't know," she said honestly. "I've never made it so mild before."

He felt a chill. "You do not know whether it is a lethal dose?"

"Oh, I'm sure it isn't. See? They aren't turning blue, like all the others. But maybe, if one drank more than the other . . ." A sudden thought: "That would simplify everything. Maybe if I go and mix up something stronger—"

"Stop," Fat Jow said crisply. "Occupy yourself instead with the ropes."

Soon Sarazin and George were twin hempen cocoons, lying peacefully side by side beneath the crystal chandelier.

Fat Jow stood and brushed off his hands. "Mr. Haskins will remain here, but Mr. Sarazin and I have further business elsewhere." He stepped to the window. The fog had closed until the car was but a dim suggestion of darker gray, the street light a diffused aura that impaired rather than aided visibility. "When Mr. Haskins stirs, you may use my telephone to call the police."

"What if he doesn't?"

"Then—follow your best instincts. The police may confirm the kidnapping of Mrs. Charles Low by interviewing Mrs. Collins, the apartment manager. I hope to have more information for them later."

First Son arrived, and Fat Jow directed him to drive Sarazin's car up to the side door. First Son asked no questions; he knew both his old friend and Clifford Sarazin. It was enough that they acted for Low Kan. Between them they carried Sarazin to the car, propped him in a corner of the rear seat, and locked him in.

Driving was slow, as they could see no more than a dozen feet ahead. The fading rows of street lights were their only reference points. Despite the relative youth of the evening, the streets were deserted. Foghorns shook the deadened world.

The central California coast presents to the sea a thousand-foot barrier of dark hills whose roots are scoured by water and wind into naked cliffs rising from tumbled rocks and narrow crescent beaches. State Highway One, sightseer's dream and acrophobe's nightmare, follows these rugged contours well above cliffs and crashing surf, descending only rarely to sea level. When visibility is limited, whether by fog or darkness or both, this road becomes as remote as deep wilderness, although it is but a few miles from the centers of population. Its more precipitous stretches, those closed most frequently by slides, are by habit largely unused, because of a lingering aversion of the driving public to being swept into the sea with a fragment of the landscape.

As they rounded a tight curve skirting a rock buttress, Fat Jow said suddenly, "Stop here." The headlights revealed a strip of earth-and-gravel shoulder, a dusty fringe of weeds along the broken rocky edge and, beyond, the blank fog curtain throwing back the glare. "Pull off the pavement."

"On the outside?" First Son asked nervously, squinting ahead past the flopping windshield wipers.

"Where else?" For the buttress rose almost sheer from the inner side of the curve.

"It's a downgrade."

"Yes," said Fat Jow.

With slow caution First Son edged over as far right as he dared, set the hand brake firmly.

"Lights off," said Fat Jow; "engine off."

Darkness closed in, slowly softened as their eyes adjusted, and they became aware of the restless soughing of the unseen surf below. They were beyond the foghorns' range.

From behind the glass screening the rear compartment came a bored drawl. "Would you mind filling me in on the plot of this farce?"

Fat Jow turned. "Ah, welcome back, Mr. Sarazin. Rather melodrama than farce."

"Melodrama is out of date," said Sarazin.

"My entire existence rests upon out-of-date standards." Fat Jow waved First Son out of the car, climbed out after him. The opening of the door snapped on the dome light, and a small, fuzzy globe of gray light permeated the fog beside the car. He said to First Son, "I presume that you are familiar with that adjustment of the hand brake which holds the car unless slight motion causes slippage?"

First Son displayed his first resistance. "I can't be a party to this," he declared.

"Let us walk aside and talk," said Fat Jow, taking his arm. They withdrew into the fog until the gray glow was almost swallowed up behind them, Fat Jow speaking softly and earnestly, not to persuade but to explain.

First Son left him and stalked alone down the shoulder of the road.

Fat Jow returned to the car. "He is a sensitive person—which is good. He has gone off to wrestle his conscience."

Sarazin was testing the ropes, but Adah Baxter had wrapped well. "Assuming that you plan to see this through, just how will you explain it away for the police?"

"Who but one with imagination of sheerest fantasy could consider this decrepit Oriental a threat to Clifford Sarazin? The facts will be evident to establish the 'accident': a dangerous road, a heavy fog, a sharp curve."

"And these ropes?"

Fat Jow shrugged. "Rope is combustible. We shall let the engine idle, and increase the probability of fire."

Sarazin managed a harsh laugh. "You're a cool one . . . but I don't think you have the nerve."

"I wield no weapon, administer no blow. I but set the stage, but you are chief performer. While you sit relaxed, the car will stand. But no one can remain motionless indefinitely. A single answer will suffice to set the hand brake again."

First Son, hands in pockets, feet scuffing the dirt, came slowly out of the fog ahead. "I think I'm ready."

Sarazin blazed, "Aren't you going to show more sense than this old fool?"

First Son gave him a long look. "Nope."

Fat Jow said, "We are not constituted precisely as is your average law-abiding citizen. By ancient custom, friendship and loyalty are strong influences, superseding our habitual restraints. If one is not a person of violence, he must improvise, with the first instruments to come to hand."

Sarazin surged forward, fell back. "Suppose I don't know a thing about Sallie Low?"

Fat Jow bowed. "Then I now offer my apology, for what will have been my regrettable error." He directed First Son to enter the car. "Please start the engine." The powerful engine throbbed into life. "Now the hand brake—gently."

First Son eased forward the lever notch by notch, until the heavy car stirred with a groan that reverberated through the frame. He pulled back, and the groaning stopped. A notch forward . . . another . . . they waited.

"Get out," said Fat Jow. Tentatively he rocked the car with one hand. The brakes slipped a little, caught again. "Excellent. We may now leave Mr. Sarazin to his meditation." He moved away, beckoning First Son to follow.

Sarazin neither moved nor spoke. At a little distance they squatted down, prepared to wait with the infinite patience of their people. The surf roared, shattering upon the rocks below, transmitting its strength in a mild trembling of the ground.

They did not measure time, for time measured is

slow to move. They only waited, without words. A groan came from the brake drums, amplified through the open door of the car. After another wait the next slippage endured longer, and ticked on slowly, undecided when to stop. A last tick . . . and the brakes held again.

Well into the following silence came Sarazin's low call, tense, controlled: "You there?"

Fat Jow did not move. "Yes, Mr. Sarazin."

"Say it occurred to me where she might be."

"We would know not where she might be," said Fat Jow stolidly, "but where she is."

A spark of anger: "Okay! Say she is, then!" Sarazin's vehemence started a small slippage, and his voice became very low, very quiet. "Come here and set this brake, and we'll talk about it."

"First," said Fat Jow, rising, "we shall talk—and then decide whether to set the brake."

Sarazin seemed to have shrunk into himself. He was huddled into the corner, staring at the floor. He said in a rush. "There's an abandoned ranch house down below Half-Moon Bay—rustic brushwood arch over the gate. The sheriff will know it."

"She is there?" persisted Fat Jow.

"Yeah!" snapped Sarazin. "Now get that lousy brake."

First Son would have reached into the car, but Fat Jow held him back. "She is guarded?"

"One man, and he's not expecting trouble, so he won't raise a fuss. He's got orders—no rough stuff." Sarazin grimaced. "Please?" An unaccustomed word for Clifford Sarazin.

First Son jerked back firmly upon the hand brake, and cut the engine.

Sarazin was limp, his voice weak. "You drive a hard bargain. Now how about these ropes?"

Fat Jow climbed into the front seat. "Until we have confirmed your information, the stage remains set. First Son—the radio, please. Can you reach the city police for me?"

"Sure." First Son switched on the set. "They can zero in on our location once we're on the air."

"Then we shall not remain long on the air. For the present."

First Son did not ask for Detective-Lieutenant Cogswell, but the name of Fat Jow brought the lieutenant on immediately. "I might've known you'd be in on the Low case somewhere," said Cogswell. "Where are you? Half the department's out hunting you. Where's Sarazin? Are you okay?"

Fat Jow took the microphone. "None of this is important. Your first concern is to fetch Sallie Low from the place where she is held."

"You know where she is?"

"Mr. Sarazin has proved most informative."

"Cliff?" A growing note of exultation: "But—this ties him in with the whole business!"

"I am sure Mr. Sarazin is well aware of that."

Cogswell sounded worried. "What'd you *do* to him? No, don't tell me. Where's the girl?"

Fat Jow repeated Sarazin's directions, heard Cogswell relay them to someone. Cogswell was in midsentence when Fat Jow signaled First Son to cut him off.

They broke radio silence at irregular intervals, and little more than an hour later came the welcome word that Sallie, unharmed, was on her way to a hospital for observation. Her bewildered guard was in custody.

"Now then," said Cogswell ominously, "we got a fix on you. Will you come in, or will we go out there to get you?"

"We shall not move," said Fat Jow, to the accompaniment of a long sigh from Sarazin, "until you arrive to relieve me of the burden of guaranteeing Mr. Sarazin's safety."

Cogswell mumbled something unintelligible. "He's all right, isn't he? I mean, he'd better be."

Fat Jow held the microphone over his shoulder, against the glass between compartments. "Tell him, Mr. Sarazin."

Sarazin said sarcastically, "Oh, I'm fine. What'd you think?"

Cogswell said, "That sounds like him. Stay right there. We're on our way."

The radio went dead, and Fat Jow returned the microphone to First Son. He rested his head against the seat back. "A long night. An old man misses his sleep."

Sarazin said, "I think I've been infinitely patient with you. Cut me loose."

Fat Jow did not stir. "We shall not come near you. The police will see to your improved comfort."

"And I'll have a thing or two to tell them," Sarazin said darkly. "Harassment, intimidation."

Fat Jow smiled a little. "I wonder exactly what you will tell them. And how would the national press present the story, Mr. Sarazin? The potential variety is endless. You do have an image to maintain."

After a pause Sarazin grumbled, "The first stray thread . . . now the unraveling begins."

Sirens echoing among the sea cliffs announced the coming of the authorities. Out of the fog materialized three cars: two from the San Mateo county sheriff's office, one from the city, Fat Jow noted.

Cogswell came first, assessed the situation at a glance, bent with hands on knees to look in at Sarazin. "You don't look too chipper, Cliff. You seem to have got yourself tangled up in something. Any complaints?"

"I'll have to think about it," Sarazin said glumly.

Cogswell beckoned his men. "Get the ropes off him and take him downtown. Conspiracy and kidnapping will do for a starter."

Fat Jow and First Son emerged from the car. Fat Jow handed Cogswell the notebook. "This may be of use," he said.

Sarazin shouted past the men working on his ropes, "Illegal search and seizure!"

"I was merely keeping it for Mr. Sarazin," said Fat Jow. "When he was feeling drowsy earlier this evening, he dropped it."

Cogswell handled it as he might an art treasure. "Don't you worry, Cliff, you can have it back after we've copied it." He tilted it to the light and glanced through it. "We'll take the best care of it." He gave it to one of his men. "Round up everybody in this book, and check out all the license numbers with Motor Vehicles. The bank accounts we'll go into in the morning."

They conducted Sarazin from the car. He stretched cramped muscles, turned to look at the cliff's edge, and saw for the first time the several heavy rocks which First Son, laboring on hands and knees and under cover of fog, had maneuvered into the path of the front wheels.

Slowly Sarazin turned to Fat Jow. "You—old—fraud!" he said grudgingly. "It's high time I retired. This pace could be too much for my heart. I may even turn state's evidence. After tonight I'll be safer on the inside looking out. Several gentlemen are going to resent the attention of the police." He looked again at the rocks. "And there are certain explanations I doubt I'll ever be able to make."

The two sheriffs' cars departed with Sarazin, and Cogswell directed the remaining man to deliver Sarazin's car to the police garage. He waved Fat Jow and First Son toward the waiting city car. "I'll give you a lift home. I know it's foolish of me to ask—but you wouldn't just know where Charles Low is, too?"

Fat Jow got into the rear seat. "If you care to make a small detour to my shop, you may then take Low Kan to Sallie at the hospital."

Cogswell stopped where he was. "That's what I thought." He slid in behind the wheel. "Sallie Low, Cliff Sarazin, Charles Low—a fair night's work. While we're at it, is there anything else you have for us?"

A vague discomfort suggested caution. Fat Jow asked, "And how was Miss Baxter when you left her?"

Cogswell pulled out upon the pavement. "We only talked to her on the phone. And we wouldn't have believed her at all, if we hadn't already heard about Sallie from Mrs. Collins. Who ever believes anything Adah Baxter says? Some wild story about a kidnapping, and Cliff Sarazin taking you for a ride. She was worried about you—that was the only reason she called."

A statement, not a question: "You did not go out to the house."

"No reason, was there?" Cogswell chuckled. "Old faithful Adah . . . she was in rare form tonight. After telling us all that, she had to look important, too. 'Oh, by the way,' she says, 'there's something else. I've had to dispose of somebody—in the usual manner.' What an imagination! By now, I suppose there's a nice neat new patch in her cellar floor."

Fat Jow refrained from inquires about George Haskins, and spoke no further word all the way downtown.

THE LONG WAY DOWN
by *Edward D. Hoch*

Many men have disappeared under unusual circumstances, but perhaps none more unusual than those which befell Billy Calm.

The day began in a routine way for McLove. He left his apartment in midtown Manhattan and walked through the foggy March morning, just as he did on every working day of the year. When he was still several blocks away, he could make out the bottom floors of the great glass slab which was the home office of the Jupiter Steel & Brass Corporation. But above the tenth floor the fog had taken over, shrouding everything in a dense coat of moisture that could have been the roof of the world.

Underfoot, the going was slushy. The same warm air mass which had caused the fog was making short work of the previous day's two-inch snowfall. McLove, who didn't really mind Manhattan winters, was thankful that spring was only days away. Finally he turned into the massive marble lobby of the Jupiter Steel Building, thinking for the hundredth time that only the garish little newsstand in one corner kept it from being an exact replica of the interior of an Egyptian tomb. Anyway, it was dry inside, without slush underfoot.

McLove's office on the twenty-first floor had been a point of creeping controversy from the very beginning. It was the executive floor, bulging with the vice-presidents and others who formed the inner core of Billy Calm's little family. The very idea of sharing this exclusive office space with the firm's security chief had repelled many of them, but when Billy Calm spoke, there were few who openly dared challenge his mandates.

McLove had moved to the executive floor soon after the forty-year-old boy genius of Wall Street had seized control of Jupiter Steel in a proxy battle that had split stockholders into armed camps. On the day Billy Calm first walked through the marble lobby to take command of his newest acquisition, a disgruntled shareholder named Raimey had shot his hat off, and actually managed to get off a second shot before being overpowered. From that day on Billy Calm used the private elevator at the rear of the building, and McLove supervised security from the twenty-first floor.

It was a thankless task that amounted to little more than being a sometime bodyguard for Calm. His duties, in the main, consisted of keeping Calm's private elevator in working order, attending directors' meetings with the air of a reluctant outsider, supervising the security forces at the far-flung Jupiter mills, and helping with arrangements for Calm's numerous public appearances. For this he was paid fifteen thousand dollars a year, which was the principal reason he did it.

On the twenty-first floor, this morning, Margaret Mason was already at her desk outside the directors' room. She looked up as McLove stepped into the office and flashed him their private smile. "How are you, McLove?"

"Morning, Margaret. Billy in yet?"

"Mr. Calm? Not yet. He's flying in from Pittsburgh. Should be here anytime now."

McLove glanced at his watch. He knew the directors' meeting was scheduled for ten, and that was only twenty minutes away. "Heard anything?" he asked, knowing that Margaret Mason was the best source of information on the entire floor. She knew everything and would tell you most of it, provided it didn't concern herself.

Now she nodded and bent forward a bit across the desk. "Mr. Calm phoned from his plane and talked with Jason Greene. The merger is going through. He'll announce it officially at the meeting this morning."

"That'll make some people around here mighty sad." McLove was thinking of W. T. Knox and Sam Hamilton, two directors who had opposed the merger talk from the very beginning. Only twenty-four hours earlier, before Billy Calm's rush flight to Pittsburgh in his private plane, it had appeared that their efforts would be successful.

"They should know better than to buck Mr. Calm," Margaret said.

"I suppose so." McLove glanced at his watch again. For some reason he was getting nervous. "Say, how about lunch, if we get out of the meeting in time?"

"Fine." She gave him the small smile again. "You're the only one I feel safe drinking with at noon."

"Be back in a few minutes."

"I'll buzz you if Mr. Calm gets in."

He glanced at the closed doors of the private elevator and nodded. Then he walked down the hall to his own office once more. He got a pack of cigarettes from his desk and went across the hall to W. T. Knox's office.

"Morning, W.T. What's new?"

The tall man looked up from a file folder he'd been studying. Thirty-seven, a man who had retained most of his youthful good looks and all of his charm, Knox was popular with the girls on twenty-one. He'd probably have been more popular if he hadn't had a pregnant wife and five children of varying ages.

"McLove, look at this weather!" He gestured toward the window, where a curtain of fog still hung. "Every winter I say I'll move to Florida, and every winter the wife talks me into staying."

Jason Greene, balding and ultraefficient, joined them with a sheaf of reports. "Billy should be in at any moment. He phoned me to say the merger had gone through."

Knox dropped his eyes. "I heard."

"When the word gets out, Jupiter stock will jump another ten points."

McLove could almost feel the tension between the two men; one gloating, and the other bitter. He walked to the window and stared out at the fog, trying to see the invisible building across the street. Below, he could not even make out the setback of their own building, though it was only two floors lower. Fog . . . well, at least it meant that spring was on the way.

Then there was a third voice behind him, and he knew without turning that it belonged to Shirley Taggert, the president's personal sceretary. "It's almost time for the board meeting," she said with that hint of a southern drawl that either attracted or repelled but left no middle ground. "You people ready?"

Shirley was grim-faced but far from ugly. She was a bit younger than Margaret Mason's mid-thirties, a bit sharper of dress and mind. But she paid the penalty for being Billy Calm's secretary every time she walked down the halls. Conversations ceased, suspicious glances followed her, and there was always a half-hidden air of tension at her arrival. She ate lunch alone, and one or two fellows who had been brave enough to ask her for a date hadn't bothered to ask a second time.

"We're ready," Jason Greene told her. "Is he here yet?"

She shook her head and glanced at the clock. "He should be in any minute."

McLove left them grouped around Knox's desk and walked back down the hall. Sam Hamilton, the joker, passed him on the way and stopped to tell him a quick gag. He, at least, didn't seem awfully upset about the impending merger, even though he had opposed it. McLove liked Sam better than any of the other directors, probably because at the age of fifty he was still a big kid at heart. You could meet him on even ground, and, at times, feel he was letting you outdo him.

"Anything yet?" McLove asked Margaret, returning to her desk outside the directors' room.

"No sign of Mr. Calm, but he shouldn't be long now. It's just about ten."

McLove glanced at the closed door of Billy Calm's office, next to the directors' room, and then entered the latter. The room was quite plain, with only the one door through which he had entered, and unbroken walls of dull oak paneling on either wall. The far end of the room, with two wide windows looking out at the fog, was only twenty feet away, and the conference table that was the room's only piece of furniture had just the eight necessary chairs grouped around it. Some had been heard to complain that the room lacked the stature of Jupiter Steel, but Billy Calm contended he liked the forced intimacy of it.

Now, as McLove stood looking out the windows, the whole place seemed to reflect the cold mechanization of the modern office building. The windows could not be opened. Even their cleaning had to be done from the outside, on a gondolalike platform that climbed up and down the sheer glass walls. There were no windowsills, and McLove's fingers ran unconsciously along the bottom of the window frame as he stood staring out. The fog might be lifting a little, but he couldn't be certain.

McLove went out to Margaret Mason's desk, saw that she was gathering together her copy books and pencils for the meeting, and decided to take a glance into Billy Calm's office. It was the same size as the directors' room, and almost as plain in its furnishings. Only the desk, cluttered with the trivia of a businessman's lifetime, gave proof of human occupancy. On the left wall still hung the faded portrait of the firm's founder, and on the right, a more recent photograph of Israel Black, former president of Jupiter, and still a director though he never came to the meetings. This was Billy Calm's domain. From here he ruled a vast empire of holdings, and a word from him could send men to their financial ruin.

McLove straightened suddenly on hearing a man's muffled voice at Margaret's desk outside. He heard her ask, "What's the matter?" and then heard the door of the directors' room open. Hurrying back to her desk, he was just in time to see the door closing again.

"Is he finally here?"

Margaret, unaccountably white-faced, opened her mouth to answer, just as there came the tinkling crash of a breaking window from the inner room. They both heard it clearly, and she dropped the cigarette she'd been in the act of lighting. "Billy!" she screamed out. "No, Billy!"

They were at the door together after only an instant's hesitation, pushing it open before them, hurrying into the directors' room. "No," McLove said softly, staring straight ahead at the empty room and the long table and the shattered window in the opposite wall. "He jumped." Already the fog seemed to be filling the room with its damp mists as they hurried to the window and peered out at nothing.

"Billy jumped," Margaret said dully, as if unable to comprehend the fact. "He killed himself."

McLove turned and saw Knox standing in the doorway. Behind him, Greene and Hamilton and Shirley Taggert were coming up fast. "Billy Calm just jumped out of the window," McLove told them.

"No," Margaret Mason said, turning from the window. "No, no, no, no . . ." Then, suddenly overcome with the shock of it, she tumbled to the floor in a dead faint.

"Take care of her," McLove shouted to the others. "I've got to get downstairs."

Knox bent to lift the girl in his arms, while Sam Hamilton hurried to the telephone. Shirley had settled into one of the padded directors' chairs, her face devoid of all expression. And Jason Greene, loyal to the end, actually seemed to be crying.

In the hallway McLove pushed the button of Billy Calm's private elevator and waited for it to rise from the depths of the building. The little man would have no further use for it now. He rode it down alone, leaning against its padded walls, listening to, but hardly hearing, the dreary hum of its descent. In another two minutes he was on the street, looking for the crowd that would surely be gathered, listening for the sounds of rising sirens.

But there was nothing. Nothing but the usual mid-morning traffic. Nothing but hurrying pedestrians and a gang of workmen drilling at the concrete and a policeman dully directing traffic.

There was no body.

McLove hurried over to the police officer. "A man just jumped out of the Jupiter Steel Building," he said. "What happened to him?"

The policeman wrinkled his brow. "Jumped? From where?"

"Twenty-first floor. Right above us."

They both gazed upward into the gradually lifting fog. The police officer shrugged his shoulders. "Mister, I been standing in this very spot for more than an hour. Nobody jumped from up there."

"But . . ." McLove continued staring into the fog. "But he *did* jump. I practically saw him do it. And if he's not down here, where *is* he?"

Back on twenty-one McLove found the place in a state somewhere between sheer shock and calm confusion. People were hurrying without purpose in every direction, bent on their own useless little errands. Sam Hamilton was on the phone to his broker's, trying to get the latest quotation on Jupiter stock. "The bottom'll drop out of it when this news hits," he confided to McLove. "With Billy gone, the merger won't go through."

McLove lit a cigarette. "Billy Calm is gone, all right, but he's not down there. He vanished somewhere between the twenty-first floor and the street."

"*What?*"

W. T. Knox joined them, helping a pale but steady Margaret Mason by the arm. "She'll be all right," he said. "It was the shock."

McLove reached out his hand to her. "Tell us exactly what happened. Every word of it."

"Well . . ." She hesitated and then sat down. Behind her, Hamilton and Shirley Taggert were deep in animated conversation, and Jason Greene had appeared from somewhere with a policeman in tow.

"You were at the desk," McLove began, helping her. "And I came out of the directors' room and went into Billy's office. Then what?"

"Well, Mr. Calm came in, and as he passed my desk, he mumbled something. I didn't catch it, and I asked him what was the matter. He seemed awfully upset about something. Anyway, he passed my desk and went into the directors' room. He was just closing the door when you came out, and you know the rest."

McLove nodded. He knew the rest, which was nothing but the shattered window and the vanished man. "Well, the body's not down there," he told them again. "It's not anywhere. Billy Calm dived through that window and flew away."

Shirley passed Hamilton a telephone she had just answered. "Yes?" He listened a moment and then hung up. "The news about Billy went out over the stock ticker. Jupiter Steel is selling off fast. It's already down three points."

"Good-bye merger," Knox said, and though his face was grim, his voice was not.

A detective arrived on the scene to join the police officer. Quickly summoned workmen were tacking cardboard over the smashed window, carefully removing some of the jagged splinters of glass from the bottom of the frame. Things were settling down a little, and the police were starting to ask questions.

"Mr. McLove, you're in charge of security for the company?"

"That's right."

"Why was it necessary to have a security man sit in on directors' meetings?"

"Some nut tried to kill Billy Calm a while back. He was still nervous. Private elevator and all."

"What was the nut's name?"

"Raimey, I think. Something like that. Don't know where he is now."

"And who was usually present at these meetings? I see eight chairs in there."

"Calm, and three vice-presidents: Greene, Knox, and Hamilton. Also Calm's secretary, Miss Taggert; and Miss Mason, who kept the minutes of the meeting. The seventh chair is mine, and the eighth one is kept for Mr. Black, who never comes down for the meetings any more."

"There was resentment between Calm and Black?"

"A bit. You trying to make a mystery out of this?"

The detective shrugged. "Looks like pretty much of a mystery already."

And McLove had to admit that it did.

He spent an hour with the police, both upstairs and down in the street. When they finally left just before noon, he went looking for Margaret Mason. She was back at her desk, surprisingly, looking as if nothing in the world had happened.

"How about lunch?" he said. "Maybe a martini would calm your nerves."

"I'm all right now, thanks. The offer sounds good, but you've got a date." She passed him an interoffice memo. It was signed by William T. Knox and it requested McLove's presence in his office at noon.

"I suppose I have to tell them what I know."

"Which is?"

"Nothing. Absolutely nothing. All I know is a dozen different things that couldn't have happened to Calm. I'll try to get out of there as soon as I can. Will you wait for me? Till one, anyway?" he asked.

"Sure. Good luck."

He returned her smile, then went down the long hallway to Knox's office. It wasn't surprising to find Hamilton and Greene already there, and he settled down in the remaining chair feeling himself the center of attraction.

"Well?" Knox asked. "Where is he?"

"Gentlemen, I haven't the faintest idea."

"He's dead, of course," Jason Greene spoke up.

"Probably," McLove agreed. "But where's the body?"

Hamilton rubbed his fingers together in a nervous gesture. "That's what we have to find out. My phone has been ringing for an hour. The brokers are going wild, to say nothing of Pittsburgh!"

McLove nodded. "I gather the merger stands or falls on Billy Calm."

"Right! If he's dead, it's dead."

Jason Greene spoke again. "Billy Calm was a great man, and I'd be the last person in the world to try to sink the merger for which he worked so hard. But he's dead, all right. And there's just one place the body could have gone."

"Where's that?" Knox asked.

"It landed on a passing truck or something like that, of course."

Hamilton's eyes widened. "Sure!" he remarked sarcastically.

But McLove reluctantly shook his head. "That was the first thought the police had. We checked it out and it couldn't have happened. This building is set back from the street; it has to be, on account of this sheer glass wall. I doubt if a falling body could hit the street, and even if it did, the traffic lane on this side is torn up for repairs. And there's been a policeman on duty there all morning. The body didn't land on the sidewalk or the street, and no truck or car passed anywhere near enough."

W. T. Knox blinked and ran a hand through his thinning, but still wavy, hair. "If he didn't go down, where did he go? Up?"

"Maybe he never jumped," Hamilton suggested. "Maybe Margaret made the whole thing up."

McLove wondered at his words, wondered if Margaret had been objecting to some of his jokes again. "You forget that I was out there with her. I saw her face when that window smashed. The best actress in the world couldn't have faked that expression. Besides, I saw him go in—or at least I saw the door closing after him. It couldn't close by itself."

"And the room was empty when you two entered it a moment later," Knox said. "Therefore Billy must have gone through the window. We have to face the fact. He couldn't have been hiding under the table."

"If he didn't go down," Sam Hamilton said, "he went up! By a rope to the roof or another window."

But once more McLove shook his head. "You're forgetting that none of the windows can be opened. And it's a long way up to the roof. The police checked it, though. They found nothing but an unmarked sea of melting snow and slush. Not a footprint; just a few pigeon tracks."

Jason Greene frowned across the desk. "But he didn't go down, up or sideways, and he didn't stay in the room."

McLove wondered if he should tell them his idea, or wait until later. He decided now was as good a time as any. "Suppose he did jump, and something caught him on the way down. Suppose he's hanging there now, hidden by the fog."

"A flagpole? Something like that?"

"But there aren't any," Knox protested. "There's nothing but a smooth glass wall."

"There's one thing," McLove reminded them, looking around the desk at their expectant faces. "The thing they use to wash the windows."

Jason Greene walked to the window. "We can find out easily enough. The sun has just about burned the fog away."

They couldn't see from that side of the building, so they rode down in the elevator to the street. As quickly as it had come, the fog seemed to have vanished, leaving a clear and sparkling sky with a brilliant sun seeking out the last remnants of the previous day's snow. The four of them stood in the street, in the midst of digging equipment abandoned for the lunch hour, and stared up at the great glass side of the Jupiter Steel Building.

There was nothing to see. No body dangling in space, no window-washing scaffold. Nothing.

"Maybe he took it back up to the roof," Knox suggested.

"No footprints, remember?" McLove tried to cover his disappointment. "It was a long shot, anyway. The police checked the tenants for several floors beneath the broken window, and none of them saw anything. If Calm had landed on a scaffold, someone would have noticed it."

For a while longer they continued staring up at the building, each of them drawn to the tiny speck on the twenty-first floor where cardboard temporarily covered the shattered glass. "Why," Jason Greene asked suddenly, "didn't the cop down here see the falling glass when it hit? Was the window broken from the outside?"

McLove smiled. "No, the glass all went out, and

down. It was the drilling again; the sound covered the glass hitting. And that section of sidewalk was blocked off. The policeman didn't hear it hit, but we were able to find pieces of it. You can see where they were swept up."

W. T. Knox sighed deeply. "I don't know. I guess I'll go to lunch. Maybe we can all think better on a full stomach."

They separated a few moments after that, and McLove went back up to twenty-one for Margaret Mason. He found her in Billy Calm's office with Shirley Taggert. They were on their knees, running their hands over the oak-paneled wall.

"What's all this?" he asked.

"Just playing detective," Margaret said. "It was Shirley's idea. She mentioned about how Mr. Calm always wanted the office left exactly as it was, and with the directors' room right next door, even though both rooms were really too small. She thought of a secret panel of some sort."

"Margaret!" Shirley got reluctantly to her feet. "You make it sound like something out of a dime novel. Really, though, it was a possibility. It would explain how he left the room without jumping from the window."

"Don't keep me in suspense," McLove said. "Did you find anything?"

"Nothing. And we've been over both sides of the wall."

"They don't build them like they used to in merrie old England. Let's forget it and have lunch."

Shirley Taggert smoothed the wrinkles from her skirt. "You two go ahead. You don't want me along."

She was gone before they could protest, and McLove wasn't about to protest too loudly anyway. He didn't mind Shirley as a co-worker but, like everyone else, he was acutely conscious of her position in the office scheme of things. Even now, with Billy Calm vanished into the blue, she was still a dangerous force not to be shared at social hours.

He went downstairs with Margaret and they found an empty booth at the basement restaurant across the street. It was a place they often went after work for a drink, though lately he'd seen less of her outside of office hours. Thinking back to the first time he'd become aware of Margaret, he had only fuzzy memories of the tricks Sam Hamilton used to play. He loved to walk up behind the secretaries and tickle them—or occasionally even unzip their dresses—and he had quickly discovered that Margaret Mason was a likely candidate for his attentions. She always rewarded his efforts with a lively scream, without ever really getting upset.

It had been a rainy autumn evening some months back that McLove's path crossed hers most violently, linking them with a secret that made them drinking companions if nothing more. He'd been at loose ends that evening, and wandered into a little restaurant over by the East River. Surprisingly enough, Margaret Mason had been there, defending her honor in a back booth against a very drunk escort. McLove had moved in, flattened him with one punch, and they left him collapsed against a booth.

After that, on different drinking occasions, she had poured out the sort of lonely story he might have expected. And he'd listened and lingered, and sometimes fruitlessly imagined that he might become one of the men in her life. He knew there was no one for a long time after the bar incident, just as he knew now, by her infrequent free evenings, that there was someone again. Their drinking dates were more often being confined to lunch hours, when even two martinis were risky, and she never talked about being lonely or bored.

This day, over the first drink, she said, "It was terrible, really terrible."

"I know. It's going to get worse, I'm afraid. He's got to turn up somewhere."

"Dead or alive?"

"I wish I knew."

She lit a cigarette. "Will you be blamed for it?"

"I couldn't be expected to guard him from himself. Besides, I wasn't hired as a personal bodyguard. I'm chief of security, and that's all. I'm not a bodyguard or a detective. I don't know the first thing about fingerprints or clues. All I know about is people."

"What do you know about the Jupiter people?"

McLove finished his drink before answering. "Very little, really. Except for you, Hamilton and Knox and Greene and the rest of them are nothing more than names and faces. I've never even had a drink with any of them. I sit around at those meetings, and, frankly, I'm bored stiff. If anybody tries to blame me for this thing, they'll be looking for a new security chief."

Margaret's glass was empty too, and he signaled the waiter for two more. It was that sort of a day. When they came, he noticed that her usually relaxed face was a bit tense, and the familiar sparkle of her blue eyes was no longer in evidence. She'd been through a lot that morning, and even the drinks were failing to relax her.

"Maybe I'll quit with you," she said.

"It's been a long time since we've talked. How have things been?"

"All right." She said it with a little shrug.

"The new boyfriend?"

"Don't call him that, please."

"I hope he's an improvement over the last one."

"So do I. At my age you get involved with some strange ones."

"Do you love him?"

She thought a moment and then answered, "I guess I do."

He lit another cigarette. "When Billy Calm passed your desk this morning, did he seem . . . ?" The sentence stopped in the middle, cut short by a sudden scream from the street. McLove stood up and looked toward the door, where a waiter was already running outside to see what had happened.

"What is it?" Margaret asked.

"I don't know, but there seems to be a crowd gathering. Come on!"

Outside, they crossed the busy street and joined the crowd on the sidewalk of the Jupiter Building. "What happened?" Margaret asked somebody.

"Guy jumped, I guess."

They fought their way through now, and McLove's heart was pounding with the anticipation of what they would see. It was Billy Calm, all right, crushed and dead and looking very small. But there was no doubt it was he.

A policeman arrived from somewhere with a blanket and threw it over the thing on the sidewalk. McLove saw Sam Hamilton fighting his way through the crowd to their side. "Who is it?" Hamilton asked, but he too must have known.

"Billy," McLove told him. "It's Billy Calm."

Hamilton stared at the blanket for a moment and then looked at his watch. "Three hours and forty-five minutes since he jumped. I guess he must have taken the long way down."

* * *

W. T. Knox was pacing the floor like a caged animal, and Shirley Taggert was sobbing silently in a corner chair. It was over. Billy Calm had been found. The reaction was only beginning to set in. The worst, they all realized, was still ahead.

Jason Greene glared at Hamilton as he came into the office. "Well, the market's closed. Maybe you can stay off that phone for a while now."

Sam Hamilton didn't lose his grim smile. "Right now the price of Jupiter stock happens to be something that's important to all of us. You may be interested to know that it fell fourteen more points before they had to suspend trading in it for the rest of the session. They still don't have a closing price on it."

Knox held up both hands. "All right, all right! Let's everybody calm down and try to think. What do the police say, McLove?"

Feeling as if he were only a messenger boy between the two camps, McLove replied, "Billy was killed by the fall, and he'd been dead only a few minutes when they examined him. Body injuries would indicate that he fell from this height."

"But where was he for nearly four hours?" Greene wanted to know. "Hanging there, invisible, outside the window?"

Shirley Taggert collected herself enough to join the conversation. "He got out of that room somehow, and then came back and jumped later," she said. "That's how it must have been."

But McLove shook his head. "I hate to throw cold water on logical explanations, but that's how it *couldn't* have been. Remember, the windows in this building can't be opened. No other window has been broken, and the one on this floor is still covered by cardboard."

"The roof!" Knox suggested.

"No. There still aren't any footprints on the roof. We checked."

"Didn't anybody see him falling?"

"Apparently not till just before he hit."

"The thing's impossible," Knox said.

"No."

They were all looking at McLove. "Then what happened?" Greene asked.

"I don't know what happened, except for one thing. Billy Calm didn't hang in space for four hours. He didn't fall off the roof, or out of any other window, which means he could only have fallen from the window in the directors' room."

"But the cardboard . . ."

"Somebody replaced it afterward. And that means . . ."

"It means Billy was murdered," Knox breathed. "It means he didn't commit suicide."

McLove nodded. "He was murdered, and by somebody on this floor. Probably by somebody in this room." He glanced around.

Night settled cautiously over the city, with a scarlet sunset to the west that clung inordinately long to its reign over the skies. The police had returned, and the questioning went on, concurrently with long distance calls to Pittsburgh and five other cities where Jupiter had mills. There was confusion, somehow more so with the coming of darkness to the outer world. Secretaries and workers from the other floors gradually drifted home, but on twenty-one life went on.

"All right," Knox breathed finally, as it was nearing eight o'clock. "We'll call a directors' meeting for Monday morning, to elect a new president. That should give the market time to settle down, and let us know just how bad things really are. At the same time we'll issue a statement about the proposed merger. I gather we're in agreement that it's a dead issue for the time being."

Sam Hamilton nodded, and Jason Greene reluctantly shrugged his assent. Shirley Taggert looked up from her pad. "What about old Israel Black? With Mr. Calm dead, he'll be back in the picture."

Jason Greene shrugged. "Let him come. We can keep him in line. I never thought the old guy was so bad anyway, not really."

It went on like this, the talk, the bickering, the occasional flare of temper, until nearly midnight. Finally McLove felt he could excuse himself and head for home. In the outer office Margaret was straightening her desk, and he was surprised to realize that she was still around. He hadn't seen her in the past few hours.

"I thought you went home," he said.

"They might have needed me."

"They'll be going all night at this rate. How about a drink?"

"I should get home."

"All right. Let me take you, then. The subways aren't safe at this hour."

She turned her face up to smile at him. "Thanks, McLove. I can use someone like you tonight."

They went down together in the elevator, and out into a night turned decidedly coolish. He skipped the subway and hailed a cab. Settled back on the red leather seat, he asked, "Do you want to tell me about it, Margaret?"

He couldn't see her face in the dark, but after a moment she asked, "Tell you what?"

"What really happened. I've got part of it doped out already, so you might as well tell me the whole thing."

"I don't know what you mean, McLove. Really," she protested.

"All right," he said, and was silent for twenty blocks. Then, as they stopped for a traffic light, he added, "This is murder, you know. This isn't a kid's game or a simple love affair."

"There are some things you can't talk over with anyone. I'm sorry. Here's my place. You can drop me at the corner."

He got out with her and paid the cab driver. "I think I'd like to come up," he said quietly.

"I'm sorry, McLove. I'm awfully tired."

"Want me to wait for him down here?"

She sighed and led the way inside, keeping silent until they were in the little three-room apartment he'd visited only once before. Then she shrugged off her raincoat and asked, "How much do you know?"

"I know he'll come here tonight, of all nights."

"What was it? What told you?"

"A lot of things. The elevator, for one."

She sat down. "What about the elevator?"

"Right after Billy Calm's supposed arrival, and suicide, I ran to his private elevator. It wasn't on twenty-one. It had to come up from below. He never rode any other elevator. When I finally remembered it, I realized he hadn't come up on that one, or it would still have been there."

Margaret sat frozen in the chair, her head cocked a little to one side as if listening. "What does it matter to you? You told me just this noon that none of them meant anything to you."

"They didn't; they don't. But I guess you do, Margaret. I can see what he's doing to you, and I've got to stop it before you get in too deep."

"I'm in about as deep as I can ever be, right now."

"Maybe not."

"You said you believed me. You told them all that I couldn't have been acting when I screamed out his name."

He closed his eyes for a moment, thinking that he'd heard something in the hallway. Then he said, "I did believe you. But then after the elevator bit, I realized that you never called Calm by his first name. It was always Mr. Calm, not Billy, and it would have been the same even in a moment of panic. Because he was still the president of the company. The elevator and the name—I put them together, and I knew it wasn't Billy Calm who had walked into that directors' room."

There was a noise at the door, the sound of a familiar key turning in the lock. "No," she whispered, almost to herself. "No, no, no . . ."

"And that should be our murderer now," McLove said, leaping to his feet.

"Billy!" she screamed. "Billy, run! It's a trap!"

But McLove was already to the door, yanking it open, staring into the startled, frightened face of W. T. Knox.

Sometimes it ends with a flourish, and sometimes only with the dull thud of a collapsing dream. For Knox the whole thing had been only an extension of some sixteen hours in his life span. The fantastic plot, which had been set in motion by his attempt at suicide that morning at the Jupiter Steel Building, came to an end when he succeeded in leaping to his death from the bathroom window of Margaret's apartment, while they sat waiting for the police to come.

The following morning, with only two hours' sleep behind him McLove found himself facing Greene and Hamilton and Shirley Taggert once more, telling them the story of how it had been. There was an empty chair in the office, too, and he wondered vaguely whether it had been meant for Knox or Margaret.

"He was just a poor guy at the end of his rope," McLove told them. "He was deeply involved in an affair with Margaret Mason, and he'd sunk all his money into a desperate gamble that the merger wouldn't go through. He sold a lot of Jupiter stock short, figuring that when the merger talks collapsed, the price would fall sharply. Only Billy Calm called from his plane yesterday morning and said the merger was on. Knox thought about it for an hour or so, and did some figuring. When he realized he'd be wiped out, he went into the directors' room to commit suicide."

"Why?" Shirley Taggert interrupted. "Why couldn't he jump out his own window?"

"Because there's a setback two stories down on his side. He couldn't have cleared it. He wanted a smooth drop to the sidewalk. Billy Calm could hardly have taken a running jump through the window. It was far off the floor even for a tall man, and Billy was short. And remember the slivers of glass at the bottom of the pane? When I remembered them, and remembered the height of the bottom sill from the floor, I knew that no one—especially a short man—could have gone through that window without knocking them out. No, Knox passed Margaret's desk, muttered some sort of farewell, and entered the room just as I came out of Calm's office. He smashed the window with a chair so he wouldn't have to try a dive through the thick glass, head first. And then he got ready to jump."

"Why didn't he?"

"Because he heard Margaret shout his name from the outer office. And with the shouted word *Billy*, a sudden plan came to him in that split second. He re-crossed the small office quickly, and stood behind the door as we entered, knowing that I would think it was Billy Calm who had jumped. As soon as we were in the room, he simply stepped out and stood there. I thought he had arrived with the rest of you, and you, of course thought he had entered the room with Margaret and me. I never gave it a second thought, because I was looking for Calm. But Margaret fainted when she saw he was still alive."

"But she said it was Billy Calm who entered the office," Greene protested.

"Not until later. She was starting to deny it, in fact, when she saw Knox and fainted. Remember, he carried her into the next room, and he was alone with her when she came to. He told her his money would be safe if only people thought Calm dead for a few hours. So she went along with her lover; I needn't remind you he was a handsome fellow, even though he was married. She went along with what we all thought happened, not realizing it would lead to murder."

Sam Hamilton lit a cigar. "The stock did go down."

"But not enough. And Knox knew Calm's arrival would reactivate the merger and ruin everything. I don't think he planned to kill Calm in the beginning, but as the morning wore on it became the only way out. He waited in the private elevator when he knew Billy was due to arrive, slugged him, carried his small body to that window while we were all out to lunch, and threw him out, replacing the cardboard afterward."

"And the stock went down some more," Hamilton said.

"That's right."

"She called him Billy," Shirley reminded them.

"It was his name. We all called him W.T., but he signed his memo to me *William T. Knox*. I suppose the two of them thought it was a great joke, her calling him Billy when they were together."

"Where is she now?" someone asked.

"The police are still questioning her. I'm going down there now, to be with her. She's been through a lot." He thought probably this would be his final day at Jupiter Steel. Somehow *he* was tired of these faces and their questions.

But as he got to his feet, Sam Hamilton asked, "Why wasn't Billy here for the meeting at ten? Where was he for those missing hours? And how did Knox know when he would really arrive?"

"Knox knew because Billy phoned him, as he had earlier in the morning."

"Phoned him? From where?"

McLove turned to stare out the window, at the clear blue of the morning sky. "From his private plane. Billy Calm was circling the city for nearly three hours. He couldn't land because of the fog."

THE FLY SWATTER
by Frank Sisk

Twice a day nearly every day Sr. Giampietro Saccovino—*l'Americano ricco,* as the Portofinese referred to him—descended from his villa in the pine-shrouded foothills above the Via Roma and refreshed himself for a while at a table on the piazza outside the Trattoria Navicello.

He came first in the morning not long after the *carabiniere* had unpadlocked the heavy chain that stretched across the narrow road at the town's entrance from one stone post to another—about seven-thirty. He came again late in the afternoon, a few hours before sunset. Generally he was alone, although there were those rare occasions when he might be accompanied by a woman—one of a number who visited the villa with some degree of regularity; women who, in the eyes of the parochial natives, looked suspiciously like high-priced *sgualdrine* down from Genova. The *signore* nevertheless was adjudged *il gentiluomo,* for man is not born to be a saint.

Besides, Sr. Saccovino tipped most handsomely all who served him.

Also he wore shimmering silk suits of a conservative cut. The third finger of his left hand shone with a stone worth perhaps two million lire or more. Another fortune was represented by the ruby-studded clasp formed like a scimitar that adorned a succession of hand-painted cravattes. Then there was the thin gold watch, not much larger than a Communion wafer, which told not only the hour down to the split of a second but the day of the week as well. Not to be overlooked either was the slender pen of (some said) platinum that the *signore* employed with a smile and a flourish to sign the presented chits, never failing to write down that generous gratuity. Then—the pearl-handled fly swatter.

This fly swatter was final proof, if ever such proof were needed, that Sr. Saccovino was not only a rich American gentleman but *eccentrico* in the bargain, and this could be the very best kind to have around.

He entered Portofino toward the middle of March on board the yacht *Santa Costanza*. The *marinai* who operate the taxi craft in the harbor quickly learned that he had chartered the yacht at Bastia in Corse and had sailed here by way of Livorno and La Spezia.

Five boat-taxi and three mulecart trips were required to transport the *signore*'s luggage from the yacht, which soon thereafter raised anchor, to the villa that had been unoccupied since the previous spring when the owner, a crusty old port-drinking *inglés,* had succumbed to *il colpo apopletico* while watching, as was his diurnal wont, the evening sun sink like a big orange into the Ligurian Sea.

Sr. Saccovino made his first exploratory visits to the quayside a few days after settling in. Flies being scarce at this time of the year, he came armed only with his warm, engaging smile and his soft but authoritative voice. His *"Buon giorno,"* his *"Buona sera,"* his

"Venga qua, per piacere," his *"Mille grazie,"* were all uttered without the trace of a foreign accent. When he ordered lasagna al pesto (a regional manifestation of squared pasta covered with a green sauce in which basil is prominent, and sprinkled with grated goat cheese and crushed pine nuts), he obviously knew exactly what to expect.

These pleasant aspects of the man, combined with the dignified swaths of gray in his sleek black hair and the corded wrinkles in his mastifflike face, earned him immediately a certain homage from the townspeople.

The pearl-handled fly swatter didn't appear until the last days of May. By then the *mosce* were growing bold and bothersome. While strolling from shop to stall and along the quays, the *signore* carried the fly swatter as inconspicuously as possible. Often as not he concealed the greater part of the beautiful handle up the sleeve of his jacket in the fashion of a professional knife thrower, but whenever he sat at a table, he always laid it out in plain view on the cloth to the right of the place setting, ready for instant use, and he could use it with remarkable accuracy.

Each morning the *signore* broke his fast with the same nourishment—caffe ristretto, warm rolls with sweet butter and tart marmalade, a bottle of mineral water, more caffe ristretto. Mercia was usually the *cameriera* at his table and she batted her brown eyes outlandishly as she served him. She was a plump young widow with two small children.

In the evening, when he consumed a bottle of white wine with perhaps pasta con frutti di mare, he was most respectfully attended by a gaunt, middle-aged bachelor named Silvestro, whose voice and mien were as funereal as an undertaker's at the obsequies.

During the noontime repast in the trattoria's aromatic kitchen, these two—Mercia and Silvestro—were forever dissecting and analyzing every nuance of Sr. Saccovino's utterances and behavior. The following colloquy, typical in mood, occurred one day in July:

"This morning the *signore* praised the cool breeze coming in from the harbor."

"Last evening he spoke well of it too."

"Did he dine alone?"

"As if you didn't already know, Mercia."

"What did she look like?"

"Her hair was as black as a raven's wing . . ."

"You have a poet's tongue, Silvestro."

". . . Her eyelids were tinted green. A tiny black star occupied her left cheekbone. Her skin was the color of fresh cream. She possessed a pair of *mammelle* the like of which you see on—"

"Ah, one of that type again."

"What else?"

"What else indeed. He is a man with blood in his veins. His nature is affectionate."

"Last evening he ordered two bottles of Cinque Terre and permitted the lady to drink a bottle and a half."

"He is an abstemious man. His name is a gross misnomer. What did he eat?"

"Fish soup with an extra pinch of basil. Squid simmered in oil and garlic. Anchovies and capers in lemon juice. Bearded mussels in mustard. Pasta with clam sauce. Wild strawberries in brandy."

"The food of love."

"I must say he appeared to be wonderfully prepared for the lady by the time she had finished the last of the wine."

"I can well believe it. Did he kill many flies?"

"Only three in my presence. The lady was a powerful distraction."

"And the gratuity, it was generous?"

"More than generous. Eight thousand lire."

"So it goes. This morning he presented the *carabiniere* with two long cigars and bought a dozen lace handkerchiefs from old Camilla."

"The dark hours of night rewarded him."

"Over coffee he inquired after my *bambini* by name."

"He is a most courteous gentleman."

"He asked why I do not marry again."

"How do you reply to such a question?"

"To the *signore* I said that a good man is not to be found in the market as readily as a good fish."

"Alas, that is the truth."

"And he answered—do you wish to hear what the *signore* said to that, Silvestro?"

"I think so."

"He said that many a sweet-fleshed fish is overlooked because it is thought to be not fat enough or young enough."

"That also is true."

"Such a fine fish is Silvestro, he said."

"He actually said that, Mercia?"

"I swear on the cross."

"Ah."

"He spoke in jest, of course."

"Of course."

"Then with his platinum pen he wrote out a gratuity of thirty-five hundred lire on a chit of half that sum. A night of love is a wonderful experience, Silvestro."

Toward the latter part of September—*sabato, settembre ventisimo primo,* as it would be remembered locally—the Hairy Tourist arrived in a rented Fiat just as the *carabiniere* was making fast the chain across the Via Roma. The time was 10:04 A.M.

"What's the big idea?" the Hairy Tourist asked as the *carabiniere* snapped shut the padlock. "I want to drive this heap into town." He spoke abominable Italian with an atrocious foreign accent.

"No motor vehicle is allowed in the town, *signor*," said the *carabiniere,* whose name was Umberto. "Except between the hours of seven and ten o'clock in the morning. And then we allow only those vehicles authorized to make deliveries of essential commodities."

"What the hell kind of a town is this anyway?"

"An old town, *signor*. A peaceful town. A town as yet unblessed by the fumes of *benzina*."

"Okay, admiral. Where do I park the heap?"—using the word *mucchio*.

"You may park the *mucchio* where the *mucca* grazes," Umberto said, pleased at the way he had worked a cow into the conversation.

It was Sr. Daddario, manager of the Hotel Nazionale, who dubbed this man the Hairy Tourist. The proffered passport identified him as Henry A. Scotti of St. Louis, Missouri, U.S.A., but Sr. Daddario was more impressed by the bushy black eyebrows, the sweeping black mustachios, the dense black beard, and the flowing black hair that fell nearly to his shoulders.

"You are fortunate, *signor*," Daddario said. "Because of a late cancelation we have a single room available."

"I'll take it," the Hairy Tourist said, setting his luggage, an airlines flight bag, on the counter as he signed in.

"On the other hand, you are not so fortunate. This room is available for three days only."

"That's all right with me, captain. I'll be checking out early tomorrow morning."

"In that case, *signor,* you must pay in advance."

The room, a small one as are all the rooms in the Hotel Nazionale, was situated on the second floor and overlooked the town square. The Hairy Tourist remained in it just long enough to drop the flight bag on the bed and then he was outside wandering around the town and asking questions of everyone about everything.

Where is the Church of San Martino? Who lives in the Castello Brown? Are there dolphins in these waters? Where is the Church of St. George? Is the fishing good outside the harbor? How cold does it get here in the winter? How old are some of these old arches? Do many tourists come here? Where do most of the tourists come from? Are there any Americans in town now? Has Sr. Giampietro Saccovino been living here long? Where does he live? When he dines here in town, does he dine alone? How many miles is it to Rome? How much is a kilometer?

Sr. Saccovino strolled down from his villa an hour before sunset, graciously greeting all whom he met on the way, and finally settled down at a table outside the Trattoria Navicello. The chair he sat in, his favorite, afforded him a view of the harbor, with its flotilla of pleasure craft, impeded only by an occasional passerby. He enjoyed the warm, glittering look of the water at this time of day.

Silvestro materialized at his side with a mournful *"Buona sera"* and *"Desidera, signor?"*

The *signore* ordered a bottle of Cinque Terre and the antipasto and placed the pearl-handled fly swatter on the table. The flies of September are obnoxious and hardy. In a moment one of the creatures buzzed past his ear and settled on the corner of a folded napkin. The *signore*'s veined right hand moved stealthily toward the pearl handle, grasped it firmly, lifted it slightly, slapped it down unerringly.

The crumpled fly left a spot of black blood on the white napkin. Using the rubber palm of the swatter, the *signore* meticulously shoved the small corpse off the table onto the cobbles.

"This I had to see with my own two eyes," twanged an American voice close by. "Old J. P. Sacco killin' flies for his kicks."

The *signore* raised his eyes from the spot of blood and saw the Hairy Tourist standing where Silvestro normally stood, with what appeared to be an exultant grin breaking its way through the hirsuteness. The *signore*'s eyes grew suddenly slitted but his voice, when he spoke, was toned to its usual softness. *"Buona sera, signor. A que ora c'è l'omicidio?"*

"Let's talk United States," the Hairy Tourist said.

"As you wish," said the *signore*. "Since you probably plan to stay awhile, take a seat."

The Hairy Tourist, sitting in a chair that placed his back to the harbor, said, "You got a very quaint scene here, J.P."

"It's restful."

"I guess. A man could rest in peace here. Forever."

"There are worse things. What is your name?"

"What's the diff? We ain't gonna know each other long enough to get acquainted."

"We're already acquainted," the *signore* said, lifting the swatter and striking down a fly in mid-air. "You're acquainted with me by sight and reputation. I'm acquainted with you because I've known a dozen of your kind."

"It takes one to know one," the Hairy Tourist said.

"Don't equate me with yourself, young man. I never did a thing in my life just for money alone."

"Oh yeah."

Silvestro arrived with the wine and cast a look of sad inquiry at the newcomer.

"*Bene, grazie.* Silvestro," the *signore* said. "*Un altro bicchiere, per favore.*" To the Hairy Tourist: "What will you drink?"

"What's good enough for you is good enough for me."

"Would you care for an antipasto?"

"Why not?"

The *signore* gave instructions to Silvestro, who left for a moment and returned with another glass. He poured a dram for the *signore*'s taste of approval and then filled the Hairy Tourist's glass to the brim.

"Can this ginzo understand English?" the Hairy Tourist asked after Silvestro's departure.

"No more than ten or twelve simple words," the *signore* replied, his attention on a fly that had landed a few inches from the tip of his fork.

Taking a swallow of wine, the Hairy Tourist watched the *signore* slap the insect fatally and flick it from the table. "What's all this business with the fancy fly swatter?" he asked.

"Swatting flies is second nature to me," the *signore* said. "The first money I ever made was paid to me for swatting flies."

"You're tryin' to put me on, J.P."

"Not at all."

"This is Cutter Moran you're talkin' to."

The *signore* took a thoughtful sip of the wine. "I knew a Cutie Moran back in the old days."

"None other than my old man."

"You don't say. Like father like son. As I remember, Cutie got too cute for his own good. And suddenly he wasn't around anymore."

"Just like you, J.P. Suddenly you weren't around

nomore and one hell of a lot of bread went with you."

"I took my retirement fund, Cutter. That's all."

"I ain't interested in the details, man. All I'm gettin' paid for is findin' you and finishin' you."

"How did you find me, by the way?"

"It wasn't easy."

Silvestro served the antipasto and asked whether there would be anything else. The *signore* thanked Silvestro and promised to signal when further service was required. Silvestro bowed somberly and left.

The Hairy Tourist fingered a slice of red peperoncino from the dish in front of him and popped it into the whiskery opening in his face. "One thing's for sure, J.P.," he said, chewing, "you got off the beaten track when you picked this burg. They don't even let cars inside. Wow, these peppers are hot!" He downed a big draft of wine. "Now, if you'd gone to Rome or Naples, we got connections there and could've dug you out in a couple a weeks. In fact that's where I was goin' first, to Rome, but then I decided I better see an uncle a mine in Corsica I hadn't seen in four–five years, a nice old guy retired like you but clean, and that's where the old coincidence come in. I'm in a waterfront joint outside Bastia a couple nights ago and I get talkin' baseball with this cat speaks United States pretty good and it turns out he goes to sea whenever a job turns up, except he ain't been to sea since way last spring when he gets a berth on a yacht chartered by a rich American named Saccovino, this cat says—Jampeetro Saccovino—and I think to myself, I wonder. Plain dumb luck, but here I am, two days later, drinkin' wine with old J.P. Sacco himself."

"Do your employers in St. Louis know about this

dumb luck?" the *signore* asked, laying another fly low.

"Not yet. Until I seen you in person I wasn't a hundred percent sure you'd be the same cat who chartered that yacht. Besides, I hate to use the phones in this damn country. I don't trust the damn phones, you know what I mean."

"And quite right too, Cutter."

Beads of perspiration began to form on the bare area of the Hairy Tourist's face, that space between the bushy eyebrows and the low bangs. "That pepper was *hot*." From the lapel pocket of his jacket he flicked a handkerchief embroidered with a blue *M* and patted his brow. "Do you eat these damn peppers as a regular thing?"

"Yes," the *signore* said. "I find they sharpen my wits."

"Like swalleyin' a lighted match."

"Well, you've got to be properly dressed to eat these peppers."

"Oh, sure you do."

"That turtleneck sweater you're wearing, for instance, and the tweed jacket. Absolutely no good for anyone who plans to eat a few red peppers."

"Yeah, you gotta be naked to eat them."

The *signore* chuckled. "It might help at that, yes it might. But I can promise you one thing, Cutter, you'll definitely be more comfortable without that heavy wig and those phony whiskers."

The Hairy Tourist registered confoundment, at least to the degree that it was able to seep through the camouflage, and then tried to cover it up by pouring more wine into his own glass. Finally he said, "A real sharpie, ain't you? They told me that about you—a real sharp cookie. Don't ever rate him low, they said. He's got a sharp eye for a lot a little things nobody else notices. That's why he live so long. He keeps an eye open for the—"

The *signore*'s swatter took toll of another fly.

"Flies they failed to mention. Little things like flies. What's this fix you got on flies, man? You act like a cat with a bad habit."

"It's an old habit, anyway," the *signore* said. "I've already told you that."

"Yeah, you made money at it. Tell me more."

"Are you really interested, Cutter?"

"Until the sun goes down, J.P., you're my main interest in life."

"That's very flattering, Cutter. *Silvestro!*"

"Keep it cool, man."

"That's why I'm ordering more wine."

"Whatever you do, you talk United States."

"That wouldn't be cool at all, Cutter. I always converse with Silvestro in Italian."

"Then keep it short. My old lady was Italiano and I capeesh and don't you forget it."

Silvestro materialized and leaned deferentially toward Sr. Saccovino, who ordered another bottle of wine and two plates of lasagna al pesto. The Hairy Tourist followed every word with the big-eyed concentration of a bloodhound.

"My first flies," the *signore* said as Silvestro withdrew. "I was eight or nine at the time, a small boy, small for my age, my father already dead, my dear mother forced to work long hours in sweatshops . . . Are you sure you want to hear this, Cutter?"

"With violins it would be better, but keep talkin'."

"My mother had a younger brother, Isacco—Ike to all who knew him—and somehow he got enough money together to rent a small shop in our neighborhood. Much later I was able to guess where the money came from. Anyway, for sale in Ike's shop were olive oil, cheeses, prosciutto, sardines, salami, tomato paste, figs, mushrooms, peppers hotter than even these in this antipasto, braciole—"

"Skip the Little Italy part, man, and get to the flies. That's the part I'm interested in. How you started out makin' money by killin' flies."

"Of course. Well, my uncle's inventory attracted flies in the warm weather. And although this inventory was merely a front for his real stock in trade, he had a fussy prejudice against—"

"You mean he was like hustlin' somethin' else out of the back room there, I guess. Right, man?"

"That's right, Cutter. This was during the time of the Eighteenth Amendment. Ever hear of it?"

"Sure, the no-booze bust."

"Right again. Uncle Ike didn't sell enough Italian food to pay the rent. He moved what was known in those days as hooch. Still, he had a certain number of food customers, old-country people, who came in for a pound of provolone or something like that, and he honored them by keeping the front of the store neat and clean. No flies allowed. He let me hang out there after school and on Saturdays for the express purpose of keeping the place free of flies. I used a rolled-up newspaper to kill them and earned a penny a corpse. At the end of a good day I often collected as much as . . ."

While the *signore* was talking, Silvestro served the lasagna and more wine and the sun slipped into the shimmering sea and violent shadows crept rapidly over the pines on the uplands behind the town. Soon the darkness lay everywhere outside the meager light from the old-fashioned street lamps and the boats moored in the harbor.

The Hairy Tourist washed down the last morsel

with the last of the wine. "I feel so good right now," he said, "that I almost might grab the check right off the waiter."

"Don't strain yourself," the *signore* said. "I have a weekly account here."

"This could be the week it don't get paid." The Hairy Tourist chortled mirthlessly in his beard.

"That depends on how well you do your job."

"I ain't flubbed a job yet, J.P."

"*Silvestro!*"

The Hairy Tourist, sobering, leaned across the table. "Watch yourself with the waiter, man. One word outta line and I'll put a shiv in your gut so fast you won't have time to say *scusa*."

"Don't worry, Cutter. I have due respect for any man with a name like yours." The *signore* took the proffered tray from Silvestro and signed the chit with his renowned pen, adding a fat gratuity.

"*Mille grazie, signor,*" Silvestro said.

"*Prego, Silvestro,*" the *signore* said benignly.

"*Buona notte, signor.*"

"*Arrivederci*, Silvestro."

A few minutes later the *signore* and the Hairy Tourist passed from the town square side by side. The *signore* was carrying the fly swatter, pearl handle up, under his right arm, much in the manner of an NCO with a baton on parade. The Hairy Tourist was smoking a cigarette silently, all talked out.

As they proceeded around one of the stone posts that held the chain across the Via Roma, the *signore* said conversationally, "Did you come by car?"

"Yeah, that's right."

"Where did you park it?"

"You'll see soon enough."

"You plan to give me a ride?"

"Just a short one."

Out in the darkness, away from the lights of the town, a thousand stars became visible around a nearly full moon. In a moment the *signore's* searching eyes caught a metallic glint ahead on the side of the road—a steel wheel disc.

"Do you have another cigarette?" he asked.

"Sure do," the Hairy Tourist said.

"I could use one."

"Okay, but no tricks." The Hairy Tourist took a pack of cigarettes from one pocket of his tweed jacket and a switchblade knife from the other. "Just in case," he said, snapping out the business end of the knife.

With his left hand the *signore* pulled a cigarette from the pack. "Do you have a match?"

"You want me to spit for you too?" Returning the cigarette pack to his pocket, the Hairy Tourist came up with a butane lighter. "Here you are, man," he said, clicking a blue flame into life. "Enjoy it. You got time for maybe five good drags."

The *signore* was standing ramrod straight, a few inches shorter than his companion. He still held the fly swatter tucked under his arm like a baton. As the Hairy Tourist leaned forward to touch the cigarette in the *signore's* mouth with the shimmying flame, the *signore's* left hand went swiftly to the pearl handle and gave it a double twist. There was a vibrating sound—*piiing-giing-giing*—and the lighter shook convulsively.

"Aaah gug ach," the Hairy Tourist said, dropping the switchblade and reaching for his throat. In a few seconds he got down on his knees and in another few seconds he prostrated himself at the *signore's* feet.

After rolling the body over on its back, the *signore* squatted beside it and began to remove the wig, the eyebrows, the beard, the mustache. The face thus re-

vealed struck a chord of memory. Cutie Moran all
over again, twenty years later, with a few minor
variations. Still stupid, still inept. Like father like
son.

He raked the nearby ground with his fingers until
he located the butane lighter. Then with the lighter's
help he explored the throatal region until he found
what he was looking for—the tip of a narrow, stain-
less-steel shaft protruding a tiny fraction of an inch
from the folds of the turtleneck sweater. With a pair
of jeweler's pliers taken from the pocket of his silk
coat, he grasped the tip of the shaft and gently
pulled, presently extracting a needle six inches long.
He wrapped it carefully in the monogrammed handkerchief which he took from the breast pocket of the
dead man's jacket and set it on the ground next to the
fly swatter for reloading at a later time. He stripped
off the jacket and went through the pockets. Wallet,
money, traveler's checks, *two* passports.

The first passport, containing a photograph of the
Hairy Tourist, identified him as Henry A. Scotti of
St. Louis, Missouri; the second, depicting a living
likeness of the hairless corpse, was issued to Charles
Moran, also of St. Louis.

"*Addio,* Enrico," the *signore* muttered. "*Addio,*
Carlo."

He spread the tweed jacket on the ground. Onto its
lining he dropped the passports and the switchblade.
The turtleneck sweater followed. Next went the slacks,
in the hip pocket of which he found the car keys.
When the corpse was stark naked he dragged it several yards off the road and propped it in a sitting
position with its back against a boulder.

He made a bundle of the tweed jacket by tying its
arms together. He carried the bundle to the car—a
rented Fiat, he noticed—and locked it in the trunk.

He climbed into the driver's seat and drove the car in the direction of Paraggi until he reached a place where the road hung recklessly over the Golfo Marconi. He got out of the car, its motor idling, and walked it with some effort to the brink of doom. As it began its irreversible tilt, he lit the butane lighter and tossed it into the front seat. Then he began the longish walk—three kilometers, at least—back to the villa, reloading the pearl-handled fly swatter en route.

The next day was *domenica*, God's day, but the Portofinese weren't talking about God. The main subject of conversation was the discovery of the nude body of an unidentified man on the Via Roma outside the town. The man was generally assumed to have been an Italian because of the tattoo on the left forearm—a serpent (evil) climbing a cross (good). Though not yet officially determined, the cause of death was attributed by Umberto the *carabiniere*, who had seen such things, to a fishbone's lodgment sidewise in the man's gullet. Nobody seemed to wonder why a naked stranger would be eating bony fish out there at night.

A minor topic of conversation that same morning concerned the fact that Henry A. Scotti had departed unseen from the Hotel Nazionale without taking along his airlines flight bag which contained, according to the manager, Sr. Daddario, a safety razor, a package of razor blades, an aerosol can of shaving cream and a bottle of lime-scented lotion.

"Why should such a hairy devil carry around articles like these?" Sr. Daddario was fond of asking whenever the subject arose, which was not often.

On this same day Sr. Saccovino killed twenty-seven flies.

DOUBLE ZERO
by Robert Colby

At breakfast that Friday in June, Anita Waldron merely toyed with her food and waited with growing impatience for her husband to complete some notes he was jotting down between sips of coffee. These were notes for one of the eternal staff meetings Mark now held since he had been elevated from program director to manager of a television station in San Diego. Although he loved Anita more than all else, at thirty-four Mark was a dedicated career man with a feverish sense of responsibility.

Anita was six years younger. Small and trim; with black hair and dark eyes, she had the intense, exotic attraction of the most elegant Latin women, a quality inherited from her Mexican mother. Although her English was flawless, so was her Spanish, spoken with the accent of a native.

The couple had met at a broadcasters' convention in Los Angeles little more than a year ago. At the time Anita was giving Spanish lessons on TV over a PBS station. They had commuted back and forth to spend alternate weekends with each other. A few such weekends and they were married.

They were still passionately in love. Mark told Anita that their present life together seemed no less ecstatic than their honeymoon, though of course they had minor disagreements and a few stormy arguments. The latter usually ended when Anita would laugh suddenly and inappropriately at the peak of one of Mark's executive-type lectures.

As Mark tucked his notebook into a pocket and looked up, Anita said, "Darling, Iris Landry just called me from L.A. You were in conference with your notes and I suppose you didn't even hear the phone. But I've been trying to get in touch with you ever since."

He smiled. "Sorry about that, honey. I've got an early meeting and I'm a bit fogged under. Who's Iris—what's her name?"

"Landry. I used to consider her my best friend. Remember?"

He nodded. "You spoke of her, yes. But I never got to meet her."

Anita nibbled her English muffin. "That's because Iris moved to Las Vegas and got married."

Mark puffed his cigarette and made a face. "I always thought people went to Vegas for a divorce."

"Iris did both. She got married *and* divorced in Vegas. Now she's back."

"I feel sorry for people who don't have what we have to make it stick," Mark said earnestly.

"Yes, well, Iris was simply crushed by the divorce. She's very down right now. Terribly lonely and depressed. Almost—"

"Suicidal?"

Anita chewed her lip, shrugged. "Who knows what

people will do under deep stress? Anyway, she needs me desperately. And—and impulsively I agreed to fly there for the weekend, to see if I can help her put the pieces together again. It would be rough for both of us and I'd miss you. But would you mind, darling, under the circumstances?"

His uneven, homely-handsome features darkened, the gloomy prospect of her absence hollowing inside him. Then, abruptly, to hide his dismay, he smiled. "Under the circumstances, I think you should go," he said. "And I only mind losing you for a while."

"How sweet," she said with a flash of brilliant teeth against café au lait skin. "Theres's a plane I could take at eleven-thirty."

Mark rejected the thought of fixing a lonely meal at their suburban home that evening. He had dinner in town, then drove home to watch the Box, faithfully dialing in his own channel. At ten o'clock, when Anita had not yet called him from L.A. as promised, he lost his concentration, cut the set and went to the kitchen for a beer. He carried it out to the patio at the edge of a spacious backyard adorned by towering old trees, shrubs and flowers. He set the extension phone on a table beside him and gazed at it with annoyance as a symbol of rejection.

His irritation was replaced by a small current of anxiety when by eleven the indifferent phone still remained silent. Anita was not casual about keeping in touch. She would usually be eager to exchange a few intimate words to bridge the distance. At midnight, his imagination constructing any number of possible calamities and intrigues, he fought the urge to call her for assurance.

It seemed a childish indulgence, an alarmist reaction. Further, it might appear that he was checking on her. On occasion she had put him down hard for being unreasonably jealous, finding cause for jealousy where none existed. Nothing provoked her quite so much as a display of mistrust.

He went to their bedroom and tried to sleep. Without Anita nestled beside him, the king-sized expanse seemed a vast, chilly wasteland. Through the night he merely dozed, often waking to reach for the bedside lamp and squint at the time.

Saturday dawned with a sense of unreality, a depressing malaise. He got up and dressed unnecessarily —top management had weekends off—made a careless breakfast and read the paper from front to back.

At nine o'clock, congratulating himself upon a masterpiece of self-control, he snatched up the phone, got the number from L.A. information, and dialed Iris Landry.

The signal pulsed on and on, sounding as distant and lonely as Mars. As he was about to hang up, a female voice, wrapped in the fuzz of sleep, finally tiptoed across the line.

"Is this Iris—Iris Landry?" He was almost shouting.

"Yes. Yes, it is." She sounded more alert, but wary.

"May I speak with Anita?"

"Anita?"

"That's right, Anita!" he said acidly. "This is Mark Waldron, her husband—Anita's husband."

An unbelievable silence threatened his sanity. Then Iris said, "Anita isn't here just now. Could you call back?"

"Whatta you mean she's not there! It's nine in the morning. All last night I waited for a call from her. So where in hell is she?"

"It won't help to scream at me, Mark. Iris went out and she hasn't come in yet."

"She hasn't been there all night?"

"Well, uh—I've been asleep, so I couldn't say just when she—"

"Now—now wait a minute. Please don't bull me, Iris. This has the stink of trouble and I want it right on the line. Just tell me the truth. Otherwise—"

There was a pause. "Very well, then, Mark. Anita is out with a friend—an old friend of sorts. She left with him yesterday afternoon."

"What friend? A man! I thought she went there to see you, desperate situation and all that. Now you tell me she took off with some guy. What've we got here—an arrangement?"

"I had nothing to do with it, believe me, Mark."

"You didn't, huh? Does this character she's with have a name?"

"Yes, and not a very good one. You may not remember because it was some time back, but Anita said she told you about this creep. She used to go with him. She had a very big thing for him before he was sent to prison for smuggling hard dope across the Mexican border by the bushel. His name is Rick Conway."

He remembered at once. "Iris, are you saying that Conway is out? I thought he had years more to serve."

"He did, oh, he did! But his shyster lawyer got him a new trial on a technicality."

"I see. Yeah, I get the picture, but I just can't believe it." His voice faded. He was stunned, felt as if he were falling in a runaway elevator. "So yesterday this Conway met Anita at your place. Then they simply picked up the pieces and buzzed off together. Is that it?"

"No. That's not the way it was at all. She went with him under some rather peculiar circumstances."

"What does *that* mean?"

"Well, for one thing there was some heavy cash involved, money he'd left with Anita. You know about that?"

"Yes, but Anita said she turned his money over to you a long time ago."

"Uh, that's true, she did. But—listen, I don't want to talk about it on the phone. Maybe it would be best for you to get up here, soon as you can."

"That's exactly what I had in mind. I'll be on my way in a few minutes. Iris—do you have an idea in the world where I can find them?"

"Not one. I can't even guess."

"Think about it. Try to come up with a lead."

"I'll do that, Mark. Now let me give you the address . . ."

He decided not to wait for a plane, for he could drive it in a couple of hours. On the way out he crossed to a desk in the living room and lifted his .38 from a drawer. He examined the load, hesitated. If he caught up with Conway, in his present frame of mind the gun would be a dangerous temptation. If needed, he had over six feet and just under two hundred pounds of solid beef to deal with Conway. It wouldn't be the first time he had flattened some joker who was asking for trouble—and Rick Conway was just begging for it.

Mark returned the gun to the drawer and hustled out to his car. He drove briskly, the heavy traffic of the hour taking his attention until he left the city behind. Then he began to prod his memory for those details Anita had volunteered concerning her involvement with Conway.

She had related the story briefly and reluctantly, as if it were a happening she felt obligated to confess. She had met Conway while browsing through a Mexican import shop he owned in L.A. She believed him to be precisely what he appeared to be—an importer who sold odd pieces of furniture, native art, leather goods and other items he bought during frequent trips to Mexico. He was young and friendly and nice-looking. When she learned that he spoke Spanish almost as fluently as she did, they became friends. No doubt they became a lot more than friends, but Anita was careful not to arouse Mark's excessive jealousy with explicit details.

In any case, Anita went to work for Conway in his store and was soon such an asset that he put her in charge while he was on buying trips in Mexico. Returning from one of these trips, Rick and a confederate were arrested on the American side for smuggling a large quantity of hard drugs concealed with the imports they were hauling.

Out on bail and sure of his impending conviction, Rick told Anita that he would need a stake when he was released. For some such emergency he had a cache of $140,000 that he wanted her to hold for him.

At first Anita refused. The money would tie her to Rick, and at this point she was ready to break with him permanently. Conway pleaded that she was the only person in the world he could trust, and more, he was positive that he was being tailed by detectives and he was afraid that they would confiscate his loot.

Anita believed him. Out of sympathy and a mistaken sense of loyalty, she took the money and placed it in a safe-deposit box at an L.A. bank, but when she and Mark began to talk marriage, Anita had a change of heart. She wanted to be rid of the money so that one day Rick would not be coming to collect it, perhaps upsetting her life with Mark in the bargain. So Anita turned the money over to Iris Landry, and Iris promised to visit Conway at the prison to inform him that his money was safe in her hands. The two girls had dreamed up a remarkable reason for the switch: that Anita had married a Latin gentleman who had taken her to his home somewhere in Mexico.

That was the way the matter stood, complicated by Conway's unexpected freedom years ahead of schedule, as Mark sped toward Los Angeles and Iris Landry.

Iris lived on the twelfth floor of a high-rise building near Griffith Park. Overlooking tree-lined, flower-decked walks, a tennis court and swimming pool, it had the lush flavor of casual elegance. If Iris suffered, it apparently was not from the sting of poverty.

Mark left his car in one of the visitors' parking slots and rode the elevator aloft. In the discreet silence of the corridor outside Iris Landry's door, he poked the button. Waiting tensely, absently punching a fist into his palm, he was caught up now in the torment of anger and frustration. In the orderly, self-governing pattern of his life, he could not bear to be confronted by any crucial situation over which he had no control.

A stealthy flutter behind the door was followed by another wait and he knew that Iris must be peering at him through the spy window. When the door opened cautiously, he announced his name and she let him in quickly, almost as if there might be someone at his heels.

Iris was a petite, beauty-parlor blonde who looked to be at the gateway of thirty. Her features were so tiny that her wide, startled green eyes seemed to overwhelm her face. She wore a tailored beige linen suit with brass buttons—and a hectic smile.

"Any news?" he said. "Have you heard from—"

"I'm sorry, nothing yet," with a nervous shake of her head.

He charged past her into the living room—woodsy-rustic with beamed ceilings, a Swedish-modern fireplace. A picture window overlooked the azure oval of the swimming pool, where bright clusters of umbrellaed tables blossomed in the sun between redwood lounges decorated by indolent girls in bikinis, hardly a man in sight.

"Would you like a drink?" Iris was saying, her words laboring to reach him through frantic rapids of thought.

"A drink? No, no thanks," he answered with a wave of dismissal as he dropped to the edge of a chair and bent toward her. "Now listen, Iris, what's this all about? As you can imagine, I'm wound tight. So give it to me fast, right from the top."

Perched on the arm of a chair, Iris studied her nails, flicked her eyes up at him. "Conway came here early yesterday morning," she began. "He was fresh from prison and wild because he didn't know where to find Anita. Said she hadn't written or been to see him in going on two years and it looked to him like he'd been crossed. When he couldn't locate Anita, he went on the hunt for me because he figured I'd know the answers. Like where was she, and what did she do with his hundred and forty grand?

"I snowed him with the story we once cooked up—that she married some guy from Mexico, went there to live with him. Then I said I didn't have an inkling about his money. Maybe Anita took it along with her to Mexico and was keeping it there for him. Sure, because how could she know he was gonna be set free so soon? But I was fumbling around, coming on scared, and he wasn't buying it. Then he—"

"Wait a minute—hold it right there!" Mark snapped. "Why didn't you tell Conway that Anita turned his money over to you? I thought you were supposed to get word to him at the prison."

Iris lowered her head. "That's the rub," she said in a woeful voice. "Anita did give me his money to hold and I had every intention to. But then I married this fellow—Damon Kimbrell, same one I divorced in Vegas. Damon is a big gambler; he's won and lost a couple of small fortunes. So when I mentioned the business about Conway's money, well, Damon—"

"Now you're gonna tell me he lost the whole bundle at the tables in Las Vegas." Mark made a hopeless gesture.

She nodded. "All but five thousand that I kept. For expenses, you know. He had this system, Damon. He wanted to just *borrow* the money and double it. He double *zeroed* it, that's what he did! He was a gem. Oh, he was a prize, all right."

"Incredible!" Mark said with a face of disgust. "And being a friend to end all friends, you finally told Conway that Anita was actually in San Diego, and agreed to phone her with a sad tale that would get her here on the run."

Iris flamed a cigarette and puffed furiously. "No, no," she denied. "I stuck to my story. But then he went crashing around the apartment searching through everything, and he came up with a letter that Anita had written me—with her return address. I only called her with that sob story because Rick had a knife at my throat—my own carving knife. Can you believe it?

"I lied about the money, though—said she still had it in that safe-deposit box in L.A. That's why he wanted to get Anita here, I guess. When she arrived, I was out of my mind because I hadn't gotten around to breaking the news that Rick's bread was gone—the whole loaf. Then I lucked out. Anita hadn't been here two minutes when the boy who delivers my newspapers came to collect what I owed him from way back. Rick didn't trust me; he went to the door himself and paid the bill when the kid kept insisting. Just to be rid of him, you know.

"That gave me a chance to whisper the score to Anita—like a telegram. Her chin fell a yard, but then she said she would stall Conway on the money bit until she could get away from him, make a run for it. Anyhow, when he got an eyeful of her after those years in a cage, he had more on his mind than money. And by the time he got around to pressing her for it, I imagine the banks were closed. Until Monday. Sharp gal like Anita, she'd use that excuse to stop him from going ape, long enough to escape."

There was a silence as Mark considered the implications of Conway keeping Anita prisoner somewhere over an entire weekend. "Anita just went along quietly?" he said. "She didn't put up any resistance?"

"At first she made a loud noise about being married, wanting nothing more to do with Rick. But when she saw it was useless, that he was gonna get physical, she played it cozy by pretending to give in." Iris sighed heavily. "Oh, it was a nightmare. I'm so afraid that Rick will learn the truth about what happened to his money that I'm getting ready to skip town, get lost permanently. Because he'd kill me. I mean it, he would."

"Yeah?" said Mark. "Well, you haven't earned any sympathy from me. I blame you for most of this." He got up and began to pace. "I should go to the police, but by the time they did anything—Where would a punk like that take Anita?"

"I've been pondering that one for hours off and

on," Iris said. "For what it's worth, I could give you a long-shot possibility. Just this minute while we were talking, it hit me that Rick used to own a cottage. Really just a spooky shack off Topanga Canyon Road in the hills. He bought it so his brother would have a place to flop other than wino alley. The brother, one of those terminal alcoholics, died there. That was just before Rick went to prison and there's a chance that he didn't get around to selling it."

"That's a chance I'll take!" said Mark. "You've been there?"

"Just once. To help Rick and Anita clean it up after the brother died. What a mess! You never saw such—"

"Never mind that, can you tell me how to get there?" he asked.

Iris pursed her lips, nodded. "Better still, I'll draw you a map."

Mark wound his car over the narrow, twisting canyon road at reckless speed. He had been climbing steadily but now the road leveled off and continued through a rugged terrain of steep, rocky cliffs and stands of tall, ragged trees. Though it was yet early afternoon he encountered less than half a dozen cars. If there were houses, they were so remotely placed that he had noticed none at all. It seemed a parched and forbidding territory, an enclave between sea and valley where none but the most confirmed alien of society would care to exist.

Indeed, Iris had told him that it had been a kind of retreat for the most lawless among the hippie elements, cycle gangs and outcasts of all kinds; though a few merely eccentric citizens in love with isolation had also braved the place. From time to time there had been a murder in the area, and most people who were not just passing through, en route to the ocean or valley, did not linger long, especially after dark.

In a couple of miles he began to glimpse an occasional battered wood-frame house poking forlornly through distant trees. Then there was a sagging barn-like structure topped by a faded sign that identified it as Wendy's Tavern. Wendy's had long since become a mortality, its windows boarded up, paint peeling, beer cans and bottles littering the grounds.

On the map given him by Iris, Wendy's was a landmark, and now Mark slowed somewhat to search for an access road off to the right. He found it in half a mile, a rutted dirt trail slicing through open land for a space, then vanishing into a dense tangle of trees.

Braking beside a rural mailbox, Mark squinted at the dusty face of it until he caught the dim block printing of a name: G. CONWAY. That would be Rick Conway's brother Gilbert, the one who had followed a long chain of bottles to oblivion.

Mark turned and thumped over the trail, then nosed into the trees. He eased down a gradual incline for perhaps a hundred yards, entered a clearing and saw the house just ahead. It was a weathered and dejected cottage of wood frame, only a few patches of scabby white paint still clinging to it here and there. Dying shrubs and withered flowers hemmed the place. Wild grass and weeds overran the tree-ringed grounds.

Left of the cottage an ancient, rusting station wagon squatted on bald, flat tires. No doubt it had once belonged to "G. Conway," and toward the end had slowly died apace with its owner.

Mark cut the engine and sat listening. There was the leaden, torpid silence of desertion. He got out and waded through the high grass and weeds to the door.

A rusty knob resisted entry. The windows were curtained with a shabby material that looked as if it had been made from red-checkered tablecloths.

He circled the cottage and tried the back door. It too was locked. He pounded the door with his fist, then listened with an ear against it for a sound of movement inside.

There were a rusted rake and shovel leaning against the rear of the house beneath an old-fashioned window of four small panes. He got the rake and tapped one of the panes with the handle to shatter it. The center pieces fell inside with a minor tinkle. Using a handkerchief, he carefully removed the remaining shards and reached in, turned the lock and tried to hoist the window. It refused to budge but he applied muscle until it slowly gave upward.

He climbed in awkwardly, squeezing his massive bulk through the small opening. Then he closed the window, put the curtains back in place, and moved from a tired kitchen of relic appliances to the living room. Made dusty-dim by the drawn curtains, it was furnished with sagging junk in pitiful disrepair. There was about it a faint odor of decay.

He crossed to a door and entered the bedroom. The lumpy double bed, with twin pillows and rumpled, graying sheets, had a look of recent use. There was a bureau, a table supporting an unshaded lamp, and a closet, door slightly ajar.

He yanked the door open. A man's zipper jacket hung from a rack, a terry-cloth robe dangled from a hook. A pair of new slippers were on the floor. In a corner of the closet there was one other item—a powder-blue suitcase. Knowing instantly that the case belonged to Anita, Mark felt a pang of despair, then a rush of anger and the excitement of discovery.

He snatched up the case, brought it to the table

and thumbed the lamp switch as he opened it. The contents were familiar. There was the green dress with the burnt-orange design, a sweater, underwear, robe and slippers, and cosmetics, all typically arranged in fussy order.

Gently fingering the green dress with a feeling that in a moment he was going to weep, he made instead a bellowing sound of rage and slammed the case closed. With it he thundered to the front door and, bursting outside, locked the case in the trunk of his car. Then he drove the car around to the rear of the cottage, out of view.

Returning, he pulled a chair up to a window by the door and sat down to wait. As the hours passed his mood darkened, violence gathering in him as a storm builds for destruction. Night came and another sluggish span of waiting was filled with the lonely orchestration of insects. Then a dancing, feeble glow of light fell upon the curtains of the front window. With it came the murmur of engine sound. Folding back an edge of curtain, Mark peered out cautiously.

A deep-green sedan braked near the front door. A tall man, wiry and dark-haired, climbed out. Moving through a shaft of moonlight, he had the brooding, heavy-featured good looks described by Iris Landry. Mark saw at once that Conway was alone, and had a moment to wonder if Anita had escaped.

Conway keyed the door open and entered. He reached for a wall switch and the room was then somewhat wanly illuminated.

"Conway," Mark said softly from just behind him, and when Conway turned abruptly, Mark belted his jaw, then planted a fist in his gut. Conway doubled up and Mark gave him a giant shove with his foot that sent him sprawling precipitately to the floor.

Conway recovered quickly and sprang up, but when

he saw that Mark was merely standing stonily with his arms folded across his chest, he wiped blood from his chin and said, "Even if you got a warrant, that's no excuse to maul me, pig." He shook his fist.

"My name is Waldron," Mark announced, "and I came for my wife."

Conway sent him a look that was more relief than surprise. "Is that all?" he said with a mocking twist of smile. "Well, you came too late, buddy. I drove her to the airport and put her on a plane to San Diego tonight."

Mark shook his head. "Your luck ran out, Conway. I found her suitcase in your closet. Lie to me again and I'll cripple you."

Conway shrugged. "All right, I got her locked away somewhere. You want her, it'll cost you a hundred and forty grand that she stole from me."

Mark advanced, a crouched animal stalking with savage eyes and terrible purpose. Conway turned and bolted for the bedroom.

Mark caught up with him as he scooped a sawed-off shotgun from behind the bureau. By that time Mark was on top of him, pounding his face, hammering it with heavy, methodical blows until Conway sagged and went to the floor.

Even then, his eyes peering up from the crimson mash of his face, he was trying to raise the hand that still held the gun. Mark easily twisted the weapon from his grasp and sent it flying across the room. Then he set his big foot firmly upon Conway's windpipe. Pressing down with the force of his weight, he asked the question, then eased the pressure to allow for an answer.

"You—you bring the cash—" Conway choked, and I'll tell you where she—"

Mark repeated the process, his foot grinding brutally. "One more time," he said. "Where is she?"

Conway made a sound in his throat but couldn't speak until Mark lifted his foot. Then he said hoarsely, "You don't scare *me*, big man." He winked slyly. "You want her, she's for sale."

That was when the long-tormented, raging thing inside him broke loose. That was when his big body-weighted, fury-driven foot came crashing down, smashing fragile bones, crushing windpipe—again—and again; and then again—the mindless overkill of hate unchained.

In the trance of aftershock, Mark sat on the edge of the bed and stared at the body. Then, swept by the enormity of what he had done, with the desperate question still unanswered, he lowered his head to his hands. Overcome by an oppressive, morbid sense of guilt and remorse, he told himself that he had been pushed too long and too far, beyond human endurance to withstand.

Yet another voice, the one that never lied, argued that he was seething with jealousy, that he had wanted to kill the man almost from the beginning, to punish him for the intimacy he must have shared with Anita. When he saw the unmade bed and the suitcase, wasn't that the moment he decided? Didn't he wonder then if, in the need to play the game to the limit, she had found it not too difficult to rationalize giving herself for the sake of disarming her captor?

Yes, in that very moment, he had known he would kill the man.

Now there was only the wall to survive and the need to cope. So he gathered the body into his arms and carried it into the woods behind the cottage. He used the rusted shovel to bury it, the rake to comb the surface of the ground, then rested a thick branch over the spot.

He wiped his prints from the tool handles and everything he had touched in the house, at the same time restoring it to order. With the keys taken from Conway's pocket, he started Conway's green sedan and burrowed it deeply into a screen of trees. He remembered to erase his prints from the steering wheel and door handle.

Driving into town, he paused at a gas station to phone Iris. He wanted to feed her the lie that he had given up on the cottage as a hideaway after finding it locked and deserted. He would then beg her to pound her memory until it gave up some other hideout where Conway might be holding Anita.

Iris did not answer, and it occurred to him that perhaps she had already skipped town in fear of Conway. If so, with her went about the only chance of uncovering the place where Anita was being kept prisoner.

For a foolish moment as he approached the house in San Diego, Mark allowed himself the feeble hope that Anita had escaped after all and was waiting there to greet him; but the house was dark from without, mournfully silent and empty when he entered it.

He was undressing for bed when he observed for the first time that his tan suit was dirt-caked and stained with dried blood. His shoes were also covered with dirt and dried blood. If the body were found and despite all precautions he were to become a suspect, his suit and shoes would accuse him. Dry-cleaning clerks had memories and trash collectors had been known to turn bloody clothes over to the cops. He decided to bury everything, even his shoes, but certainly there was plenty of time. He'd let it go until tomorrow after dark.

In the morning he phoned Iris again: no answer. So then he went to the police station and reported Anita missing. He gave an accurate account of the circumstances, but for his trip to the cottage and the killing of Conway. The cops had ways beyond knowing. If they poked around long enough questioning the hoods, the dope peddlers who knew Conway's haunts and habits, they could quite conceivably locate that unthinkable, unimaginable place where Anita was imprisoned, perhaps with an accomplice to guard her. In the process they might also stumble upon Conway's grave site, but that did not mean the murder could be tied to him, and it was well worth the risk.

A couple of weeks crawled by in which the police of both San Diego and Los Angeles came up with not a single clue. Meanwhile, Mark was in such a dreadful state of mind that once he even got the .38 from his desk and sat for a long time, holding it in his lap, but it was only a passing temptation. Life was like a tragic and pointless novel, which nevertheless one was compelled to read to the end, just to see how it all turned out. One could not shorten it.

Then late one afternoon as he was leaving the studio, a couple of homicide detectives approached and placed him under arrest.

"On what charge?" he asked, though he knew well enough.

"Suspicion of murder," said one of the cops.

"What murder?" he bluffed.

"The murder of your wife, Anita Waldron. Her body was removed today from a grave in your backyard, along with your bloodstained suit and shoes." The cop studied Mark with wry amusement as his partner searched and cuffed him. "You want another cincher, pal? The slug that killed her matches the .38 we took from your desk. The gun is registered in your name and the only print our boys could lift is yours.

"Now, before you make any statement, sir, let me inform you of your rights . . ."

Waiting in a holding cell for his lawyer, Mark tried to put it together the way it could have happened. Obviously, Anita had lured Conway to the house. Perhaps she had told him that her safe-deposit-box key had been left at home in a drawer of the desk, something like that. Conway drove her to San Diego, and after he checked to be sure that Mark was absent, they entered the house. Whatever her excuse, Anita had probably gone to the desk and reached in for the gun she knew was there.

Then, before she could fire it, Conway grabbed the gun and shot her—or the gun went off as they struggled for it. No matter; she was dead. Then Conway buried her with the same shovel Mark had used to bury his suit and shoes beneath the garden off the patio. Mark had concluded that it was better to plant guilty evidence where it was least apt to be unearthed by strangers who came upon it by accident.

What a bitter joke that was! When the cops could not locate Iris Landry to back up his story, they began to wonder if Mark were covering the murder of his wife with a missing persons report. They figured he could have killed her in a jealous rage as she was about to leave him in favor of her ex-con lover, Rick Conway. So while Mark was at work they swarmed in and hunted for signs of digging. They uncovered his clothes first and then naturally they pulled the whole yard apart in further search . . .

In the conference room of the jail, Mark's lawyer said, "I must tell you frankly from the outset that on the face of the unshakable evidence against you, your conviction appears certain." The lawyer sighed, his expression a pronouncement of doom. "But despite the odds against proving it, Mark, do you still insist that Rick Conway killed your wife and planted the evidence?"

Mark nodded vigorously. "Yes, yes, absolutely! Since I know that *I* didn't do it, that's the only possible solution."

"Well, then," said the attorney with a smile of encouragement, "we've got to run him down, no matter what it takes. Once the police have him in custody, I'm sure they'll be able to get him to talk. Don't you think?"

"Yes," Mark said carefully, "perhaps. But first they have to find him."

"Oh, they will, they will!" said the lawyer. "They never give up. In any case, it's the only hope I can offer you."

A woman's touch may be all that is needed to insure instant success.

YOU AND THE MUSIC
by John Lutz

The surf booms with a certain rhythm, and as I drew nearer the cottage, the deep, booming bass speakers of Natalie's expensive stereo setup seemed to become an extension of the roaring surf. Anyway, that's how I remember it.

My bare feet felt comfortable in the still-warm sand as I walked up the beach at sundown toward the front door of the cottage. It wasn't much of a cottage, really—one of those angled, small, unpainted structures that seemed to be trying to outwait the sea. I didn't make much as a junior accountant, and almost everything I did make went into Natalie's music hobby—or, more accurately, music obsession.

Not that I minded her spending the money on tapes and stereo equipment; I knew when we were married a year ago how important music was to her. "Life is really music, if you just listen," she often told me. I suppose she's right. The surf has its rhythm; hearts beat in rhythm; and the deep, vibrant chords of Natalie's music have rhythm. Maybe it is all really the same rhythm, and maybe death is a part of it; and maybe only certain people can tune in.

I wonder if you'll be able to tune in on what you're about to read. I doubt it. It's too true to be believed, and that's why I can tell you. Of course the names have been changed to protect me. (Would I pull a switch now and use real names?) It all happened because what I felt for the dark-eyed, dark-haired, music-souled Natalie was genuine love, and you know what that can change into. Now I'm horrified sometimes that it might change back.

Oh, she was a sound freak! I recognized that more strongly than ever as I glanced into the front window of the cottage and saw Natalie dancing almost unconsciously to the deep, driving rhythms that seemed now to run in currents through the formless sand beneath my feet. She was listening to *Blood and Love*, a recent Doug Hall tape, a mixture of violent orchestration and throaty screaming, a sound that you'll never hear on the Top Ten but, according to Natalie, a sound of genius nonetheless. Hall was still simply "undiscovered."

I opened the front door of the throbbing cottage and stepped inside. The artist in person was slouched on the worn sofa. Doug Hall (whose performing name was Mad Dog Howl) was drawing languidly on a suspicious-looking cigarette and observing Natalie through slitted eyes. He'd been a friend of Natalie's for years, and now had become by degrees one of those ever-present family friends.

"How was your swim, Benton?" he asked as I closed the door behind me. He had to shout to be heard above the blasting music. His hoarse voice had a way of always blending with the music, as if it were accompaniment to whatever he had to say. Talent, I suppose.

"Cold and wet," I shouted in answer. I watched Natalie's lithe, bikini-unclad figure lurch and sway with the music. She was too deeply entranced to notice me at present.

The music ended with a high, wavering, mournful note and, as if drained and vowing subservience to a god, Natalie bowed until her long dark hair swayed gently to touch the floor. For once, the rest of her body was still.

The tape went into a more subdued, simple, repetitive rhythm, and Natalie suddenly jerked upright, smiling. "It's terrific, Doug—it really is! I mean, how can it miss? Oh, hi, Benton."

I nodded, then stepped over and kissed her forehead, which was cool and moist.

"Question is," Mad Dog answered hoarsely, "will the damn geeks out there have sense enough to understand it?" He waved a long, braceleted arm to indicate the general public.

"They'll have to!" Natalie said with great conviction. She aimed her perfect, encouraging smile at him. "Someday you'll have a hit! I just know it!"

That was all they talked about, this will-o'-the-wisp future hit. Sometimes it was all for which either of them seemed to live. Long into the night, while the three of us sat over a bottle of red wine, I would lapse into silence while they talked reverently of gold records, Grammy awards, Hall's picture in various hard rock publications, all of the various monetary and spiritual rewards that "the hit" would bring. Both of them took for granted that it was simply a matter of time before his genius was recognized. After almost a year of this, it became hard for me to share in their constant enthusiasm, and sometimes I became irritable. I never actually wanted to become a part of that kind of world.

The tempo of the music, pulsating from the speakers set at strategic points about the cottage, began to pick up, grow in intensity, and Natalie began to sway again.

"There's sandwich stuff in the kitchen, Benton," she said loudly. "We ate while you were gone."

Before walking to the kitchen I looked to see if Hall were going to join me, as he usually did for any kind of meal, but his pink suede boots were propped up on the scarred coffee table, his head thrown back and his eyes closed. I noticed that his hair, wildly curly and probably longer than Natalie's, cascaded halfway down the back of the sofa. When he performed, the hair was strung with a hundred tiny blinking lights.

Even in the kitchen there was no escaping the booming music. I made a ham salad sandwich, sat down and watched the beer can I'd gotten from the refrigerator dance wetly on the slick tabletop. I felt like stomping into the other room and switching off the stereo—but I didn't. One of my troubles was that I never quite did what I felt like doing.

Still dancing, Natalie appeared in the doorway. "Doug's flying to Memphis tomorrow to push his new sound," she said. "One of the big record companies is all twisty about it!"

I knew better. Hall was always on the verge of success. He'd flown to Memphis, or hitchhiked or rode a bus, more times than I could recall with the music beating in my ears. I felt like telling this to Natalie, but I didn't, quite.

A number of times recently I'd almost, but hadn't quite, told her that we'd have to use some of my salary to finance a better car if I could expect to keep my job. I'd been warned several times about absenteeism. I thought about how things might have been changed if I had told her, and if (small chance) she'd listened. When it happens, it's hard to tell good luck from bad, but I do know our ten-year-old convertible wouldn't have broken down half a mile from the cottage when I was on my way home from work that next evening.

It was Friday, so I wasn't too upset. I'd have all weekend to get the car running again; and it was a pleasant—though a bit warm—evening for a walk.

Long before I reached the desolate cottage, I could hear the boom of the music, and I wondered idly how far out to sea it could be heard on a calm night.

When I opened the cottage door I was surprised to find that the front room was empty but for the throbbing, dizzying music. Curious, I looked into the kitchen. It, too, was empty. Then I checked the one bedroom, and it wasn't empty. Mad Dog Howl hadn't flown to Memphis at all.

They hadn't seen me, and the deafening music had prevented them from hearing me. I backed away through the hallway, through the cottage's front door, through the raucous rhythm into the suddenly furious heat of the sun's orange, slanting rays.

I ran then, back toward the car, the frantic music still pounding in my brain. Finally, exhausted, I stopped and leaned on a rough wooden railing and stared out to sea, at the now visible tiny lights of the distant ships whose oil contaminated the seaweed that drifted to shore. The music had changed now to the relentless beating of the surf, but it was the same. As I stood and watched the sea in the fading light I could see slimy, reaching things washing darkly onto the beach. That's what I could see in the fading light.

I didn't go home that night. I got the car running somehow and drove to a phone, where I called and told Natalie I'd had car trouble and would be staying with friends in the city. Over the music, she expressed disappointment, and I felt like screaming what she was into the phone. That's what I felt like doing, but I didn't quite do it. Instead I told her not to worry, that I'd be home as early as possible Saturday. I slept in the car, awakening several times with the mistaken notion that the radio was blaring.

When I arrived home Saturday, the cottage was blaring as usual. The very air shimmered with deep, rhythmic sound. Natalie looked up at me from where she was seated cross-legged on a cushion in the middle of the floor and pressed her index finger to her lips in a signal for silence. Then those same lips told me in silent, exaggerated speech that she was taping Mad Dog Howl's latest song.

I could see how important that was to her, and for once I did exactly what I felt like doing.

Mad Dog came by the cottage later that evening to see Natalie, but I told him she'd had to go to New Mexico to visit her sister who was unaccountably ill. He looked at me with his slitted eyes, then shrugged, told me he'd come back later to see her and get some tapes she had, and left.

Natalie's relatives weren't put off as easily, so here I am, but unworried.

Why unworried? Because I know they'll let me out of here soon. They'll have to conclude that Natalie simply left me and disappeared. If they wait too long, I'm sure Mad Dog Howl will get me out somehow, even though they say I'm different from the way I was. Isn't everybody different from the way they were?

The idea of their finding Natalie doesn't worry me, either. Usually the police identify a body that's been in the sea a long time by dental work or fingerprints, but I took care of those possibilities even *before* I killed her. Not that I'm squeamish, but would you like to do that sort of thing to a corpse?

As it happened, everything worked out perfectly, because *Soul in Pain,* Mad Dog's latest, is a gigantic, ambition-fulfilling hit that rocketed to the top on all the charts to garner praise and riches. They say it's not only the frenzied, beating music that makes the record great, but the almost inhuman screams and howls of anguish that make up the background. The public seldom really knows what goes into creating a popular recording. But the point is, this one's a hit.

THE IMPOSSIBLE FOOTPRINT
by William Brittain

Matt Kehoe leaned his hunting rifle against one of the small pine trees that encircled his hiding place in the still woods and beat his mittened hands together to get some circulation stirring in his fingers. Even through the two sweaters and the thick parka he was wearing, the icy cold crept up his spine and made him shiver uncontrollably. His snowshoes creaked loudly as he shifted his weight from one foot to the other.

"Mister Kehoe, will ye hold still, if ye please? Oi'm a guide, sor, not a worker of miracles. If ye expect a deer to pass this way so's ye kin get a shot at it, ye've got to stop soundin' like a boiler factory at full production."

The whispered voice with its rich Irish brogue conjured up visions of the morning sun rising over the green fields of County Cork and the smoke of peat fires issuing from the chimneys of sod huts in Galway. Kehoe looked at his companion and shook his head in amazement.

For the man who had spoken, crouched down on

his snowshoes in a position Kehoe would have sworn it was impossible to achieve, had the swarthy skin, high cheekbones and thin, hawklike nose of a full-blooded Indian. His blue denim jacket could provide little in the way of warmth, while his wide-brimmed hat was perforated with several bullet holes as well as a few larger openings which looked suspiciously as if they had been made by human teeth. Yet the cold didn't seem to affect him at all. The look of repose on his face might have been graven from stone.

"Joshua, I'm going to freeze to death if we don't start moving around," Kehoe said through chattering teeth. "Wouldn't it be better to go looking for deer instead of just waiting for them to come to us?"

Joshua Red Wing shook his head slowly and looked up at Kehoe with reproachful eyes. "Yesterday when I agreed to guide ye in yer huntin'," he said, "I understood ye wuz one o' them detective chaps like oi've read about in the penny-dreadful magazines. Oi thought ye'd be used to a bit uv hardship, what with runnin' down alleys an' climbin' fire escapes like I see on the tellyvision. It's a sad disappointment to discover yer as soft as the rest uv the hunters from the city. Next oi'll be findin' out ye can't shoot worth a damn, neither."

Joshua reached into a pocket and drew out a dented tin flask. "Here," he said, passing it to Kehoe, "this'll warm yer blood a bit."

Kehoe grasped the flask, removed the top and took a single long swallow, then suddenly jerked the flask from his lips. Strange gasping sounds came from his throat, and his face turned bright red as the liquid, which felt as if it had been produced from sulfuric acid liberally laced with ground glass and old razor blades, streaked down his gullet.

"Luscious, ain't it?" asked Joshua, retrieving the

flask. "It's from an old family recipe me sainted mother gave to me at the time of—"

"Joshua," Kehoe said, tears streaming from his eyes, "I'd pull you in right now for attempted poisoning if I hadn't seen you drink that stuff yourself. Is it that brew that makes you sound like an Irish Geronimo?"

"No," replied Joshua with a twinkle in his eye. "Fact is, oi spoke nothin' but Injun up to the age uv four. At that point oi began workin' at a church in the village in exchange fer an eddication. Me English wuz learned from a Father McGrath and a cook named Bridget O'Toole. They wuz both first-generation Irish, which accounts fer me way uv speakin'. If it offends ye, why oi kin do 'ugh' and 'how' ez good ez any Injun ye'll see in the movies."

Before Kehoe could reply, Joshua stood up, gripping his rifle in one hand and motioning for silence with the other. "Oi heard somethin' off in the woods," he whispered to Kehoe. "Comin' this way, it wuz. Now ye sees the wisdom uv me ways. Let the other hunters drive the game ahead uv 'em. We'll be here to greet it when it arrives."

Kehoe nodded, pumping a cartridge into the chamber of his own gun.

"Wait fer a good shot, an' try to drop the animal in its tracks," Joshua breathed. "Old Karl Spearing's land begins about two hundred yards over to the left. If a wounded deer makes it that far, no sense chasin' it. Spearing's a mean one an' won't have anybody comin' on his land to hunt. The few who tried hev wound up with a rump full uv buckshot."

"I think I see something off there in the woods," Kehoe said, pointing. "I'll just—"

"Don't be too hasty," Joshua warned. "It could be

anything. Mebbe a black bear that got up too early from its winter nap."

A loud shout established the inaccuracy of the bear theory. "Help! Is anybody around? Help!"

Through the trees Kehoe caught sight of a man headed toward them at a dead run. He envied the man's ability to handle snowshoes without tripping over them.

"It's Tip Spearing, Karl's lad." Joshua said. "Over this way, young fella."

Joshua stepped out of the grove of pines. As the running man approached, he tripped and would have fallen if the Indian hadn't caught him in his arms.

"Take it easy, lad," Joshua said to the gasping man. "Now then, Tip, what's the trouble?"

"Josh, I—I—" Tip Spearing was in his mid-twenties, at the peak of his manhood, but judging from the ghastly expression on his face, he had looked into the deepest pit of hell itself.

"It's terrible," Tip went on. "I can't believe—"

"Calm down," whispered Joshua soothingly. "What is it now?"

"It's Dad. He didn't come back home last night. I've been out looking for him and—" He gulped convulsively. "I'll take you to where he is."

Beckoning to them. Tip turned and retraced his tracks. Joshua followed at an easy trot, while Kehoe stumblingly brought up the rear. They passed through a large clearing where the ground had been blown free of snow, and Kehoe almost tripped as twigs and leaves caught at the webbing of his snowshoes.

Reentering the forest, the men finally reached a vertical mass of shale that jutted upward like some monstrous grave marker. Tip signaled for Joshua and Kehoe to stop. "Over . . . over there."

Leaning their rifles against a tree, the two men left Tip and moved off in the direction that he had indicated. The white snow on the ground caught the sunlight that filtered through the branches and threw it back into their eyes so they squinted from the glare. They burst out onto what appeared to be a game trail amid the trees—and suddenly the snow wasn't white anymore.

It was red. The bloody, frozen circle was almost six feet in diameter.

Kehoe had seen dead men before, but he clamped his teeth together and swallowed loudly as he beheld the body of Karl Spearing spread-eagled in the snow, its lower part across the bloody stain. The body's left foot was shod in a calked boot with the letter *S* worked into the sole—but all that was left of its right leg was a stump, ending in a raw, open wound.

"Cut clean through the leg bones, just below the knee," Kehoe said to Joshua. "Knife's missing from the sheath at his hip, too. What do you suppose happened?"

"Oi've got a fair idea," replied the Indian. "Not too pretty, either. Oi've heard about such things often enough in this country, but this is the first time oi've seen it. Would ye mind followin' me? An' hev a care where ye step, if ye please, so's not to destroy tracks. Eventually we'll hev to call in the local law. No sense ruinin' all such things for 'em."

They moved off down the trail, keeping well clear of the wide swath in the snow where Karl Spearing had evidently dragged his tortured body in a desperate attempt to seek help. The trail led past a thick stand of willow shoots. Joshua pulled aside the leafless branches.

"Yonder's the trap, Mr. Kehoe. Hev a look."

Kehoe gaped at the shiny-toothed jaws of the bear

trap in the midst of the white snow of the willows. They were clamped inexorably together on a bloody booted leg.

His eyes riveted on the leg, Kehoe spoke to Joshua. "You said you knew what happened here. What was it?"

Quickly the Indian sketched in the story. A lone man in midwinter, the chance misstep, and the heavy jaws of the trap, chained to a thick tree, leaping up out of the snow to grip the leg. In such a fix there was only one desperate chance, to be taken before cold seeped too deeply into the bones and blood.

A tight tourniquet was applied, after which the imprisoned limb was packed with snow to numb it as much as possible. Then, in a grinding hell of shock and pain, the pinioned man performed an amputation—on himself. Finally, if cold and loss of blood did not take their toll, it might be possible to make one's way to where help was available. A slim chance at best, but Karl Spearing knew what must be done. He had tried—and he had lost.

"Spearing's house is but a short ways beyond the trees there." Joshua said, pointing. "Great big stone buildin' it is, with a telephone line down to the village. If he'd been able to get it to it, he might be alive now."

"Rotten business," added Kehoe. He pointed to a bone-handled hunting knife lying on the flattened snow. "Must be what he did the operation with. The poor devil hardly had a chance, did he? Well, what now?"

"We'd best get back to Tip and take him to the house. Oi'll call Vern Lefner from there."

"Lefner? Who's that?"

"He's our sheriff. When he's done makin' out his reports on this—that'll take several hours, ez Vern loves to scribble on official papers—the two of ye kin talk about police work fer the rest uv the day. What with all our shoutin' and hollerin', oi doubt there's a deer left in the whole county."

"Do you think it'll be okay to leave the body unguarded? I mean, couldn't it be mutilated by wild animals?"

"Oi'd doubt it. There's some bears ez travels this game trail during the summer, but they're all hibernatin' now. Besides, they're not too partial to human flesh. And the body's too cold and stiff to attract wolves."

The two men flanked the wide trail in the snow that led back to Karl Spearing's body. Kehoe gave the corpse a wide berth, but Joshua seemed intent on examining it at close range. Suddenly he paused, peering quizzically at a spot on the ground.

"There's a queer thing," he breathed softly.

"What's the matter?" called Kehoe, who had moved a few paces ahead.

"Oi've found a bit uv an oddity here. Yer the detective. Come and tell me what you make uv it."

Kehoe padded closer on his snowshoes.

"Hev a care," Joshua said. "Ye'd not want to destroy evidence, would ye?"

"Evidence? What evidence?"

Joshua pointed to a spot near the toe of the left snowshoe. "What hev ye to say about that?"

"Karl Spearing's footprint, that's all. There's no mistaking that *S* from the bottom of his boot. He probably tried to stand before he became too weak to do so, and—"

"Mister Kehoe, would ye take note uv the fact that the print wuz made by the right foot? An' the leg to which that foot's attached is now caught fifty yards back down the trail in a bear trap."

"Why yes, that's true, but—"

"Then tell me, sor, how did the print get up here next to the body?"

"Well, it . . . that is . . . Oh, there's got to be some simple answer."

"Then would ye care to offer an explanation? Is it yer contention that the severed leg, takin' on a life uv its own, somehow got out uv the trap an' then hippety-hopped down here to the body like a pogo stick? An' then later returned and put itself back into the trap?"

"No, of course not. But . . . well, maybe Karl Spearing left the print several days earlier. If there was no new snow since then . . ."

"He just happened to be in the area, I suppose? An' how would you suggest he arrived here that first time? There's no second set of footprints. Just the ones that lead to the thicket where the trap is."

"Oh. Then perhaps Spearing walked ahead on the trail a little way and came to this spot. He went back for some reason, and that's when he got himself caught. Dragging his body along, he'd have covered up the other tracks he made."

"Oi see." Joshua's voice dripped sarcasm. "He walks up to here. 'Oh my!' he sez, 'oi've forgotten somethin'.' So he turns about, walks back down the trail and thrusts his foot into a trap he'd set hisself. After cuttin' off his own leg he crawls back, destroyin' all tracks except this one by the body, which he leaves to confound us. No, Mr. Kehoe. There's more to Karl Spearing's death than meets the eye."

"Josh, according to what you told me yourself, this whole thing is open and shut. Karl Spearing cut off his leg and then bled—or froze—to death. Stop trying to make such a big deal out of it. Why, if you hadn't seen that footprint—"

"Ah, but I did see it, Mr. Kehoe. An' so did you."

"Yes, and I'll bet when this Lefner fellow gets here, he'll have a dozen logical explanations for how it got there. Better leave detective work to the police, Josh."

"Very well. But oi'll hev no part uv any explanation uv Karl Spearing's death that doesn't take that footprint—that damned impossible footprint—into account."

The two men returned to where the weeping Tip Spearing was waiting and half-led, half-carried him through the woods to his house. While Kehoe looked for the telephone to put in a call to the village, Joshua laid logs in the huge fireplace and soon had a roaring blaze going. From the liquor cabinet he took a bottle and administered a healthy tot of whiskey to Tip as well as taking a mammoth swig for himself. Then he laid Tip on the couch and repeated the dosage. Within half an hour the bottle was nearly empty, Tip was asleep, and Joshua was honoring Kehoe with a nasal rendition of "The Rose of Tralee."

It was almost noon when Sheriff Vernon Lefner's jeep stopped at the edge of the dirt road that ran past the house. Matt Kehoe met him at the door.

"Glad to know you," Lefner said when Kehoe had introduced himself. "Always good to meet another cop. How's the hunting been going?"

"Got me a new guide this time," Kehoe said. "His name's Joshua Red Wing. He looks Indian but talks like he was mayor of Dublin. Do you know him?"

"Know him?" was the reply. "I've run him in for hunting and fishing out of season more times than I can remember. He's a good guide, though, at least when he's sober. By the way, what's that sound? Is somebody using a chain saw out back?"

In reply Kehoe opened the door to the living room.

In front of the embers of a dying fire Joshua was sprawled out in a leather easy chair. His eyes were closed, but his open mouth resembled the entrance to a mine shaft. The gargantuan snores coming from his throat reverberated from the room's beamed ceiling.

Lefner, considering the empty bottle on the floor near the Indian's right hand, said, "He'll be out for quite a while, but it's just as well. It'll give the two of us a chance to examine Karl Spearing's body."

"Fine." Kehoe hauled his parka from the closet. "By the way, Josh found a footprint down there. A little strange, its being where it is, I guess. But he's trying to make a big thing of it."

"Between his police magazines and what he sees on TV, Josh considers himself another Sherlock Holmes," Lefner commented. "C'mon. Maybe we can get back before he wakes up and decides he's being attacked by a herd of pink elephants."

It was almost sundown when Joshua woke. He got up from his chair, holding his head as if it were about to burst, and gingerly walked to the kitchen.

"Cold lamb," he groaned, looking from the two men at the table to the platter in front of them through bloodshot eyes. Within the Indian's head a gang of tiny miners seemed to be excavating his brain with pickaxes and dynamite.

"We found it in Karl's refrigerator," Lefner said. "I had some men come up and take the body to Dr. Fanchion's in town for a medical examination, but I wanted to be here to ask Tip a couple of questions when he wakes up. I thought we might as well eat while we're waiting. Slice some off, Josh, and dig in."

"No sense me even tryin' to eat," moaned Joshua softly. "With a bit o' luck, oi'll be dead within the hour anyway."

He shuffled to the door, threw it open, and took several deep breaths of the cold, clear air. Slowly his eyes focused, and the mining operations within his head closed down. "An' what, Vernon, is yer conclusion ez to Karl Spearing's death?"

"An accident, no question about it, Josh. Spearing did everything he could to save himself. If he hadn't cut off his leg he'd have frozen to death right there in the trap. As it was, well, at least he went a lot more quickly his way."

"An' the footprint? Ye did see it, didn't ye?"

Lefner nodded. "I saw it, Josh. It's gone now, of course. When the men came for the body they scuffed up the area pretty badly."

"So it's gone, eh? An' with it, any embarrassin' explanations ye'd hev to make about it."

Lefner gestured toward Kehoe. "We both saw it, Josh. We admit it was there. It's just that we don't think it's that important."

"Oh." Joshua slumped into a chair. "Oi see. Then how d'ye explain its presence by the body?"

"I don't know, Josh, but . . ." Lefner shook his head in annoyance. "Kehoe, talk to this knothead, will you? Tell him what police work is really like."

Joshua turned to Kehoe, a look of intense interest on his face. "Do that, Mr. Kehoe," he said. "Talk to me about how the police ignore clues that's right in front of their noses."

Kehoe cut himself another slice of lamb, the knife grating on the bone of the roast. "What Lefner is trying to say," he began, "is that real police cases aren't like the shows on TV. On the crime shows everything's neatly wrapped up at the finish. But in real-life criminal cases there are a lot of loose ends—"

"Ez the police," interrupted Joshua, "oi merely want yez to explain how that one footprint got up

THE IMPOSSIBLE FOOTPRINT

by the body, when the foot that made it wuz fifty yards away, caught tight in a bear trap. Is that too much fer a taxpayin', law-abidin' citizen to ask?"

Lefner was taken with a sudden fit of coughing. "Josh, we've got to be getting back to town," he said finally, getting control of himself. "Now we're going to have to wake Tip, and when we do, I don't want to hear anything more about that footprint. The boy's been through enough for one day."

"Then ye wouldn't be interested in me theory."

Kehoe and Lefner looked at one another and then both stared at Joshua. "What theory?" asked Kehoe.

"About the footprint, uv course. But if you two detective gintlemen are too busy, why . . ."

Lefner, red-faced, began rising from his chair. Kehoe restrained him. "Just a minute, Vern. How long will this take, Josh?"

"P'rhaps thirty minutes. Oi'm sure Tip'll sleep that much longer. He drank almost ez much ez oi did from that bottle, an' he ain't had near the practice."

"Okay!" Lefner pounded the table. "Okay, Josh. We'll hear you out. But it had better make sense. And after this, no more talk about that blasted footprint. Agreed?"

"Yer charmin' manner puts me completely in yer power," Joshua said. "Agreed."

The Indian stood up and dug a hand deep into a trousers pocket. Then he held the hand over the table and allowed three scraps of grimy paper to fall lightly in front of Lefner. "Oi ask yez to look at these," he said. "Meanwhile oi'll be outside, lookin' about a bit."

As Joshua left the room, Lefner took one of the bits of paper and passed another to Kehoe. "Looks like an IOU," Lefner said. "From Tip Spearing to Joshua. Seven dollars and eighteen cents."

"Mine's the same," Kehoe said. "But the amount's different. A dollar and a quarter."

"Less than a week old, both of them. The third's for five dollars even. Josh probably got 'em in one of those poker games they hold at the hotel. Everybody in town knows Tip gives IOUs. But he always makes good on them."

"But what's this got to do with the footprint?" Kehoe asked. "I still don't see—"

He was interrupted by the thump of something being deposited on the back porch. Then the outside door burst open, and amid a blast of frigid air Joshua entered, smiling broadly at the two.

"We saw the IOUs, Josh," Lefner said. "What's the matter, don't you think Tip will make good, now that his father's dead?"

"Oi'll disregard yer remark ez unworthy uv ye," Joshua said, grinning expansively. "Fer while yez two were sittin' here stuffin' yerselves, oi've been solvin' the murder of Karl Spearing."

"Murder!" Lefner's face turned a beet-red. "Josh, I've heard enough already. Nothing's been said at all about Karl Spearing's being murdered."

"Yes there has. Oi just said it meself. Now if ye'll calm down a bit, oi'll elucidate fer ye."

Lefner turned to Kehoe, shaking his head.

"Ye see, Vernon," Joshua began, "there wuz somethin' about Karl Spearing lyin' there in the snow that disturbed me from the first. In addition to the footprint, oi mean. A couple of things, in fact. In the first place, while the snow around the body itself wuz drenched with blood, there wuz none to speak uv back at the trap. What oi mean to say is, the leg wuz covered with it, but none at all on the snow. Even if Karl had wrapped his tourniquet to the tightest, seems ez if there'd be a drop or two, don't it?"

Kehoe was seeing the Indian through new eyes. "You know, you're right," he said. "But that's still not conclusive, Josh."

"P'rhaps not. But try this. Karl Spearing had a sheath knife to do his cuttin' with. The blade wuz mebbe six inches long. Oh, t'was sharp enough, and he could hev performed the amputation with it. But only if he'd cut off his leg at the knee where the joints come together. But no. The bones wuz sheared through cleanly, a few inches below the joint. An' ye just can't cut a bone like that with a knife without doin' a good bit o' hagglin' at it. Ye kin experiment on the lamb roast right now, if ye'd like."

Both Kehoe and Lefner let their confusion show in their faces. Their preconceived notions were trickling out of their minds like sand through an hourglass.

"Karl Spearing's leg," Joshua went on, "wuz cut off with the one weapon an outdoorsman might carry that could slice through bone with a single cut—a finely honed ax."

"Wait a minute," protested Lefner. "Karl Spearing didn't have an ax with him."

"Ah." Joshua held up a finger triumphantly. "So finally yer comin' round to me way o' thinkin', eh? Ye'll admit, then, the presence uv a second party?"

"Well . . . yeah, I suppose so," Lefner said. "But I still don't see how the other person got there. I mean, there were no tracks around except Karl's."

"But there wuz other tracks, don't ye see? Don't forget the trail Tip Spearing, Mr. Kehoe an' me made when we went to view the body."

"Why, sure we did," Kehoe said. "But neither of us killed—" He stopped abruptly.

"Yer beginnin' to see what oi'm drivin' at, ain't ye?" Joshua said, smiling.

Kehoe jerked a thumb in the direction of the living room. "Are you saying you think Tip killed his own father and then retraced his trail back to where we were?"

"Somethin' like that. O' course the killin' wuz probably done a day or so ago. But ez long ez Tip walked in the tracks he'd first made, there'd be just the single trail. When Tip located us in the woods an' took us to the body, we figured the tracks had been made when he discovered his father. But they could just ez easy uv been put there a day or two before, when the killin' wuz done."

"Josh," Lefner said, "I don't care when the trail to the body was made. I still can't see that Tip's guilty of murder. I mean, what motive did he have?"

"Karl Spearing owns this house and a good deal uv the land around here. A man uv considerable means. An' yet Tip, his own son, wasn't allowed to have enough pocket money even to play a few hands uv penny-ante poker. He had to use IOUs an' then account to his father for every cent he lost. A most degradin' situation fer Tip. Might it be that he went searchin' fer his father to ask fer money to pay his debts? Tempers flared, an' there wuz a fight, with Karl comin' out the loser. Oi tried to point out this possible motive by presentin' yez with them IOUs uv mine, but I suspect ye wuz hard put to divine their true meanin'."

"So you think Tip killed his father, eh?" asked Lefner. "Well what about the foot in the trap? And that footprint by the body?"

"All right, let's sum up the whole operation. At some time yesterday—or p'rhaps the day before, I dunno, what with the body bein' froze the way it wuz—Tip is out in the woods, carryin' an ax. He sees his father on the game trail an' decides to ask fer money. There's an argument, ez I said, an' a brief struggle.

Tip loses his temper an' swings the ax, takin' off Karl's leg. Karl falls to the ground, fast bleedin' to death, right at the spot where we seen his body. Out there in the woods, who wuz to hear his cries of pain?

"But Tip's mind is on other things. He knows if the body is found in its present condition, he'll be the number-one suspect.

"Then, an inspiration. Tip's heard stories, ez oi hev, about men bein' caught in a trap an' what they had to do to save themselves. He knows the bear trap's nearby. So he picks up the bloody leg, and off he goes down the trail. Once in the willow thicket, he jabs around with that grisly member 'til he hits the pan uv the bear trap under the snow. The jaws crunch together on the leg. Then Tip drops Karl's sheath knife by the trap to complete his alibi and muckles up the trail between the trap an' the body so it'll look like a man's dragged himself along it. All the footprints are destroyed, or so Tip thinks. But there's still one uv Karl's near the body that he overlooked an' oi found."

Joshua leaned back in his chair and spread his hands expansively. "An' that's the way it wuz, ez they say on the tellyvision. This mornin' Tip went lookin' fer someone to be witness to Karl bein' dead with one leg cut off an' caught in the trap. He found Mr. Kehoe an' me. If we didn't immediately assume what Tip wanted us to, oi'm sure he stood ready to point out what he wished us to believe. Ye must, uv course, give Tip credit fer his actin' ability. He'd uv succeeded, too, if me sharp Injun eyes hadn't spotted that footprint in the snow by the body."

"He could beat the rap yet," Kehoe said. "You've got an interesting theory there, Josh, but no real proof."

"Would the murder weapon do?" Joshua asked. "Oi found an ax out in the shed. Somebody did a hurry-up job uv tryin' to wipe it clean, but there's still some reddish stains on the handle an' blade. Oi dropped it off on the steps on me way in from outside. Could yer police chemists make somethin' uv them stains, Vern?"

"Yeah." Lefner got up and peered into the living room to check on Tip Spearing. "If the stains are human blood, we'll have a pretty tight case."

"Well," Joshua said, "at least ye'll hev it easy apprehendin' yer suspect. Oh my, the hangover he'll have when he wakes. Oi hope, Vern, that ye won't be too severe with him."

"Hell, Josh, he killed a man—his own father."

"True. But what kind uv a man wuz the father? Seems to me the milk uv human kindness might uv turned to gall in the man's veins."

"Look, just because he didn't give Tip any money—"

"No, oi wuz thinkin' about how that bear trap wuz placed. It's winter. No need fer a trap with the bears all hibernatin'. Besides, no bear's about to hide in a thicket. That'd be the place where the hunters would lurk, waitin' fer game to pass by on the trail. Like we wuz doin' this mornin', Mr. Kehoe."

Kehoe stared wide-eyed at Joshua. "You mean . . ."

Joshua nodded. "Karl Spearing couldn't stand to hev people huntin' his land. He'd do anythin' to keep 'em away, even shoot at 'em. So I don't believe he wuz after bear when he set that trap.

"It wuz put there to catch a man."

FIRST PRINCIPLES
by Donald Honig

Parker, the deputy, walked across the office to the window. With his fingers he parted two slats of the blind and peered outside.

"What are they doing?" Thomson asked. He was sitting behind the desk, carefully and meticulously cleaning his nails with the point of a long hunting knife. He was a brawny man in his late thirties, his powerful biceps filling the short sleeves of his shirt. A polished, five-pointed star with "Sheriff" printed across it was pinned to his breast pocket.

"Still out there," Parker said. "Milling around."

"How big are the groups?" Thomson asked.

"Threes and fours, most of them."

Thomson grunted and went on with his nail-cleaning. It would be all right as long as they remained fragmented in small groups. It was when one or two fire-eaters began haranguing them and pulling them together into a mob that the trouble would start. At the moment they were merely sullen and dissatisfied, not hostile and menacing.

"What do you think they're gonna do?" Parker asked.

"Dunno," Thomson said.

"Most of them are across the street in front of the hardware store, talking among themselves and staring over here."

"Let 'em talk, let 'em stare," Thomson said laconically.

"You think they'll try and take him?" Parker asked.

The knife in Thomson's hand stopped moving, its point poised over his thumbnail. His lowered eyes contemplated the blade.

Parker moved away from the window, walked halfway toward the desk and stopped. "You'd like them to, wouldn't you?"

Thomson's eyes came up and languidly he raised his head and gazed thoughtfully at his deputy. "Like them to what?" he asked quietly.

Parker jerked his thumb toward the rear of the building, where the cells were; the only jail in Brownstown, the only jail for thirty miles around, and a flimsy one, vulnerable to departures from within and assaults from without.

"Like them to take him," Parker replied.

"He's my prisoner," Thomson said. "*Nobody* is going to take him away from me. My personal feelings about him have nothing to do with it."

Parker shrugged.

"Anybody thinks they're going to move into my area of responsibility without invitation," Thomson continued, "will find his damned skull full of lead."

"Okay by me." Parker returned to the window and looked out again. "They're gathering," he said ominously, surveying the scene under the street light.

There were town men out there, and men in from

the outlying farms and down from the mean little hardscrabble hills; the town men in their conventional trousers, white shirts and fedoras, the others in overalls or denims, wearing caps; mingling together, smoking cigarettes, talking quietly. Pickup trucks kept cruising past—these were the teenagers, exhilarated by the "excitement." Parker knew them all—they were his neighbors, his friends, and he believed he understood them perfectly. As a matter of fact, he knew that if he weren't wearing a deputy's badge, he would doubtless be standing out there with them.

"If you want my opinion on it," Parker said, and paused—the sheriff didn't want his opinion, he knew, but he went on nevertheless, "you're foolish to be moving him at night. Morning would be better."

"First of all," Thomson said, impatience making his voice inordinately polite, "I was told to bring him to Glensburg tonight, that they want him there first thing in the morning, to charge him. And second of all, this jail is a cracker box and you know it and they know it out there just as well."

"It's a lonely drive at night," Parker said.

"You needn't fret," Thomson said caustically, "you're not coming along, so just forget about it."

"I would if you asked me," Parker murmured.

Thomas emitted a loud, harsh laugh. "You're damn right you would. But I ain't asking you. If I can't handle this job by myself, then I may as well hang it up."

Thomson put down the knife, pushed back his chair and got to his feet. He put his thumbs into his belt and hoisted his khaki trousers more securely around his thickening middle.

He walked back to the cells. There were only four, and they seldom held anyone, and even then it generally was someone sleeping off a drunk. Tonight, however, cell number one held someone special: a murder suspect.

Thomson stood before the cell, gazing impassively through the bars at the occupant. The young man within was sitting on the cot, which was suspended out from the whitewashed concrete wall by a pair of taut, diagonally poised chains. The prisoner was twenty years old, slight of build, with short, curly hair. The expression on his face was of despair, and of mute, almost ingenuous appeal, as of someone hoping for compassion and understanding from strangers. He was wearing a long-sleeved white shirt, corduroy trousers and desert boots. He had the soiled, weary look of the informal traveler.

His name was Earl Johnson. He had been passing through Brownstown, heading for Miami, he said, to look for work. Late in the afternoon of the day before, he was seen approaching the house of an elderly widow, Mrs. Norris. His purpose, he said, was to see if he couldn't contribute a few hours' work in order to earn a meal. No one had answered his ring, he said, and he had gone away. Some hours later a neighbor found Mrs. Norris strangled.

Earl Johnson was picked up on the highway at midnight, his thumb in the air. The car he had thumbed down was Sheriff Thomson's, who by that time had Johnson's description burned into his mind.

Johnson stuck to his story, under the sheriff's relentless and menacing interrogation. He had done nothing more than mount the porch steps of Mrs. Norris's house, he claimed, ring the bell, wait, and then go away. To his disadvantage, however, was the fact that two people had seen him approach the house and none had seen him go away, the witnesses being a man and a woman in a passing car.

Word of what had happened spread quickly through the town and its environs. People didn't like what they heard. Mrs. Norris had been a particularly popular and well-liked old woman, and the accused was a stranger. At five o'clock the men began gathering outside the jail, not belligerent, not noisy, but simply there, brooding and restive.

When Sheriff Thomson telephoned the county prosecutor at Glensburg to ask for instructions, he was told to bring the prisoner there.

"Can you do that?" the prosecutor asked.

"I can do it," Thomson said. "But I can't guarantee anything. The people around here are pretty upset over it."

"Do you want me to send some state troopers to give you a hand?" the prosecutor asked.

"No," Thomson said. "I can handle it myself," and he hung up. With his hand resting on the telephone, he thought: *I can handle it myself.*

Now he lifted a key from the chain that hung from his belt and unlocked the cell door and swung it slowly back.

"Get up," he said to Johnson.

"Why?" Johnson asked. "What's happening?"

"I'm taking you to Glensburg."

"Why?"

"Because it's the county seat."

"Can I see a lawyer there?" Johnson asked.

Thomson wet his lips, studying the young man with flat, expressionless eyes. "Sure," he said.

He entered the cell and handcuffed Johnson's hands in front of him. Then he took his prisoner by the elbow and walked him out to the office.

"I heard you talking," Johnson said. "There's a mob outside, isn't there?"

The deputy grinned at him. "You scared?" he asked.

"Sure I'm scared," Johnson said. "Wouldn't you be?"

"Not if I had a clear conscience," the deputy said. "I wouldn't be scared of anything, if I had a clear conscience."

Johnson turned to the sheriff. "What's going to happen?"

"I told you," Thomson said. "I'm taking you to Glensburg."

"What about them?" Johnson asked, indicating with a lift of his head what was outside.

"Parker," the sheriff said, "take a rifle and cover us. Stand in the doorway until we're in the car."

The deputy unlocked a wall cabinet and took down a rifle, grabbed some cartridges from a box and loaded it.

Thomson went first, unlocking the door and opening it. At the sight of the big, broad-shouldered sheriff standing in the lighted doorway, one hand on his holster, the men in the street stopped talking, paused in their gestures and became quite still.

"Come on," Thomson said over his shoulder.

At the appearance of the prisoner, the men in the street became animated with pent-up anger, outrage.

"Give him to us, Sheriff," one shouted.

"Hand him over, Tommy, and take the night off!"

Thomson ignored them. The car with the big, encircled star on either door was parked directly in front of the office. As Thomson led his prisoner to the car several of the men began crossing the street toward them. Without hesitation Thomson lifted his .45 free of its holster and held it belt high.

The men stopped.

"Not another step," Thomson said quietly.

One man, in the lead of the others, with a mean,

sun-cracked face, said in a soft, cajoling voice, "Give him over, Tommy."

Thomson studied him, almost as though giving consideration to the request. Then his lips parted in the merest smile. "I appreciate your feelings, Bob, but you boys know me well enough. You know I can't, and you know I won't."

A beefy young man with a white T-shirt covering his broad, sloping belly came forward and pointed his finger at Thomson. "You're making a big mistake, Sheriff!" he shouted.

"Not as big as the one you'll be making if you take another step," Thomson said, grinning maliciously and cocking the .45. Then, to Johnson, he said, "Follow me."

Without taking his eyes off of the crowd of men in the street, Thomson opened the door on the passenger side and pushed Johnson inside, then slammed the door shut. With the deputy standing in the doorway, rifle shouldered and aimed into the street, Thomson got into the car and slid behind the wheel. He placed the .45 on top of the dashboard, turned on the ignition and drove away.

The drive to Glensburg was thirty miles of almost unrelieved desolation, covering winding back roads. One saw an occasional farmhouse, but that was all. Thomson had made the drive countless times and knew it well. He also knew that after dark only an occasional car or truck traversed the sinewy two-lane road, which for years the old-timers had referred to as the highway, because of the white stripe painted down the middle. Depending on your purposes, the highway could be dangerous or it could be safe.

As he drove away from town, Thomson kept looking into the rearview mirror. He didn't think any of them would have the nerve to follow, to try something, but he couldn't be absolutely certain. He knew they weren't going to disband so quickly, that they were going to continue standing there, talking about it. It was quite possible one of the fire-eaters in the crowd might strike the right chord and provoke the others into doing something impulsive.

Thomson took the road's broad, sweeping curves as fast as he dared. Next to him, his prisoner sat, handcuffed, head bent, morosely silent. From time to time Thomson glanced at him. Neither man spoke.

When they were about fifteen miles out of Brownstown, Thomson began to slow down.

Johnson raised his head and stared out to where the headlights were picking up the roadside brush, the scrawny trees. "Why are we slowing up?" he asked.

Thomson didn't answer. He brought the car to a halt at the side of the road and switched off the engine, then turned off the lights. The darkness was immediate and engulfing.

"What are you doing?" Johnson asked as he gazed at the sheriff.

Thomson reached out and took the .45 from the dashboard. He swung it around and pointed it at Johnson.

"What's going on?" Johnson asked.

Thomson did not immediately answer. Only the noise of the crickets beating their rolling, twinkling sounds interminably upon the night broke the silence.

"Listen," Johnson said, fear and panic filling his voice now, "what are you doing? What's happening?"

"I want to tell you something," Thomson said. "That old lady was like a mother to me. She practically raised me, after my own mother died."

"Look," Johnson said, "I had nothing to do with it. You're making a big mistake here. I never saw her. Nobody answered the door, and I went away. I've told you that over and over. It's the truth. Why can't you believe it?"

Thomson said, very quietly, "Because I can't. Because it isn't the truth, and you know it."

"Then if I did it," Johnson said, "why didn't you find something on me? You said there was stuff taken from the house—money, jewelry. Where is it?"

"You had plenty of time to get rid of it, once you saw you weren't going to be getting out of town so fast."

Johnson closed his eyes despairingly and brought his manacled hands with some impact up to his forehead. "Oh, hell," he muttered. "Oh hell. Oh, hell."

"I've been waiting to do this," Thomson said. "Of all the people in this world, she was the only one who ever gave a damn for me."

"I never saw her," Johnson whispered, shaking his head, his hands still pressed to his forehead.

"I'll tell them you tried to escape," Thomson said.

"You'll never get away with it."

"Nobody will give a damn about you," Thomson said. "You saw those men back there. Is anybody going to give a damn?"

No one would question the incident, Thomson knew. He would tell them that his prisoner had gone berserk in the car, tried to wrest the gun away from him. There had been a struggle in the moving car, the gun had discharged. The prisoner was killed. That would be the end of it. No one would care about a murderer, a stranger.

At that moment a flash of light in the rearview mirror caught Thomson's attention. He peered into the mirror, then whirled around. Three sets of headlights were advancing along the road.

"Damn them!" Thomson said bitterly.

There was no question in his mind about who they were, what they were doing on this road at this hour. One car along this road at night was a rarity; and two or three, traveling in tandem, meant that the fire-eaters had finally got the men in the street moving.

Thomson jammed the .45 into his holster and swung back behind the wheel and got the car started.

"What's happening?" Johnson cried.

"Shut up," Thomson said furiously.

The sheriff gunned the accelerator, taking the curving road as fast as he dared. The car swung out dangerously across the road's center stripe. The roadside trees and shrubbery seemed to be lunging straight for the car as the headlights suddenly opened on them, but then, as the car followed the curving road, they seemed to leap back.

Gritting his teeth, scowling, Thomson negotiated the turns with all the skin he could. Now and then he threw a glance into the mirror: they were still behind him, still coming with a recklessness and determination equal to his own. There was no point in stopping and trying to face them down, not out here, not after they had come this far. He knew them well enough—they had guns in those cars, and they would use them. Once that kind of energy became mobilized, there was no stopping it.

Next to him, Johnson swung back and forth with every sharp snap of the wheel, like some lifeless, boneless mannequin.

Thomson hit the accelerator a shade too hard then —he knew it the moment he saw the next road bend coming up. He tried to brake, though he knew that was a mistake too. The car shuddered and swung across the road. Frantically Thomson fought the car, but it was out of control now, and there wasn't time or road enough to bring it back. It shot across the narrow shoulder and fairly leaped into a snarling tangle of stunted pine and brier thickets. Driven forward by its own maniacal momentum, the car plowed ahead for about thirty feet before coming to a halt with a thudding suddenness that tossed its passengers against the dashboard.

Thomson turned off the ignition and the lights, then jumped out. He hefted himself onto the fender, slid across the hood and got to the other side of the car. He opened the door and with one powerful hand took hold of Johnson's arms and yanked him out of the car.

"Get moving, get moving," the sheriff said. "And keep your mouth shut."

Pushing and pulling and dragging his prisoner along with him through the scratching, grasping thicket, Thomson pushed ahead into the darkness. Looking back, he could see the great fans of headlights rising into the night as the cars came forward around that last curve.

"Keep moving," Thomson said.

They kept going until Thomson heard the cars screeching to a halt, then he unceremoniously threw Johnson to the ground and crouched next to him, .45 in hand.

He saw them on the road, walking in front of their headlights. He cursed softly.

"What are they doing?" Johnson whispered.

"Shut your mouth," Thomson said.

He watched them. They were milling now in front of their headlights, with the same tentative uncertainty they had shown in the street outside the jail. They could see his car in there, but that was all they could see.

Thomson's lips moved in a churlish smile. He didn't think they would have the guts now to move in, to come maneuvering through the thicket in the dark, guns or no guns (and he could see that several of them had rifles). He would kill the first one that came close; they knew that. This was something more than simply overpowering him now. A lynch mob was capable of many things: exposing itself to gunfire was not one of them.

Through a network of thicket silhouetted by the headlights, he watched them. He was almost wishing they would come in. With those headlights behind them the damn fools would never have a chance, but they were either too dumb or too afraid to turn them off.

Then one of them called out: "Thomson. We know you're in there. All we want is that man. That's all. You know that."

Thomson bent his head low, next to Johnson, who was trembling and hugging the ground.

"All they want is you, boy," he whispered.

"Sheriff . . ." Johnson said.

"Shut up," Thomson said. "They're not gonna get you."

The men at the roadside called out a few more times, but made no forward move, even though Thomson's car was clearly visible to them, the doors hanging open.

Thomson watched them come together in a group to talk it over. A few moments later they did exactly what he expected them to—they got back into their cars and turned around and drove away.

"Are they going?" Johnson asked.

"They're going," Thomson said, a hard satisfaction in his voice. He stood up, drawing his prisoner with him.

"Sheriff . . ." Johnson said.

"Shut up," Thomson said. "We're going to Glensburg."

A look of astonished relief crossed Johnson's face. He wanted to say: *A few minutes ago you were about to kill me,* but he didn't say it; he didn't say anything. The events of the past hour had totally drained him.

They began walking. As near as Thomson could estimate, Glensburg was about ten miles along this road. They would walk it. They would get there. He was furiously adamant about it.

After walking several miles they were met by a state police car coming from Glensburg. The car pulled alongside and the trooper behind the wheel said, "Hey, Thomson, where you been?"

"Been taking our time, that's where," Thomson said.

He opened the back door and pushed his prisoner inside, then hauled himself in and closed the door, settling himself in the seat.

"You have some trouble?" the trooper asked.

"No," Thomson said, and added dryly, "just some inconvenience."

"Your deputy said you left hours ago. We've been wondering about you. The prosecutor's getting jittery."

"Then let's get moving," Thomson said.

The streets of Glensburg were deserted when they drove in. The trooper dropped them at the courthouse, where the county prosecutor was waiting. Thomson led his prisoner through the quiet corridors, to the prosecutor's office, where he entered without knocking.

"Hello, Sheriff," the prosecutor said. He was a slender man, his narrow frame slouched in a swivel chair behind the desk. "This, I take it, is Earl Johnson?"

"That's him," Thomson said.

Self-consciously, the prosecutor laughed. "I'm sorry, Sheriff," he said, "but if we'd found out earlier, we could've saved you the trip."

"What are you talking about?" Thomson asked.

"We got a call from Laurelville about an hour ago. They got the man who killed the old lady. Nabbed him in the bus terminal."

Thomson's eyes narrowed. He glared at the prosecutor. "What are you talking about?" he demanded.

"They've got the man. Found some of the old lady's jewelry on him. Got a full confession."

Thomson pointed a finger at the prosecutor. "Now you listen to me," he said angrily. "I had to fight off a lynch mob to bring this man in here. My car was wrecked. I was almost killed. And now you're telling me he's *innocent*?"

Thomson heard a thud behind him. When he turned around he saw Johnson fainted dead away on the floor.

Later, when Thomson left the courthouse to wait outside for his ride back to Brownstown, he saw his former prisoner sitting on the courthouse steps, back curved, one hand rubbing his wrist, as if trying to rub away the pain or the humiliation of the handcuffs.

Thomson came softly down the steps, ignoring Johnson, and stood at the curb, hands on hips, looking into the street. He was acutely conscious of the man on the steps, knew he was being stared at.

"Sheriff," Johnson said at last.

"What?" Thomson asked without turning around.

"Some of it I understand—some I don't. You have to explain."

Thomson said nothing, merely stood there staring

into the empty street, waiting for the state police car.

"You were about to kill me," Johnson continued. "But then you were ready to lay down your life to save me. I don't understand it."

Now Thomson turned around and looked at him.

"It's very simple," the sheriff said. "They were trying to push me around, which they had no right to do, and which you can't ever let them do."

"But you—"

"I know, I know," Thomson said with a pained expression. "I let the emotions of it get to me, that's all. And it was a mistake. Violation of first principles. Policemen are like doctors, Johnson." He turned around and finished his statement facing the empty street, "When they make a mistake, there's usually nobody to apologize to."

THE SIXTH MRS. PENDRAKE
by C. B. Gilford

The courtroom was hushed and expectant as the old man stood up and read from the paper. The words were definite, but there seemed just the slightest hint of reluctance—or perhaps doubt—in his voice.

"We, the jury, find the defendant, Arthur Pendrake, not guilty."

A few men in the rear—reporters, no doubt—slipped out quietly to file their stories. Among those who stayed there was a subdued babble, the general tone of which seemed to be dismay, but there were also many wise noddings of heads. The verdict had been rather expected.

The one most concerned sat impassive. Arthur Pendrake was a fine-looking man, slim, wide-shouldered, with wavy, silvered hair. He had been on trial for murder, but his patrician face was gentle, his blue eyes benign. He listened to the fateful decision, and by not even a flicker of a smile or a slightly more relaxed breath did he betray satisfaction or relief.

Costello, his lawyer, leaned across to him and whispered, "See, I told you, they didn't have sufficient evidence."

Pendrake nodded. He had known that.

Later, when the formalities were over and Arthur Pendrake was legally and physically a free man, Lieutenant Dunphy stopped him on his way out of the courthouse building. Dunphy was short and rotund, with the appropriate face of a small bulldog.

"Well, Mr. Pendrake," Dunphy said, "I guess you won."

Pendrake permitted himself a wry smile and extended a well-manicured hand. "Then I presume it's good-bye, Lieutenant. Since I can't be tried twice for the same alleged crime, that is."

The policeman pretended he didn't see the hand. "Maybe it isn't good-bye, Mr. Pendrake," he said instead. "The verdict today was just on wife number five. There are always the other four."

Arthur Pendrake smiled a bit wider. "Haven't the police anything better to do than the things you amuse yourself with, Dunphy? Practically your entire case was built around the coincidence that I had had four previous wives, all of whom predeceased me. Now if you couldn't come up with sufficient criminal evidence in the death of Louise, how could you hope to do it in the deaths of Cynthia, Ruth, Josephine, and Elizabeth? Besides, Lieutenant, each one of them died and is buried in a different city. That's quite a trail you would have to follow."

"You have left quite a trail, Mr. Pendrake."

"Regretfully, this is good-bye."

"There's always the future, Mr. Pendrake. You might get married again."

"I rather doubt that."

"You figure you have enough money already, is that it?"

"I have been, shall we say, fortunate in that one respect—and I certainly wouldn't look forward to a marriage in which you would be my best man and forever afterward my watchdog. And now, Lieutenant, this really must be good-bye. Don't bother wondering where I am or having me shadowed. I shall be resident at the Castle Club. That's a bachelors' establishment, you know. But of course you do."

Pendrake stepped around the policeman and walked away, out of the building, into the bright sunshine and down the broad granite steps. At the bottom of these, however, just as he was about to hail a taxi, a woman dashed directly into his path, then stood there, confronting him.

"Bravo, Mr. Pendrake!" she squealed, clapping her hands like a schoolgirl.

Yet she was considerably more than a schoolgirl. Though her skin was smooth on the planes of her face, there were telltale wrinkles in the corners and crevices. Arthur Pendrake was accustomed to measuring such items. Her waist was thin rather than matronly thick, but tight corseting might have accomplished that. A dye or rinse might have darkened her hair. Her eyes were blue, her makeup demure. Forty perhaps; not unattractive.

"I beg your pardon," he said, drawing back.

"Congratulations."

"For what?" He knew, of course.

"Your acquittal. I saw the entire trial from first to last. The prosecution had no case."

"So the jury decided." He drew back again a little, trying to go around her.

Ever so subtly, without seeming acutally to move, she still managed to bar his path. "But it was a close call, wasn't it, Mr. Pendrake? I mean, closer than the time before, anyway."

He gave her a hard stare, but her face seemed completely open and frank. "What exactly do you mean?" he asked.

"With your first three wives, nobody paid much attention. With your fourth, there was some official suspicion. Now this time you were actually brought to trial. Maybe you've gotten a little careless, Mr. Pendrake."

"I beg your pardon?"

She smiled innocently. "Or maybe it was just the coincidence catching up with you. Or the law of averages. Or maybe you've just lost your touch."

"My touch?"

"At murder."

She was faintly amusing, Pendrake thought. "You congratulated me on my acquittal, but you believe I was guilty."

"Oh, everybody is quite sure you were guilty, Mr. Pendrake. No one could prove it, that's all. You'll really have to be very careful next time."

"I don't plan a next time."

"You don't? How dreadful! What a waste! You're such a charming man, Mr. Pendrake."

He decided to play along with the game. "But my dear lady," he pointed out, "if everyone is quite convinced I'm a murderer, I shall be condemned to loneliness. No woman would dream of taking a chance on me with the reputation I have."

She surprised him completely. "How wrong you are, Mr. Pendrake," she said. "Your reputation is the very thing that many women find most fascinating about you. I myself, for one."

He stared at her.

"And I happen to have a quality that you have found fascinating in women, Mr. Pendrake. I'm rich."

He must have given some sign that he didn't believe

her, a sneering smile, perhaps, or a quizzical frown. Anyway, she accepted his challenge. Without taking her eyes from him, she waved lightly toward someone or something behind him. Over his shoulder he saw a long, black limousine approaching. It eased silently to the curb just beside them, and a liveried chauffeur hopped out and held open a door.

"May I drop you somewhere?" the woman asked him.

Almost unwillingly he accepted the invitation, found himself inside that elegant automobile, sitting beside this amazing woman, being whisked along in quiet luxury. With great reluctance he revealed his destination. "The Castle Club," he said, and he knew when he said it that he was betraying a vital secret.

Her name was Fern Spencer, and she was indeed wealthy. He verified this fact very early in their relationship. Besides, she was most eager to supply him with all pertinent information. Her father had been most successful. Was she worth a million? Oh, several. Ten, perhaps, if it were all added up. Pendrake experienced a distinct uneasiness being this close to so much money.

"Did any of your wives have that much money?" she asked him one day as they lunched together.

"I'm afraid not," he had to admit.

"Were they wealthy at all?"

"Well fixed, you might say."

"And you inherited each time?"

"Yes." He might as well tell her, since he had the feeling that she knew anyway.

"How much were they worth?"

"Louise, my last wife, left me in the neighborhood of a hundred thousand."

"And the others?"

"Somewhat less."

"Arthur dear, you sold yourself much too cheaply."

"I beg your pardon?" He didn't appreciate outspokenness on such a delicate subject.

"A man of your charm is worth a great deal more than a hundred thousand. And to commit murder for such a paltry sum . . ."

"Now, Fern . . ."

"Surely we're friends. We can be frank."

"Do you actually imagine I committed five murders?" he demanded.

"Darling, I know you did."

He shouldn't have continued seeing her. He should have broken it off. If necessary, he should have run away somewhere where she couldn't find him.

Instead, he lingered, and while he was at it, he did a bit of investigating. Fern Spencer, it turned out, was a widow.

"Whatever happened to Jeffrey, your first husband?" he asked her after a month of their friendship.

The question took her by surprise. At first she colored with embarrassment, then recovered to give him a cold, distant look, masking what, he did not know.

"He died," she said finally.

"Yes, I know that. But how?"

Her cold look became one of suspicion. "You seem to have been prying. Why didn't you pry a little further and find the answer to that yourself?"

"I did the best I could," he admitted candidly. "Jeffrey apparently died in an automobile accident."

"Yes, that's how he died. Six years ago."

"And you didn't remarry?"

"No."

He waited for the details, but they weren't forthcoming. In fact, the entire conversation was finished, the whole evening ruined. He didn't see her for almost a week afterward. Whereas before she'd been always calling him, sending him notes, invitations, even little gifts, now she withdrew completely, as if she'd moved to another planet.

Meanwhile he dug through old newspaper files. Six years ago, she had said. Anything that happened to someone with ten million dollars would surely have been reported.

It had happened in California, he discovered. Jeffrey and Fern Spencer had been driving down from one of those mountain lake resorts—too fast on an unfamiliar road. The car had skidded off the edge on a hairpin turn. Jeffrey Spencer, driving, had ridden the car to the bottom of the ravine and perished in the flaming wreck. Fern Spencer, his passenger, had been thrown clear partway down and suffered critical injuries, but was expected to survive.

Pendrake spent several days searching the files for subsequent references to the accident, but the newspapers, considering who the Spencers were, kept a rather discreet silence. Had Jeffrey Spencer, for instance, been drinking on that fatal ride? Perhaps it hadn't mattered to the authorities. After all, it was himself Spencer had killed. There was no official investigation. Jeffrey Spencer was buried in California. Six months or so later there was a brief notation that Fern Spencer had returned to the city, apparently recovered from her injuries.

Pendrake inquired in another direction. Had any part of Fern's ten million come from Jeffrey Spencer? None, as far as he could discover. Jeffrey Spencer had been an obscure young man in the employ of John Larkin, Fern's father, but he hadn't risen very far in the business, even after Larkin's death. Perhaps he'd been inadequate, or hadn't wanted to. Perhaps he'd even been a fortune hunter. Arthur Pendrake wouldn't hold that against him, of course. Jeffrey Spencer's mistake was that he had neglected to outlive his wife.

When Fern recovered from her pout eventually, she renewed her assault on Pendrake almost as if nothing had happened. "Miss me, Arthur dearest?" she asked him.

"I might have."

"Of course you did. Don't deny it. You're a man convicted of murder by public opinion if not by law. You're an outcast. Who besides me will have anything to do with you? You simply must have been lonely."

He smiled. The Castle Club, since he was not a convicted criminal, had been tolerant enough not to oust him, but people had been a bit cold, pointedly avoided him.

"Why don't you marry me, Arthur?"

"Fern!"

"Don't pretend to be surprised. You've known all along that it's what I've been leading up to."

"Well, yes . . ."

"I'm the only woman in town you'll get a proposal from. And I'm worth ten million, Arthur."

"I really don't need the money."

"Not at the moment, perhaps. But you like to live well. You appreciate the comforts. You don't know how to work. Your money won't last forever. Ten million would guarantee you luxury for the rest of your life."

He sat down beside her, taking her hand—an affectionate gesture he'd never attempted before—and looked searchingly into her eyes. "You've made something of a case for my marrying you, Fern," he said.

"But I can't understand why you should want to marry me."

She squeezed his hand, returning his gaze tenderly. Yet behind the glaze of affection that filmed her eyes, what secret lay hidden? "I'm a woman," she answered. "We women do not operate according to your masculine logic, Arthur dear. I began to admire you when you were fighting for your life in that courtroom, and I've grown terribly fond of you."

A fortnight later, and scarcely two months after he was acquitted of the charge of murdering the fifth Mrs. Pendrake, Arthur acquired a sixth.

The wedding received very good press coverage, even though they'd intended it as a very quiet, private affair. Some reporter got wind of the license having been issued, and made a headline of it. Lieutenant Dunphy of Homicide attended without an invitation.

"You're a cool one, Mr. Pendrake," he said with grudging admiration.

Arthur tried to ignore the policeman, but couldn't.

"You're pushing your luck, I want to warn you of that. Maybe it's worth it though, huh? Playing for really big stakes this time. What kind of a nut is this Spencer dame anyway? Thinks she's going to reform you, does she? Or do you plan to settle down this time and live happily ever after? Or should I ask, is the new Mrs. Pendrake going to live happily ever after? I'm real interested, and I'm going to watch—like a hawk. You're going to become my hobby, Mr. Pendrake."

Which was not an auspicious beginning.

The honeymoon was not promising, either. Fern, who before marriage had expressed a fondness for him, now was strangely distant and detached. They went on a West Indies cruise, but the romantic atmosphere failed utterly. Fern did not melt into his arms like an eager bride. Instead, rather like Lieutenant Dunphy had promised to do, she seemed to be watching him all the time. Not exactly spying, just observing with keen interest.

"Arthur," she asked him one day at the rail of the ship, "did any of your other wives know your past?"

"That I'd been married before, do you mean? Of course. I didn't lie to them."

"No, I don't mean that. Did they know how you had disposed of your previous wives?"

He was amused. "Of course not."

There was a curious brightness in her eyes—mischievous, cunning, he thought. "Then I'm the only one of your wives who was forewarned," she said.

"Forewarned? Of what?"

"Of impending doom."

This time he didn't know whether to be amused or not. "My dear," he asked her, "do you actually think I intend to murder you?"

"Don't you?"

"And you married me, courted me, thinking that?"

"Of course, darling. But this time, naturally, you'll have to be much more stealthy and careful about it, because I know what you're up to. And more important, Lieutenant Dunphy knows."

"Fern, stop it!" She sounded as if she were seriously advising him.

"What's the matter?"

"You're talking nonsense. I have no intention of harming a hair on your head."

"I really didn't expect you to come right out and announce it."

Later, still exasperated, he argued with her. "Fern, why on earth should I want to kill you?"

"Well, there were those other wives of yours . . ."

"So it's bound to happen again, is that it? I'm acting under a compulsion. A pattern of marriage and murder? I'm some sort of psychotic, is that what you think?"

"Oh dear no, Arthur. You're very cool and deliberate. You want ten million dollars."

"But I already have ten million. I'm your husband."

She arched her eyebrows. "Oh, but you don't have it. I haven't cut you in on anything. You've just taken the first step toward that ten million."

Yet on their return, and having settled into the big family mansion, the first thing Fern attended to was a legal matter. A team of lawyers labored on the project. Arthur was shown the new will and had it explained to him. He had become Fern's sole heir. On her death, he would get everything.

"Are you completely mad?" he asked Fern when he got her alone. "You've carefully arranged things so I can't touch one penny of your money while you're alive, but I become immensely rich when you're dead."

"But Arthur dear," she protested calmly, "you married me for my money, didn't you?"

"I never said that."

"And you're not so awfully fond of me that you want to share the money with me. You'd much prefer to have it all to yourself. Well, that's simply the way I've arranged it."

He couldn't fathom her. His reputation had attracted her. She'd married him with her eyes open. Now she was issuing him an invitation to try to murder her; daring him, almost.

But watching him. Or pretending to watch him. Pretending to be careful of everything she ate and drank. Pretending to be suspicious and on her guard.

It was like a game, a cat-and-mouse game, but who was the cat? And who the mouse?

Madness, yes, but in every madness there's a method. He would have to discover the particular madness of Fern Larkin Spencer Pendrake.

On Monday afternoons it was his habit to take a taxi downtown and have a personal chat with his stockbroker. Arthur was a speculator, jumping in and out of the market on a swing of a point or two. This meant keeping close tabs, and on Monday afternoons, regularly, he'd go down to the broker's office, study the board, and plot the week's strategy.

Only on this particular Monday he'd forgotten, quite stupidly, the small notebook wherein he'd jotted his inspirations of the past several days. A mile from the house he instructed the cab driver to turn around and go back. But they didn't turn in the big circular drive for, at the other end of it, Fern's limousine was just coming out. *Where could she be going?*

"Follow that car," Arthur shouted at his driver.

Their route led away from downtown, through a suburb, and seemingly toward open countryside. The chase ended abruptly when the limousine slowed suddenly, turned and entered a wide drive through an open iron gate that interrupted a low stone wall: a cemetery.

Arthur ordered his cab to halt at the entrance. Over the wall he could still see the car. It went for a hundred yards or so, finally stopped. Fern, dressed all in black, was let out of the car by her chauffeur, then walked quickly across the greensward alone.

Arthur told his cabbie to wait, slipped inside the cemetery, but stayed back close to the wall, taking a path parallel to his wife's. She walked for some distance, and since the place was heavily planted with trees, she must have almost gotten out of the chauffeur's sight. At long last she halted—at a grave, surely—seeming to hesitate for a moment, then knelt on the turf.

Arthur was too overcome by curiosity merely to remain where he was. He stalked her. She was kneeling with her back toward him, and the intervening trees more or less shielded him from the chauffeur's gaze, should that individual have been interested enough to keep a protective eye on his mistress.

Slowly, stealthily, unobtrusively, Arthur made his approach. Fern did not move, except perhaps to sink back on her heels, lower and lower, till she made only a small black lump on the green earth. As Arthur drew very close, he noticed that her face was buried in her hands and her shoulders shook. She was sobbing!

Curiosity drove him forward the rest of the way, curiosity and a dawning anger. He advanced silently over the soft ground till he stood just behind his crouching wife and read over her shoulder the name on the low, simple stone: *Jeffrey Spencer*.

Feeling somehow betrayed, victimized, Arthur found himself hating the man under the sod there, and hating too the weeping woman in widow's black, the wife they shared. With cold fury and contempt, he deliberately and loudly coughed.

Fern heard him and looked over her shoulder. Her face, he saw, was contorted with grief and wet with tears. Through her tears she recognized him, and painfully struggled to her feet. He didn't try to assist her.

It was her lack of contrition over being caught in this duplicity, her scorn of pretense, her not bothering even to look guilty, that sent him into a complete rage. He seized her shoulders and shook her, much harder than the sobs had shaken her.

"How dare you!" he shouted. "Why did you pursue me? Why did you marry me? Interested, you said. Fascinated, you said. You deceived me. Every minute was a deceit. Every word was a lie!"

She nodded convulsively, agreeing with him. "Yes ... yes ... I loved Jeffrey ... never anybody but Jeffrey ... I lied to you ... so kill me ... go ahead and kill me ..."

Later, he went to her sitting room and found her there. "What is it all about?" he challenged her. "Some terrible feeling of guilt?"

She hesitated only a moment. Then, "I killed Jeffrey."

"I thought so."

"Oh, not in any deliberate, planned way. Not the way you commit murder, Arthur, but I'm guilty nevertheless. Jeffrey and I had an awful argument. He'd been inattentive, I thought. Had too much of an eye for other women. So I accused him of having married me for my money. We had a dreadful row. Jeffrey started drinking. I should never have let him drive, but I was blinded by hatred and jealousy and hurt pride. All the way down the mountain I goaded him, said nasty things to him. I didn't even notice how fast he was driving ..."

"So you believe you killed him?"

"I murdered him."

"If you insist."

"I was thrown out of the car and badly injured. Why didn't I die then? I deserved to. I wanted to. But I was a coward. My instinct for self-preservation was too strong. I clung to life. Later on I tried to commit suicide. I was still a coward at the last moment. Since Jeffrey's death I must have tried a dozen times."

Arthur nodded. He'd been right. "Then you heard

about me. And you hired me, as it were, to be your executioner."

She looked at him, her eyes very bright. "Oh, you put it so well, Arthur. Yes, my executioner, for a fee of ten million dollars. It will be perfect poetic justice. I wronged Jeffrey by accusing him of marrying me for my money. Now to be murdered—punished by a husband who actually did marry me for that reason . . ."

She was mad, of course, as he had feared. He doubted if sessions with a psychiatrist or any other such half-measures would succeed with her. Prompted by strong feelings of guilt, she had a genuine and sincere death wish. Most extraordinary. She'd be hard to argue with.

"Quite ingenious, my dear," he said. "You hire a renowned murderer, pay him a most ample fee. Ought to get the job done. Except that you overlook one factor. Lieutenant Dunphy. Now if I disposed of you, my dear, I wouldn't stand a chance of eluding Dunphy. Even if I were very clever about it, any jury would crucify me on the mere fact of the coincidence. No, dearest. I'm afraid I'll have to disappoint you."

The madness—or whatever it was that possessed her—had begun to flicker again in her eyes. She advanced a step toward him, menacing, causing him involuntarily to retreat.

"You won't even try?"

"Fern, darling, I'd be as dead as you."

The fire in her eyes blazed even brighter. "You deceiver! You cheat! You lamb in wolf's clothing! You married me under false pretenses! You're a wife-killer; why do you stop now? You'll inherit more from me than from all the rest put together. Why do you refuse now?"

"Fern, I explained to you, I don't dare . . ."

She was in such a frenzy by then, clenching and unclenching her fists, her eyes so aflame, frothing at the mouth almost, that he was suddenly afraid that it was she who might murder him. Hastily and ignominiously he retreated to his own room, where he locked the door and found himself breathing very hard.

Arthur was still alone, and it was near midnight, when the fear seized him. He had kept to his room, pondering his situation, trying to make plans and failing, when now suddenly a new and frightful possibility occurred to him. He unlocked his door, flew down the hall, and burst into Fern's room.

What he saw there instantly confirmed his worst suspicions. His wife was sitting at her desk, and before her, littering the entire surface of the desk, was a motley array of bottles—all shapes and sizes and colors, some with their caps off, some with their contents poured into the half-dozen or so drinking glasses scattered around. She was absorbed by her collection.

He crossed the room to where she sat, seized her, lifted her from the chair, and shook her violently. "What have you taken?" he screamed at her. "For pity's sake, tell me what it was. I'll find the antidote. Hurry . . ."

She didn't struggle in his grip, but remained limp, compliant, and gradually a smile came to her lips, a smile of smugness, defiance, disdain, and she didn't answer his desperate questions.

Finally, despairingly, he let her go. She sat in her chair again, while he paced and roamed the room. Once he stopped beside her desk, and with a violent gesture of his arm, swept all the bottles and glasses off, and sent them crashing to the floor. Liquids and pills spilled everywhere, but she didn't notice. She kept right on smiling at him.

"Don't you realize what you are doing to me?" he moaned. "Lieutenant Dunphy is going to arrest me. He won't pay any attention to fingerprints or anything like that. I can go right on denying it. The jury won't listen either. This time they'll hang me. Ye gods, Fern, why did you have to drag me into your life? What did I ever do to you?"

Finally reason superseded emotion. The telephone had fallen to the floor in the midst of the debris. He knelt in the mess, grabbed the instrument, and commenced dialing frantically.

"Whom are you calling?" she asked calmly.

"The operator. She can find a doctor."

"Don't bother."

"He'll have something. Stomach pump maybe."

"It won't be necessary, Arthur. I didn't take anything."

"What!" He dropped the phone and stared at her. "I don't believe you."

"You should. I told you I was a coward. Believe me, when you refused my simple request, I was desperate. I assembled all these bottles and studied their contents. Some of them are quite poisonous, I'm sure. But I lost my nerve. I couldn't swallow anything. I'm still a coward somehow."

She was so straightforward and sincere that he couldn't help believing her. He rose from the littered floor, brushing himself off. Feeling relieved, he laughed thinly, shrilly.

"I'm glad, I'm really glad, Fern," he said. "I don't think you're a coward at all. You just have too much basic will to live, that's all. You really don't want to die. This notion of yours was a lot of nonsense, wasn't it?"

She continued to smile at him, but there was something grim in the way she shook her head in disagreement. "Not at all, Arthur. I haven't changed my mind in the least. I had a great deal of faith in you—experienced murderer and all that—but you disappointed me. You're as much of a coward as I am. You lost your nerve when the really big money was at stake. So now I'll have to look elsewhere."

Alert, with a small chill creeping up his spine, he asked her, "Elsewhere? What do you mean by that?"

"I offered you ten million to do the job. You refused. You're already too well fixed, I suppose. Now I intend to hire someone else. It'll probably cost a lot less. Should have done it that way the first time. Someone really tough. A gunman perhaps . . ."

"No, Fern!" He was on his knees again, this time directly in front of her, holding out both hands beseechingly. "They'll be sure to think it was I who hired him!"

She smiled sweetly. "Let them think it!" she said.

Arthur Pendrake sat alone again in his darkened room, deeply absorbed in a most pressing problem. He had begged, and Fern had finally relented. She would give him two weeks she'd said, and no more. Two weeks, or she'd hire someone who could really do the job.

He stared at the wall, and his brain was just as blank and empty. The question pounded dully, painfully, in his brain. *How—oh, how—does one go about committing a murder?*

A LITTLE KNOWLEDGE
by Arthur Porges

Of all teachers, a psychology professor should know better than to become emotionally involved with one of his own students. It was so obvious now that William Carson squirmed at the thought of his stupidity. In terms of experience, logic, intelligence, maturity, training and—damn it, yes—his chosen field of knowledge, there had been danger signs posted every foot of the way.

Sitting across from his wife, nodding occasionally at her amiable, harebrained comments just as though he were paying attention, Carson smoldered internally. It was all very well to look back and think, *What an ass I've been;* but when the body spoke, however voicelessly, by means of powerful ductless glands that had meant survival through ages of evolution, neither brains nor experience could ignore their commands. In every other case—and there had been many, for he was an attractive man when young, impressionable girls were involved—the professor had managed to avoid serious entanglements. This was due less to his own willpower, he now admitted ruefully to himself, than to lack of real temptation. Previously the only girls in his classes to show any interest in him as a potential seducer had been unappealing types it was easy to brush off with phony nobility. When she was skinny, wore blue-and-brown ensembles; or pimply and gauche, it was simple to say, in effect, I'm old enough to be your father, my dear; and we must be fair to my wife. So go and find a lucky boy of your own age; you deserve a better fate than this silly crush on a very ordinary man pushing fifty.

But Gloria Wells had been different. So deliciously, irresistibly different. She was like a bright, feathered bird from some tropical country, out of place among the sparrows of Marshall College, country girls from the surrounding farms. A small, dark, intense person, with blue eyes that always seemed to have some inner source of heat, suggesting sockets full of molten metal. In fact, Gloria's whole personality was high in calories; she was impetuous, passionate, a creature of whims, as became the daughter of show people. Yet in spite of such traits, she seemed more mature than most of the other girls, featherheaded creatures, pretty enough in a bucolic way, but interested only in boys, pop records, clothing fads, and some creature, shorn of his last name, they adoringly called Fabian. Gloria, on the other hand, knew Shaw and Ibsen: even Max Beerbohm, and preferred De Los Angeles to Bobby Darin.

Carson was doubly bitter about his rashness, since he had always prided himself secretly for being, under a veneer of good-humored charm, a cold, logical individual who usually got what he wanted by calculated indirection that offended nobody.

"You'll be late," his wife said cheerfully, making the first comment to pass his automatic defenses. Carson began to gulp the last of his breakfast coffee.

Next semester he'd drop this eight o'clock class; nine was early enough for anybody.

As he bucked the heavy traffic on the Harbour Freeway, the professor began to visualize himself as one of the school's laboratory mice trapped in a maze with electric shocks lurking in every passage, and no clear path to food or rest. It was easy to make even so small and unreasoning a creature as a white mouse neurotic by such tricks. For a man the dilemma was worse. But there must be a way out of this mess; and with more brains than a mouse, he would surely find it.

It was quite unfair that he should be trapped at all. Gloria had thrown herself at him with no terms of surrender implied. And now, just when they were enjoying each other to the full, came her irrational reaction to his wife, and the demand that he marry Gloria. Get rid of Jeanette, or else; that's what the ultimatum amounted to. He'd explained very patiently that however much he preferred Gloria to Jeanette, it was a matter of dollars and cents—sense, to put it even more bluntly. As long as he stayed married, Carson could share in his wife's large income; control it, in fact. It was easy enough for Gloria to talk of living with him on his salary of $7500 a year, but here her fundamental lack of maturity finally appeared. One existed on $7500, but really to live, at least $20,000 was needed. And Jeanette would enjoy, as long as she lived herself, a $35,000 annual income from her grandfather's trust. At her death, since there were no children, the money went to various charitable organizations. Carson had no claim on it at all. There was the rub. If he only could inherit that income . . . but that was definitely out. Naturally they had a decent amount saved, but even $35,000 doesn't go too far with expensive trips, frequent entertaining and, above all, taxes. What was in the bank wouldn't last him more than two years. After that he'd be a starving professor again. Not for him—he'd had enough of that before marriage.

No, he couldn't divorce $35,000 a year. He wouldn't get a dime of settlement with a girl like Gloria for the lawyers to point out. Especially since Jeanette herself was as pure as any Victorian female. Of the two women, he would infinitely prefer to eliminate his wife—brown-haired, mousy, placid and unbearably dull—but that meant giving up the $35,000. Not even Gloria was worth such a sacrifice. No, it looked as if he'd have to silence the pretty one, the lovely, fascinating girl who had brought so much delight . . . it was a ticklish situation, even for an opportunist who had deliberately extirpated his ethical roots.

For a week, while he stalled off Gloria with more— and less believable—promises, Carson tried to find an out. But the girl was adamant; there was no doubt she'd blow the whistle on him soon. Even though she loved him, Gloria made it clear she would rather destroy him utterly than share him with Jeanette.

"Then you'll lose her money for good anyway, so why not tell her the truth, and get a divorce?"

"Fine," he said ironically. "Then what? You talk about my income from teaching. Hasn't it occurred to you that I'll probably lose my job here because of the scandal? A professor seducing one of his pupils!"

"But I seduced you, darling."

"We both know that, but the regents won't buy it for a second. In their little cosmos, for a teenager to be the aggressor against a man of fifty would be like admitting the DAR was a Communist Front organization. No, I'd be type-cast as the villain. Not that it matters, except financially."

"There are plenty of other jobs. They've been after you at Midwestern for years."

She was right about that, he knew. There was a shortage of good psych men at present. Especially Ph.D.s from top schools. The scandal wouldn't mean a thing in Illinois, particularly since he would have married Gloria by then. It wasn't such a terrible prospect. For hours at a time he was tempted to abandon the money and settle for Gloria. But that meant no more flights to Paris and Tokyo. Worse, it meant a lousy pension of perhaps five thousand dollars at the age of sixty-five.

There was another aspect of the matter. Gloria had given too much too soon. While she was still exciting and desirable, it wasn't like a carrot under his nose anymore. Even a few nibbles restore perspective to a man of his age and basically cold temperament. No, Gloria had to go.

Such reasoning led inevitably to the idea of murder.

Just because Carson became infatuated against his better judgment didn't mean he was a fool. On the contrary, he had an excellent analytical mind. In addition to psychology, he taught basic criminology, although from the sociological point of view rather than the technical. So he appreciated the difficulty of getting away with murder. At the same time, he knew what every police official knows and seldom admits publicly: that many people *do* get away with murder. A large percentage of the "accidents" that happen daily are murders. Usually there is no suspicion aroused at all; sometimes there is plenty of suspicion but no proof. So the murderer goes free.

Actually Carson might never have had his brilliant idea except for a TV program; oddly enough, a Western, a type he seldom watched. The gimmick here was quite new to him, and seemed very promising. A young woman, whose husband had been goaded into a hopeless shootout with an expert gunslinger, determined to avenge the killing. While the bully was locked up pursuant to the usual farcical trial, she managed to charm a deputy into leaving her alone in the jail long enough to tamper with the killer's own guns. All she did was triple the loads in each shell, by adding powder from a handful of extra bullets. It was easy to pull out the soft lead slugs, fill the brass cartridge cases, which had extra capacity, and replace the bullets. When the killer was released, as expected, on a self-defense plea, he proceeded to pick another fight, outdrawing the victim with no difficulty. But this time the gun exploded, removing most of his right hand and large portions of his face. The occurrence was taken as an accident—a defective .44— that couldn't have happened to a more deserving fellow. Nobody in town dreamed of the widow's part in the affair.

It seemed to Carson a provocative lead. Instead of shooting Gloria, a proceeding full of risks, he would himself appear to be the victim of a disturbed girl. It should be possible to prepare a cartridge potent enough to outdo the one in the teleplay. One that could kill with metal fragments from the shattered gun. It was just a matter of persuading Gloria to aim at him and pull the trigger—with plenty of witnesses around, of course.

Then it came to him. The timing was perfect. Every semester he invited the senior psychology class to his home. There, on the huge patio overlooking the Pacific, they ate barbecued hamburgers, drank beer and shot the breeze in typical senior fashion. Lately he'd been toying with the idea of trying one of those well-known experiments involving powers of observation. You arranged to have something bizarre and exciting happen all of a sudden. Then, when the brief event was over, each student was asked to describe exactly what had happened. Very few ever seemed to agree. In this case the experiment would be an ideal backdrop for murder.

But first there was homework, lots of it, and not much time. He'd have to get a gun and see about increasing the load. A TV program is hardly a guide to ballistics.

As a Ph.D., he was well trained in research. This would be a narrow field in any case; not guns in general, but just one phase of them. It didn't take Carson long to find out (a) that a cheap pistol, preferably of foreign manufacture, was easier to blow up than a new, heavier type revolver; (b) that a high-velocity cartridge was better suited to the job than a low-powered one, such as the Army .45 automatic pistol bullet; and (c) that cheap automatics tend to jam, so that a revolver is more reliable.

There were plenty of ads for war-surplus guns, he soon discovered. He settled for a .38-caliber revolver, price $7.60. The gun had been made by a Middle East manufacturer during World War II, and was undoubtedly far more dangerous to the shooter than his target.

He was tempted to play with it by snapping the trigger a few times, but had read that such tricks might easily break the firing pin. Time was too short to risk damaging the gun. Instead he decided to make one real test in the field. For this he would use one of the ancient military cartridges that had been supplied gratis. All he wanted to do was make sure the thing really fired; it would be a mistake to use a high-powered bullet in the test, and have the pistol disintegrate.

He was afraid to hold the revolver in his hand, so after driving to a secluded spot outside of town, he fastened it to a sapling, filled all the chambers and fired the gun by means of a thirty-foot fishing line. He was pleased to find that the thing worked.

At first he hoped to use the old military cartridges to prepare the deadly one, but found that metal-jacketed slugs were hard to pull free without leaving too many scratches. So he discarded them entirely and bought fifty modern, high-velocity thirty-eights. Just as they were, these bullets could probably blow up such a gun, he reflected, but took no chances. Using plastic-tipped forceps, he removed the lead slug from one brass case, and with powder from three others filled the chamber to the very top, compacting the grains tightly with the eraser end of a pencil. Luckily there was a lot of space available in the cartridge. He estimated that the amount of powder was almost quadruple the normal load. A bullet like this one should make the old revolver into a grenade, he thought, wincing a little at the vision of Gloria's lovely face after the explosion. What a pity she wouldn't be sensible and go on just as they had for almost a year now. It was her own fault. To a murderer the victim is always guilty, otherwise deliberate killing might be impossible.

The other bullets were to be normal. Too powerful for the gun, of course, but that would be ascribed to his simple ignorance of firearms; and, in fact, he still knew very little about guns in general. Just how to make a special, deadly bullet—the specific item needed just now. When all the ordinary cartridges were in place, he rotated the cylinder a few times to make sure it turned freely, then lined up the last opening, gingerly inserting the trick bullet. The beauty of the plan was that after the tragedy any investigation would show only that this cartridge had contained the same kind of power as the others. No way to show there had been more of it by far. After all, the total amount involved was only a fraction of an ounce. It wasn't his fault that the hysterical girl had grabbed a gun unsafe to fire. He'd never dreamed the bullets were unsuited to the gun; he'd just bought it a few days earlier, and might have had to use it himself against a burglar. It was her bad luck to have been the first to fire the damned, cheap, foreign piece of junk. His intention had been only to have some protection in the house; quite a few homes had been broken into lately. Sure, it was a cheap gun, but who would believe they could openly advertise and sell one that might actually blow up when fired?

There was another advantage to this scheme. Gloria might very well survive; there was no certainty that the accident would be fatal. But she was sure to be badly disfigured. He knew her psychology perfectly. She hid from him whenever there was a little blemish on her dusky skin. With a scarred face she'd leave town and never come back. If she couldn't have him herself—and she couldn't face him with her beauty gone—Gloria would never break up his marriage. There simply was no way he could lose.

There remained the problem of getting Gloria to shoot. That was a cinch. She would naturally be at the senior class gathering. While the others were drinking their beer and solving the puzzle of Cuba, she would slip out, return with the gun and fire one shot at him from about twenty feet. No, better make it thirty; the fragments might have a long reach.

At their next meeting he briefed her carefully.

"Gloria," he said first, preparing the ground, "you win. I've thought it through, and you're right. I'm going to ask Jeanette for a divorce. She can have the money; all I want is you."

After that it was quite an afternoon. He was supposed to be at the UCLA library looking up material for a paper, but Gloria, happy and triumphant, was something you didn't find in print . . .

Then he told her about the gathering, and the part she was to play.

"It's an old psychological trick," he explained. "You'll come in, make some ridiculous accusation and pretend to shoot me dead. I'll collapse; you run out; then I'll come back to life and question the kids. It'll be a ball; you'll never hear so many different accounts of anything in your life. By the way, can you shoot a revolver?"

"Like Annie Oakley. My brother taught me. He's won medals at the big meets. Not that I've had much chance lately. I didn't dare bring my Hammerli—that's a target gun—so it's strictly archery at school." She made a grimace.

"Well, this is just a cheap pistol, but it's only loaded with blanks. No, not really blanks. I've removed the powder from the cartridges, just in case some eagle-eye misses the lead noses too soon and spoils the joke. Not that it's much of a chance; people never notice anything. But not a word to anybody; you'd be surprised how information gets around. If the kids are tipped off, they'll watch like hawks; then I'll be the only patsy."

"Who could I tell?" she said with a pout. "The girls in my dorm? I doubt if they'd even be interested. My folks don't live in town, as you very well know."

"I know," he said fervently, reaching for her.

"Thank God they don't, or we'd have to be twice as careful. And your brother a sharpshooter yet!"

"We'll be married," she sang, her eyes electric blue. "My brother will think you're great, especially when you beat him at tennis. Not many men your age can do that. And Mom will go for you; she always said I should marry a doctor or a professor—you're both." She kissed him. "What are my lines for the charade?"

He told her, and she gurgled with delight.

"How utterly silly. They'll know it's a spoof the minute they hear me."

"Like hell. Afterward they'll quote you as reciting everything from the Gettysburg Address to extracts from the Kinsey Report. That's why I used the mid-Victorian rhetoric."

"Say," she said, frowning, "what you told me about the gun just registered. You took out the powder. What about the primers?"

"What are those?" he asked, concealing a twinge of anxiety.

"They explode the powder, silly. Without them, and no powder, no bang bang, either. All you removed was powder, right?"

"That's right."

"Well, you'll get a pop—that's good enough, I suppose. But you may end up with a lead slug partway down the barrel; a primer can do that."

"It doesn't matter, he said patiently. "It's just a cheap gun I'll never use again."

"Kind of wasteful," she chided him, "but it's your problem."

"And now, my poppet," he smiled, "we'd better get dressed. I should at least go into the library for a minute."

"When are you going to tell your wife?"

"The semester ends three days after the gathering.

A LITTLE KNOWLEDGE

That will be a good time. Then we can get out of town the minute my grades are in at the college."

"I'm so glad you've finally seen the light. We'll be happy. What good is money without love?"

"Very little," he said, smiling tenderly. To himself he added: *But a whole lot more than love without money, my pet.*

At the gathering of his senior class, Professor Carson was unusually urbane and witty. Beer flowed freely, and everybody was gay except Gloria, who, according to instructions, managed to look rather wild-eyed and distraught. The other girls eyed her curiously, but said nothing. After all, she had always been rather far out.

When things were going most smoothly, Gloria unobtrusively left the room, got the revolver from a drawer in the living room, and returned, posing dramatically at the edge of the patio about thirty feet from the guests.

"William!" she cried in ringing, pear-shaped tones; and all the students gaped at her. "My William. You have never given me so much as a glance, but I love you more than life itself. I know you can never be mine—that you are loyal to your wife, poor wretch. But if I can't have you, neither shall she. I'm going to kill you, and then myself. Farewell harsh world!" Then, true to her training, she lined up the barrel with Carson's heart, and as the girls shrieked, fired once.

The professor, who a moment earlier had been congratulating himself on the stilted weirdness of the lines—not that anybody would remember them in detail; otherwise he might not have dared that "poor wretch" bit from Pepys—felt a stunning blow against his chest, and realized with horror that he had been shot for real. Something was terribly wrong; the gun hadn't exploded.

Gloria, too, saw that the charade had gone sour. She ran to him, her face chalky.

"Why didn't it explode?" Carson gasped, in no state to care about self-incrimination. "The revolver was fixed to explode; I worked on one of the bullets . . . why . . . you should be hurt, not me . . . not me . . ." He fell back. His wife, running in with a tray of snacks, saw him lying there and screamed. She was still whimpering when the doctor came, and the police; but Carson was dead.

"It was lucky for you, young lady," Captain Herrera said sternly, "that these kids all agreed pretty well on the professor's last words. If they weren't such good witnesses, I might never have thought to have ballistics check the gun. After all, your story was pretty unbelievable. You understand now that he planned to murder you?"

"But what saved me?" she asked dully. "You did find that overloaded cartridge. Why wasn't it the one that fired?"

"Carson goofed on a much lower level after doing the trick stuff very well. He read up on reloading, I suppose, but didn't understand the first thing about a revolver. I just don't see how a man would go to all this trouble and not experiment with the gun. It never occurred to him, apparently, that by putting the doctored bullet in the chamber right under the hammer, he was guaranteeing it wouldn't be fired. A little knowledge is a dangerous thing. You or I would know that when you pull the trigger of a revolver, the cylinder turns automatically to the next chamber. In this case that meant you fired a normal bullet instead of the trick one. And you can thank your lucky stars, girlie, that this cheap gun had a pretty decent barrel after all. Me, I wouldn't fire another high-speed thirty-eight in the thing for a double pension!"

ROPE ENOUGH
by Dick Ellis

So you were miles away from the Biltmore Hotel tonight, or rather last night, at eleven o'clock," Lieutenant Blanchard said thoughtfully.

" 'At's right," Tommy Horne told him. "Miles and miles. Practically on the opposite side of the city from there."

Blanchard punched out a cigarette in the ashtray atop his paper-littered desk. He glanced at the third man in the office, Detective Dominic Corsi.

"He has got an alibi, of sorts," Corsi murmured.

Horne swiveled to give Corsi a once-over. "Whatta you mean, 'of sorts'? You and that other cop checked it out, didn't you? And Shirley told you I was with her all evening?"

Corsi made no reply. He fiddled with a note pad and pencil he was holding on the arm of his big chair.

"You expect us to take the word of a broad like Shirley Yumas?" Lt. Blanchard barked. "She'd lie her head off for a dime, and give you a nickle change."

Tommy Horne shrugged heavily padded shoulders.

"Says you." His voice grew heated, "Send your stooges out to my place at one o'clock in the morning, drag me outta bed for no reason they'll give me—"

"We gave you the reason," Dom Corsi put in, "though you were so anxious to tell us about your alibi, you hardly gave me and my partner time to open our mouths."

Lt. Blanchard said, quietly, "By the way, Dom, speaking of your partner, why don't you see if Peterson is back yet from the—other matter he was going to check out."

Corsi rose with a nod of his sleek, dark head. He left the lieutenant's office for the big robbery-homicide squad room outside and pulled the door shut after himself.

"Now," Blanchard said, returning his attention to Tommy Horne, "let's go over it again. Right around eleven o'clock, about three hours ago, a couple of boys wearing masks and .45s held up the night clerk at the hotel, wanted him to open the safe where guests had left valuables—"

"Yeah, yeah," Horne said with a yawn that didn't quite match his intent gray eyes. "So you told me, already."

"Then the hotel detective came into the lobby," Blanchard went on, ignoring the interruption. "There was a fast exchange of gunfire. The two hoods took off out the door—but one of them didn't make it to the car waiting at the curb. The hotel dick put a slug through his fat head, and he dropped on the sidewalk. His buddy got in the car and sped away. Turns out the dead punk is Frenchy Raymond, an old, old friend and former cellmate of yours, Tommy. You wonder I had you hauled in?"

Horne shoved a hand through the thick mass of his

reddish hair. "You've got nothing at all to tie me to that hotel rumble. I was at Shirley's pad from seven till past midnight. Ask her, why don't you."

Blanchard leaned back in his chair and eyed the dingy ceiling of his office. The truth was that he didn't have anything, except a moral certainty, concerning Horne's part in the robbery—but he did have something else up his sleeve.

Dom Corsi came back into the office. He seemed a little excited. "Yeah, Peterson's back," he told the lieutenant. "It's official."

"Ah," Blanchard sighed with satisfaction. "What did it?"

"A knife. Six times in the back and chest." Corsi sat down and picked up his note pad and pencil.

Horne looked from one man to the other. "What's all this jazz? You cops framing some other poor guy?"

"I'm giving you a last chance to cop out," Blanchard told him. "You were with Frenchy—"

"Nuts," Horne said, "I'm leaving," and he started to get up.

"Sit back down there," Blanchard snapped. "Dom, if he makes another move, belt him one."

Horne hurriedly resumed his seat. "Cops," he muttered.

"I just want to be absolutely sure I understand you," Blanchard said. "You claim you were with this dame, Shirley Yumas, between the hours of seven and midnight—"

"After midnight. I'd just got home and into the sack, when this guy here and another one started pounding on my door along toward one o'clock," Horne said heatedly.

"Okay. You'll swear to that?" asked the lieutenant.

"Whatta I been telling you, the last half-hour?"

As he spoke, Horne was watching Dom Corsi, who

was busily scribbling notes on his note pad. Horne frowned. He crossed and recrossed his legs, obviously restless.

Blanchard directed a glance at Corsi. "Dom, you and Peterson got to the apartment where Tommy lives at one. What exactly happened?"

"He was in bed." Corsi said. "Gave us the story about the Yumas woman. We waited while he dressed, then started downtown with him. He kept yakking about his alibi, so we stopped at an all-night drugstore, and Peterson went inside and called the Yumas woman's place—"

"And she told you I was telling it straight," Horne snapped. "But you still had to drag me down here."

"Actually, Peterson didn't speak with Shirley Yumas," said Corsi smoothly. "He talked to the landlady there."

Horne gaped. "I don't get it. What—"

"Peterson couldn't reach Shirley Yumas, so he called the landlady, asked her to go check," Corsi said. Then he took his time lighting a cigarette.

"Yeah, yeah," Horne rasped. "Shirley's a heavy sleeper. But you did get to her, didn't you?"

Corsi didn't answer. He looked at Blanchard.

"Oh, yes," the lieutenant said. "Officers—reached her. Uh huh. The only thing that really puzzles us, Tommy, is why you not only admit you were at her place—you insist on it."

"What's that mean?" Horne asked. He squirmed around on his chair, ran a finger around the collar of his wilted shirt. "Course I was with her. She'll tell you."

Corsi finished writing a note. He said reflectively, "I'll tell you, Lieutenant. Probably someone saw Horne at the woman's place—and Horne knows it, so he's trying to pull a swiftie on us. By insisting he was there, he makes it look like he couldn't have—you know. He probably doesn't realize just how close the medical examiner can get, nowadays, to the exact time a person has died . . ."

Paying no attention to Horne, the lieutenant said, "Yes, that makes sense, Dom. He thinks he can bluff us into believing—"

"Wait a minute!" Horne exploded. He surged to his feet. Sweat was pouring down his narrow face. "Whatta you guys talking about here?"

"Sit down," Blanchard said. "I've got news for you, boy. You were just one of a dozen punks we talked to, about the hotel job. But you had an alibi, and it turned out to be Shirley Yumas. Detective Peterson checked it out."

Horne sat down slowly. He looked bewildered. He mopped his face on the sleeve of his flashy sport jacket. "So? I don't understand what—"

"You poor dumb slob," Corsi said. "Where do you think Peterson's been the last half-hour?"

It took Horne a moment to get it. Then he almost fainted.

"You mean—you mean this rumble about somebody getting knifed?" he croaked. "Was that—Shirley?"

Silence. Blanchard and Dom Corsi watched him squirm.

"Now, wait. Wait a minute," Horne started.

"I've been waiting, a long time," Blanchard broke in, "to nail you with a rap that'll put you away—permanently. Now I've got it. We've been feeding you rope ever since you walked in here, and now you've hung yourself."

Horne began to curse. Then he blurted, "That stupid broad. Everybody knew sooner or later some guy she's horsed around with would knock her off.

And of course it had to happen this one night out of all nights."

"Tough," Blanchard said. "Why'd you—"

"Ah, I wasn't near her place last night," Horne said. "Honest. I set it up with her on the phone, see. Yeah, yeah. It was me and poor old Frenchy pulled the hotel heist. A fat lot of good it done us. That hotel fuzz busted in before we could make the score."

Blanchard gave a loud snort. "So now you claim you were one of the bandits? Come on, boy. Sure, a fall for attempted robbery beats a murder rap, but I don't think we'll play it that way. Not when you've sworn you were at Shirley Yumas's apartment until midnight—"

"I tell you, I ain't seen her in weeks. I just talked to her on the phone. Told her how much it was worth for the alibi—don't you guys understand?"

Corsi slapped his note pad against his knee. "That isn't the way it reads here."

"Listen," Horne gulped, "I'll show you where I ditched the gun I used. That ought to prove I was there at the hotel. Slugs from my gun are splattered around the lobby there. You can match them up. I ain't taking no murder rap."

"Your proof had better be good, boy, if you want to squirm out of the Yumas deal," Blanchard said meaningfully. "Or else you're stuck with it."

Horne got up. "Listen, I'll take you right now, to where I hid the gun. Come on, gimme a break, for once."

Still the lieutenant hesitated. Finally, reluctantly, he nodded his head. "Dom, you and Peterson take this bum where he wants to go. But if he tries to pull anything—like suddenly forgetting where the gun is —you know what to do."

Moments later, when Corsi and the sweating Horne

had left the office, Blanchard suddenly burst into laughter. It wasn't often that a killer helped send himself to the chair. Of course, Horne didn't know—yet—that the hotel detective had died of wounds received in the gun battle.

He'd find out, soon enough.

Humming to himself, Blanchard got up, stalked to the corridor door and jerked it open. A uniformed cop was on post outside.

"All right," the lieutenant snapped. "Go bring that Yumas dame along from the detention cell. I want to have a chat with her. If there's anything I can't stand, it's a no-talent liar."

THE TOKEN
by Hal Ellson

Every morning at ten—no sooner, no later—Jones left the house and went off to work. On the corner he dropped a dime for the newspaper into the same dirty cigar box filled with coins at the same unpainted stand; the same bank on the opposite corner, flag hanging listless from its pole, sky above it remote. Jones barely glanced at the sky, folded the paper under his arm and went down the subway steps.

He gave up a token for the turnstile; a convenience, easier to handle than money. Rot! The tiny brass piece was another gimmick designed to deceive the public, to make the fare seem reasonable for a dirty, foul-aired trip through the underground. The token replaced the money and alleviated the pain.

The cost of living—well, you make it and they take it. We're all on the treadmill, Jones thought, shaking his head, and a rush of cold air entered the station, then the rumble of a train; the sound smothered his thoughts, rebellion died with brakes, wheels grinding to full stop.

He stepped into the train. The doors closed behind him. *Holy to mercy, a seat.* He spread his paper and the train rumbled off. Once again he was one of the eight million of the city; he couldn't escape. Long, long ago he'd given up the thought. It was all routine now—breakfast, subway, paper, office and back again to the underground with his fellow token-carriers—routine which they no longer recognized as such, miserable slaves who didn't realize they were slaves. *Really the best kind; docile, stupid and hardworking.*

"For what?" said a voice, and Jones raised his eyes, the question so clear he was certain someone had spoken, but the others, screened behind their papers, were diligently weighing yesterday's dubious history. Wheels turning furiously, the train roared on. Jones went back to his paper; the disturbing voice was silent. He spread-eagled the globe in print, the calamities of man: disturbances in Algeria, border incident in India, street riots in Iraq, a whole world seething in chaos.

He lifted his eyes, the rumbling of the train steady, drive unfaltering, passengers grimly quiet behind their papers. Nothing would stop them from reaching their destinations, no violence would intrude. *Bloody tokens,* thought Jones, *all of us.* It was the explicit sum of his revolt. He resumed reading, and the train raced on to his station.

He changed at Times Square, up the steps, into the shuttle, a brief ride across town; now the southbound local, two stations; always the same route, measured and timed to the second. He could do it with his eyes closed, without making a mistake.

Now, go through the turnstile and entry door to the basement level of the skyscraper whose marble corridors and stairs led to the street. *A robot,* he thought. *Yes, always the same corridor, same stairway, same revolving exit door and no disturbing deviation likely.* He entered the corridor. Light splintered off the marble, brass gleamed, a clock pointed the hour. No need to meet its numbered face; twenty of eleven exact.

Fifteen minutes to the office; he'd never failed to arrive, no matter how he felt. He was proud of that. "Don't you ever get sick?" his secretary once asked. Silly question. He'd smiled then; he didn't now. A distinct clicking sounded in the corridor. *Rhythm of castanets?* Not here. Up ahead he spied the girl walking on impossibly high heels.

Perfect rhythm, good legs, nice body—his eyes feasted on her. Ahead, gleaming brass doors opened to another corridor. The girl went through. He knew exactly which door she'd take. It was always the same one, then a left turn and up those stairs to vanish till tomorrow.

For a month now he'd watched her, wondering where she went, what she did. He could guess, but guessing was futile and agonizing. The agony started the moment she vanished on the stairs. Now the moment was due.

She pushed open the door, entered the next corridor and turned left. The door closed. He moved faster. The glass panel gave back a reflection, but it was a stranger he saw and he was shocked. The shock passed. He pushed open the door to see the girl mounting the stairway. He stopped, saw her vanish. The moment had come, the terrible agony; this time he couldn't take it and he started after the girl.

Her heels tapped sharply on the marble steps. Hearing them, he moved faster, mounted the steps. By this time she was out of the building. He pushed through the revolving door, stepped out onto the crowded avenue. A light rain was falling, traffic swishing on slicked asphalt. The girl was already at the corner, almost running.

Late for work, he thought, following. The lights changed. He had to wait, keeping the girl in sight. Down a side street she went, away from the dreary shadows of office buildings. Two blocks farther on she turned, entered a renovated brownstone.

Jones was completely unprepared for this. Stunned, he returned to the avenue. It was exactly eleven o'clock when he entered his office—not late, but a deviation from rigid routine; a matter of five minutes, which caused his secretary to look up in surprise. "I thought you were sick and not coming in," she remarked.

He shook his head, but he was sick—sick, foolish and stupid for following the girl, for veering off course. Only five minutes in twenty years—it shouldn't have bothered him, but did.

The rest of the day was a mess. Nothing went right. He kept thinking of the girl, the renovated brownstone. A place of rendezvous?

At five he left the office, a sick man merely because he'd turned left in the corridor that morning. Deadly sick—he was sure of that.

At six he arrived home. Dinner awaited him; he had no appetite, but he knew Cora too well by now. He ate. She noticed nothing wrong.

Leaving the table, he went directly to the living room, to the evening paper, and absolute confusion; impossible to read. It didn't matter. He had to put on a show for Cora.

Soon the dishes stopped clattering in the kitchen, the light went out. Cora entered the living room, went directly to the television set, put it on and retired to her special chair. Come hell, high water and revolution, she would neither budge from there nor brook a word of conversation in the next three hours.

Nine years like that; an insufferable sentence. Jones peered over his paper at her, saw her as a wax figure in an electric chair. *A living corpse,* he thought, and suddenly the urge took him to shout, stamp, smash the furniture!

A wild fantasy! He did nothing of the sort. The clock ticked off the minutes, images unreeled on the screen. This now was the sum of his life: dancers and cowboys, detectives and violent lady wrestlers, a legacy for all the robots like himself swarming upon the continent.

The set went off at ten. Cora mounted the stairs. The evening, which had never begun, was at an end. "Don't forget to put out the light," Cora warned from the top of the stairs.

Voice of emancipated woman, voice of waspish authority, voice of the compleat tyrant, it floated down, echoed in the living room. As if he ever forgot. As if she'd ever let him.

Like a beggar he followed her up the stairs and switched off the light. The bedroom was dark when he entered it, Cora in bed. Quickly he followed her in. Her feet were like chunks of ice; no surprise there. Later, he dreamed of the girl, the brownstone house, and groaned in his sleep.

Cora complained in the morning. Guilty, he had nothing to say, drank his juice, ate his eggs and glanced at his watch: time to leave.

He left the house, bought his paper, entered the subway and was carried off to Manhattan with his fellows. They didn't notice him, he took no notice of them, the morning paper enough. Looking up again, he found himself at his station. He made the usual changes, a routine no different from any other morning till he reached the marble corridor.

Now came the challenge, the test of his metal, for there was the girl again, walking ahead, high heels spiking frozen marble. He had no intention of following her. Yesterday's foolishness was done with.

The girl passed through the glass door, turned left, and now the glass, swinging backward, mirrored the stranger's image again. Gasping, he almost halted, then pushed open the door and was caught, taken by the same vacuous impulse which had moved him yesterday. He turned left, heard the girl mounting the stairs.

He followed, and the pattern was the same as the previous day. She hurried, as if late for work, taking the same route to the renovated brownstone, where once more she vanished.

He stood outside, gaped at the door for some minutes, then a curtain moved and he saw her at a window. She smiled down at him and nodded.

A nod, a smile and the whole city quaked, clocks stopped and a man became a man once more, and so he was late for work that morning; and late the following morning. Friday he begged the girl for a lock of her auburn hair. She refused him; he persisted. He wanted it as a token, and this amused her. She finally gave it to him.

The weekend disrupted the alliance. He went to church with Cora and took her to her mother's, a horrible visit saved by his thoughts of the redhead. He'd made up his mind about her. Monday morning he saw her again. When it was time for him to leave, he told her he was staying and the reason why.

The girl was stunned. She stared at him, then smiled and said, "Stop kidding. Now run along. I expect to be very busy today."

"Busy?"

He didn't understand. She explained quite bluntly. A few minutes later he left the house and was late for work again. This time the boss came in to see him and noticed his deathly pallor.

"Better take a few days off," he suggested. "You're coming down with something."

"No, I'm all right. Just a bit of indigestion," Jones explained. "I'll not be late again."

The next morning he was as good as his word. At ten he dropped his token in the slot and stepped on the subway platform. The morning paper was tucked beneath his arm. He opened it on the train—the usual stuff: war, threats of war, flood, famine and the inevitable daily murder, the human condition in a nutshell.

At midtown he left the train, shuttled east, localed south, and walked the marble corridor toward the door that led to the stairs. The glass panel gave back his own reflection this time. He wasn't surprised. The door swung to when he pushed it.

He turned right, mounted the stairs to the street, paused at the corner to drop his paper in a waste can and stopped his hand. There it was again, a photo of a girl, a redhead strangled in an East Side brownstone. Pretty creature, too young to die. He dropped the paper in the waste can, then a lock of auburn hair, thinking, *It's not real. It's only a token,* and walked on to his office.

SHERIFF PEAVY'S FULL MOON CAPER
by Richard Hardwick

Every time I hear an operator's voice on the telephone, particularly around the time of month when the moon is full, I wonder if she looks half as good as she sounds. This one sounded about 38-24-36, blue-eyed and blonde. She said she was the marine operator and had a call for the Guale County sheriff.

"Sheriff Peavy's out of the office right now, miss. I'm his chief deputy. Anything I can do?"

"Just a moment, sir. I'll ask my party."

I started to tell her she could just call me Pete, but the line began to hum and I knew she was gone. A few seconds later she came back.

"Sir, the captain of the yacht *Matilda J.* will speak with you. Go ahead, *Matilda J.*"

Somebody cleared his throat with a raucous sound. "Hello? Hello? Cap'n Paget here!"

"Deputy Pete Miller here," I rejoined.

"Yes! Trouble aboard ship, sir. Be tying up at a place called Swensen's Marina in about an hour. Like to have you meet us there. Know the place? Over."

"Right, Cap'n, I know the place. What sort of trouble have you got?"

"Tell you when we meet you. In an hour, sir! *Matilda J.* out!"

The line clicked and the captain was gone. "Hello?" I said. I jiggled the phone a few times. "Hello?"

"Your party has gone off the air, sir," the operator said.

"Thanks." I dropped the phone on its cradle and leaned back in the chair. Now what was that all about, I wondered. Outside I heard the swish of tires, then the slam of a car door. Sheriff Dan Peavy came in and spun his hat toward the rack, missing it by three feet.

"Anything happening, Pete?"

I told him about the call from the yacht. "The guy wouldn't tell me what was wrong."

Dan glanced up at the clock on the wall. It was one-thirty. "Well, let's go over to the Bon Air and get some lunch, then we'll run out to Swensen's."

Fifty minutes later I was trying to digest a blue-plate special while gunning the county's car out the beach road. At the Intracostal Waterway bridge I swung right on the turnoff to Swensen's. A faint whorl of white dust trailed us into the parking area. Dan and I went inside and found Swensen at his desk.

"Has a boat named the *Matilda J.* come in yet?" I asked him.

Swen shook his head. He turned and looked out the window. "That might be her coming now," he said, pointing. I went around the desk and took a look. About two hundred yards south of the marina, a big white yacht was headed our way.

The three of us went out onto the dock and waited. The boat drew closer.

"She's a big 'un," said Dan.

Swen nodded. "Good hundred feet."

A little fellow in a white jacket stood at the bow, a line in his hands. High up in the wheelhouse I could see a khaki-clad helmsman lining the boat up just right. Another man stood toward the stern, also with dock lines in his hands. On the board, awning-shaded fantail, a group of people sat in white wicker chairs. One of them lifted a glass and took a deep swallow.

The boat was warped alongside the dock, and when she was secure, the man in the wheelhouse leaned out. "Ahoy down there! You people from the sheriff's office?"

Dan nodded to him and the man came scuttling down the stairs to the main deck. The two who had handled the lines placed a gangway to the dock and Dan and I went aboard.

"Cap'n Paget," the man from the wheelhouse informed us. He was not more than five foot six, but he was the same in every dimension. His face had the appearance of having been soaked in brine for a number of weeks, and his eyes were squeezed into a sort of Teddy Roosevelt squint so that hardly any of the eyeball was visible.

Dan and I introduced ourselves. "Now, Captain Paget, what's the trouble here?" the sheriff asked.

"Blasted trouble! All there ever is aboard this blasted ship! Never did like a trouble ship! Not even in the old days aboard the—"

"Just what kind of trouble did you call us about?" Dan interrupted.

"What? Oh. Man's dead. Owner. Been shot." Paget gave a violent twist to his head. "Never liked trouble—"

"Where's the body?" I asked him.

"Body . . . yes. Stateroom. This way." Paget spun around and went through a door into the cabin. We followed down a flight of stairs, and along a deep pile carpeted corridor past a number of closed doors. At the end of the corridor, we came to another door, except this one had obviously been battered down. It hung askew on one hinge.

"Had to break in," the captain said. "Can't figure it out. How the devil—Well, you see for yourself!"

We went into the stateroom. I never saw anyplace quite like it. On the wall opposite the door was a mural, one of the impressionistic things, but somehow you got the message right away without understanding it at all. I could feel myself blushing a little. To the left there was a small bar and a settee with a large, low table before it. A hi-fi outfit stood beyond that. There were three portholes, two of them closed and dogged, and the one in the middle standing open. To our right, against the opposite wall, there was a dresser and a tremendous bed, which was neatly made up. A pair of silk pajamas was laid out on the side of the bed. The three portholes there were all closed.

Just to the left of the smashed door there was another door. It was open.

"In there," the captain nodded. "In the bath. Blasted if I can figure it out!"

We stepped into the bathroom. There were the usual fixtures, but they were nothing at all like the ones in the bathroom at the end of the hall in the boarding house where I hang my hat on off-hours. The handles were gold. The water didn't come out of faucets, but out of the mouths of grinning gold gargoyles. There was a sunken bathtub, and propped in the far corner sat a man dressed in an ornate Oriental bathrobe. There was a neat little round hole in the center of his forehead. The hole wouldn't be so neat in the back of the head, judging from the spattered tile wall behind him.

"Well," said Captain Paget. "There he is. Mr. Elliot Hocking Jenner!"

I turned and stared at the captain, "Elliot Hocking—" I looked around at the body. "The—the *playboy*?"

The captain sighed with a sound like a punctured tire. "Been called that, among other things."

Dan Peavy's eyebrows lifted.

"You know this fella, Pete?"

"Are you kiddin'? I don't *know* him, but I know *of* him! My gosh, Dan, everybody's heard of this guy!"

Dan Peavy moved slowly to the side of the tub and squatted down. He took his bulbous nose between thumb and forefinger and gave it a gentle tug. "Not everybody, Pete. I ain't ever heard of him before."

Where do you start telling someone about a man like Elliot Hocking Jenner, married a dozen or more times, apparently still going full steam ahead in his fifties or sixties, thrower of fabulous parties, leading man in a score of scandals. I briefed Dan as well as I could from my memory of newspaper items I had read over the years, and was pleased to see Capt. Paget give a curt nod of approval when I was done.

"More, of course," the captain added, "but that, sir, is the gist of it."

"Quite a fella," Dan mused. "Don't reckon it's too surprisin' for him to end up this way."

"Just it!" rasped Paget. "What the hell happened? Door locked from inside and Mr. Jenner's key still hanging there on that chain around his neck! Cabin boy and myself looked around, no gun we could see!" He waved a stubby finger into the main cabin.

"Blasted midget couldn't get through the open porthole in yonder."

"Looks like he was shot right here, and judgin' from them powder burns, from close up," said Dan. "Besides, that porthole is four or five feet outta line with the body. Woulda had to shoot a curve to hit him here." He turned to Paget. "Say that's the only key?"

The captain nodded. "And it takes the key to lock the door from the inside or the outside."

"How'd you happen to break in here and find him?"

Paget sighed and one eye pried open an eighth of an inch. "Never kept anything like regular hours, you understand. Usually count on him putting in an appearance by noon, though. Anchored last night in Kenston Sound, just off that old lighthouse on Bird Island. Mr. Jenner and his guests went ashore. Big party on the beach till the wee hours. Party every blasted night with this crowd! Anyhow, at 1300 hours today I decided to come down, see what orders he had. Stay at the blasted anchorage or sail!"

"1300 hours . . . ?" Dan started.

"That's one in the afternoon," I informed him.

"No answer to my knocking," the captain went on. "Made inquiries among the guests, nobody had seen him since they turned in around 0200 or 0300—"

"Two or three in the morning," I said in an aside to Dan.

Knocked some more. Nothing. Then lowered the cabin boy over the side for a peek in the portholes. He reported he couldn't see Mr. Jenner, and that the bed didn't look like it had been slept in." Paget shrugged.

"Only choice as captain was to force entry. Found this. Called you."

"How many people aboard the boat?" said Dan.

"Eight, if you count Mr. Jenner."

"That's includin' the crew?"

He gave a nod. "Mr. Jenner, four guests, myself, Sewell, who's engineer and deck hand, and Sammy, cabin boy and cook. Eight, all told." He looked at the dead man. "Seven now!"

"Pete," Dan said, "call the office and tell Jerry to get out here, and tell him to bring Doc Stebbins with him. Me and the captain'll meet you back there where we saw them other folks."

I went to Swensen's office, made the call and hurried back to the yacht. Dan and the captain had just gotten to the fantail. Two men and two women were sitting. A short, thin, rat-faced fellow in a white jacket was standing to one side, and next to him a stoop-shouldered man wearing a T-shirt and dungarees, and whose eyes and general appearance gave the impression of his being in the throes of a monumental hangover.

"Sheriff Peavy," Captain Paget was saying, "this is Miss Liles." He indicated a small, dark-haired woman who seemed to be in her late twenties or low thirties. She nodded and Paget continued. "Mr. Blakely." The man sitting next to her was fifty or fifty-five, I guessed, and his expression was about what you would expect to see if he had just had a straight shot of lemon juice. "And Miss Mellon—"

The blonde cut Paget off, with word and action. She gave Dan a smile that would have melted an iron ingot. I had the odd feeling that she was *jiggling*, even though she was sitting perfectly still. I also thought I recognized her from someplace. "You can just call me Honey, Sheriff. Maybe you've heard of me? Honey du Mellon? If you never saw my dance act, maybe you've seen my picture? I've had my picture in lots of magazines, the arty kind, you know?"

I swallowed hard. *Now* I recognized her. I'd seen quite a few pictures of her the last time I thumbed through the adults-only shelf of the magazine rack at the bus station. And I'd seen practically all of her, from pretty nearly all angles. None of those curves under that outfit were store-brought, I could vouch for that.

"Isn't this just terrible?" she went on, a frown passing cloudlike over her face. "You know, Poopsy and me were going to get married as soon as we got to Miami. He got his divorce just last week." She sniffled and pulled a lacey handkerchief from, well, from where properly built women carry handkerchieves, and daubed her eyes. "It's—it's like being a widow before the honeymoon, don't you know?"

The man sitting to her right concurred. "Terrible! Elliot was the best friend I ever had!"

"The best damned soft touch you ever had!" Blakely snapped.

"I resent that, Irving! I definitely *resent* that!"

"Mr. Kruger," the captain said by way of introducing the second man.

"Eric Kruger," the man added, nodding to Dan. Then he turned his gaze on the blonde. "For heaven's sake, Honey, will you please stop referring to Elliot as—as *Poop*sy? It sounds undignified, especially now that he's dead!"

"Wherever he is," she sniffed, casting a baleful glance up at the blue, blue sky, "he will always be Poopsy to me!" And she began to cry, great mascara-laden tears coursing down her creamy cheeks.

Eric Kruger sighed and shook his head. I took him to be somewhere in the mid-forties. He was immaculately dressed in white yachting shoes, duck trousers, and a lightweight turtlenecked shirt. There was no paunch about him. In fact, he seemed in excellent physical condition, almost like a man who works out regularly with weights.

The captain indicated the remaining two who stood toward the side. "Sewell," he said, nodding toward the dungaree-clad sailor. "And Sammy, the cabin boy and cook."

"Steward and cook, sir," the rat-faced little fellow grinned.

"Blasted cabin boy!" muttered Paget.

"Can Sammy get us fresh drinks now, Sheriff?" asked Blakely.

"I guess that can wait for a while. Now, as all of you know, Mr. Jenner's dead. Can anybody shed any light on what might have happened?"

There was a moment of complete silence, after which Honey du Mellon smeared her mascara further with her handkerchief and said, "We had a kind of beach party last night, you know? Poopsy made the boat stop last night because I wasn't feeling too good. I kept thinking I was going to get real sick and I told him I just *had* to get on land!"

"That's right," the captain put in grimly. "Steaming along smoothly when Mr. Jenner ordered me to pull in to shore. Said there was a good anchorage in Kenston Sound just off Bird Island. Would have been nearly to Miami by now!"

"Anyhow," the blonde went on, "we had this party on the beach last night and it was real late, around two or three, when we got back to the boat. I went to my room and went right to sleep. I didn't hear anything."

"Afraid I had a few too many Scotches last night myself, Sheriff," Eric Kruger said. "Didn't hear a peep till Sammy came knocking at my door around eleven with a little pick-me-up. Great concoction Sammy has! Tastes as though there might be a touch of tobasco in it."

"Worcestershire, sir," Sammy grinned proudly. "Also a pinch of—"

"If we can just get on with the investigation?" Dan said. "How about it? Anybody hear anything at all? Anything that might have sounded like a shot?"

I looked around at the blank faces. Miss Liles shook her head. Blakely mumbled something negative.

Sammy cleared his throat. "I—I'm not sure, sir," he said hesitantly. "I was in my bunk up forward. It was about four o'clock—" He glanced guiltily at Capt. Paget "—I mean, it was around 0400 hours. The night was quiet. No wind. I thought I heard something outside in the water. I sat up and looked out the porthole. It was just about full moon last night—"

"The moon was absolutely the most marvelous *thing* last night!" Honey du Mellon burst in. "I wish we hadn't stayed on that old island so long so I could have had my—"

"Please, Miss Mellon?" Dan said wearily.

Sammy nodded and went on. "The moon was already pretty far down and I couldn't see too well. It was a kind of splashing out there, like somebody swimming." He stopped and rubbed the back of his hand across his nose. I suddenly realized that everybody was leaning forward, waiting to hear him tell what he saw. "I could see the old lighthouse standing among the trees on shore."

"Is that all?" I asked him.

"I—I can't be real sure. I think I saw something in the water about halfway to the beach. 'Course, I could be wrong. The moon was down, like I said." He shrugged. "I just couldn't be sure."

I turned away. In the direction of the causeway, I

saw a plume of white dust. Suddenly the sound of a siren split the air. That had to be Deputy Jerry Sealey, arriving on the scene.

The siren dropped off into a mournful note as the car slid to a stop. The lean, lanky form of Deputy Sealey bounded out one door and came down the dock on the run. Trailing at a much lesser pace, black bag in hand, was the bald and somewhat roundish figure of Doc Stebbins, Guale County's coroner and medical examiner.

Dan and I went forward and met Jerry at the gangplank. He stopped short, gazed around at the yacht and finally settled a serious gaze on the sheriff. "Murder case, eh? How's it look?"

"You go back there and keep an eye on those folks," Dan told him. "Let the cabin boy get 'em whatever they want, but nobody goes ashore."

"How—" Jerry started.

But Doc Stebbins had reached the boat and Dan and Doc and myself went inside the boat and down to the stateroom. Doc examined the body.

"About how long you think he's been dead?" Dan asked.

"Autopsy'll tell closer, but I'd say, judging from what's available, that he ain't been dead more than, oh, twelve hours."

"He was seen alive about twelve hours ago," I told him.

"The bullet went through his head," Doc went on. "Looks like he was sitting right there where he is when he was shot. Bullet hit the wall tile right back of his head."

"That's what I figured," Dan said, scratching his chin. "Then it's simple," I put in. "Somebody else has a key to this cabin."

SHERIFF PEAVY'S FULL MOON CAPER 231

Doc snorted. "Seems to me if anybody did have one, you'd have one heck of a time getting 'em to admit it!" He faced around to Dan Peavy. "You ready for me to get the body outta here?"

"Soon as we mark it and get pictures."

A check with the seven survivors on board the *Matilda J.* substantiated Doc Stebbins's observation. If anyone had a key, there was no admission of it.

"I knew Elliot," Blakely said. "He was a peculiar chap in a lot of ways. I think he was always afraid of something like this, don't ask me why. He wouldn't have given his own mother a key to his stateroom."

Dan's head nodded slowly. " 'Course, there's a chance somebody coulda had one made without Jenner knowin' about it."

And if so, I said to myself, that key is somewhere out there on the bottom of Kenston Sound.

"Wouldn't say that was likely," Captain Paget rasped. "Mr. Jenner always had that chain around his neck, awake or asleep. When he was asleep he was locked in."

"He sure didn't shoot himself through the head, and then throw the gun away!" Jerry exclaimed.

Dan motioned to me and Jerry and the three of us stepped to one side of the deck. "I'm going in town to check the newspaper files on Jenner," Dan said. "I want you boys to go over this boat from one end to the other. Ain't much chance of findin' anything, but do it anyhow. Paget can show you around." He turned back to the group. "All you folks stay out here while my deputies search the boat. Nobody goes ashore till I give the word."

"See here, Sheriff!" Blakely puffed up. "I've done nothing—"

"You do what the sheriff tells you, Irving Blakely!"

Honey du Mellon snapped, eyes flashing. "If he's going to find out who killed poor Poopsy, then we have to mind him!"

Blakely sighed and picked up his glass.

It was after seven o'clock when we finished the search. A half-dozen assorted keys were found in the various staterooms, but none of them came close to fitting the lock on Jenner's door. Also, we turned up three pistols in the wheelhouse, which Capt. Paget assured us were there on Jenner's orders and, to the best of his knowledge, had never been fired.

Dan Peavy got back from town just as we were finishing our search on the little deck on top of the wheelhouse. The only thing above us at that point was the topmast.

I told him about the pistols. "None of 'em seems to have been fired anytime recently, and even if one of 'em was, it would have waked up everybody on the boat."

"Stands to reason," Jerry added, "that the killer would toss all the evidence overboard. Now how would you find a key and a pistol between here and the other side of Kenston Sound?"

The face of Sammy, the cabin boy, appeared over the edge of the canvas siding of the small top deck. "Cap'n Paget? They're getting hungry. Is it okay if I start fixing dinner?"

The captain gave Dan Peavy a questioning look, and Dan nodded. The cabin boy disappeared and we started to follow him.

"Just remembered something!" Paget said suddenly. "Don't know why I didn't think of it before. The money. And the jewelry!"

"What money and jewelry?"

"Safe. Wall safe in Mr. Jenner's stateroom."

"Let's go," said Dan.

The reason Jerry and I hadn't discovered any wall safe during our search, we soon found out, was because the thing was behind a small sliding panel located in the mural on the rear wall.

Paget pushed a finger against something that looked like a big red eye in the mural, and a little door sprung open. Dan Peavy peered into the hole in the wall. I looked over his shoulder. A round steel door was just inside the opening, and Dan took out his handkerchief and gingerly took hold of the handle. The steel door swung out smoothly.

"He always leave it unlocked?" Dan said.

"Unlocked?" the captain poked his head between us. "Blasted thing *is* unlocked!"

"What'd he usually keep in there?" I asked him.

"Fifty to a hundred thousand, plus odd bits of jewelry. Mr. Jenner depended on jewelry quite a bit in his . . . ah, romancing."

Jerry's eyes bugged out. "Fifty to a hundred thousand . . . *dollars?*"

"Whatever was in there," Dan Peavy said, "ain't in there now."

"I can't understand it!" Blakely said. He picked up another sandwich from the tray Sammy had brought into the main deck saloon and took a big bite. "How could somebody get into Elliot's stateroom without a key, shoot him without anybody hearing the shot, get into a safe that only Elliot knew the combination to, and get away with fifty to a hundred thousand dollars, plus whatever jewelry was in there, without leaving a trace?"

"Is it all right if I play some records?" Honey du Mellon said. "Everything is so awfully de*press*ing, you know?"

"Just don't play that abominable stuff you've been playing ever since we sailed!" Penny Liles said.

"Poopsy liked it!" She whirled around and looked straight at me. "Do you like to twist, Mr. Miller . . . Pete? I'll bet you're a good twister!"

She flipped a switch on the hi fi and it began blaring. Out of the corner of my eye, I saw Dan Peavy wince noticeably. "Not quite so loud, Miss Mellon," he said. He motioned to me. "Pete, we'll question these folks one at a time." He glanced toward Honey du Mellon, who was gyrating wildly. "Up in the wheelhouse. Maybe we can't hear it up there."

Capt. Paget took his seat at the helm and waited for the sheriff to begin.

"How long have you been runnin' this boat for Jenner?" Dan said.

"Little more than five years. Looks like a soft berth from the outside, but believe me, it isn't! Never know what to expect! *Never!*"

"I see. Now this trip, what can you tell us about it? And why were these particular people on the boat?"

Paget put one hand on the wheel. "Usual trip this time of year to Florida. Mr. Jenner has . . . *had* interests down there. Always took along guests. One big party all the way. Every year. Same thing, maybe a few different faces, but same blasted thing!"

"Who are the different faces this trip?" I asked him.

"Different faces . . . let me see . . ." Paget closed his eyes even tighter. Even the slits vanished. "Kruger's been along for the last three or four years. Blakely was with us last year. Miss Liles—she was the ninth . . . or was it the tenth . . . Mrs. Jenner, you know."

I stared at him in surprise.

"I found that out this afternoon," Dan said.

"Well," Paget went on, "she was on the trip the year they were married. Mr. Jenner did that quite often, took his fiancée on the Florida trip, sort of feel her out." He cleared his throat. "Didn't mean it exactly the way it sounded."

"I think we see what you mean," Dan smiled.

"Miss Mellon, this is her first time aboard. Extremely, er, vivacious young woman! Extremely!"

"And what about the crew?" I asked him.

"Well, Sewell was here when I took the berth. The man's a drunk! Been up to me I'd have put him on the beach the day I came on board! But Mr. Jenner seemed to like him . . ." The captain shrugged. "As for that blasted cabin boy, Sammy, Mr. Jenner hired him three years ago."

Dan nodded, then quietly he said, "Cap'n, you got any idea who mighta wanted Jenner dead?"

Paget pulled himself up and stared straight at Dan Peavy, "Sir, I am the master of this ship! However, the private lives of those aboard are not my business—"

"The private lives are your responsibility, Cap'n. A man's been killed."

Paget's jaw knotted and after a moment he slumped back down on the helmsman seat. "Blasted jinx ship!" he muttered. "Blasted fools! Idiots! A scheming lot, Sheriff Peavy! Every blasted one of them!"

"Let's start with Eric Kruger; what about him?"

"Leech! Plain and simple! Mr. Jenner took a fancy to him and he's been riding free ever since."

"If Jenner had showed any signs of getting rid of him," I said, "do you think that might have caused Kruger to kill him?"

"Could be the case," said Paget. "Especially since the safe was looted."

"But we're not sure there *was* anything in that safe, are we, Cap'n?" Dan mused.

The captain gave him a puzzled look, then shook his head. "No sir. We are not."

Another fifteen minutes brought out Paget's opinion that it could also have been any of the other three.

Eric Kruger shook a cigarette out of the pack. "I—I suppose I should have told you this right away, Sheriff. Yesterday . . ." He paused, clicked his lighter and touched the flame to the cigarette. "Yesterday, Elliot told me that he was afraid someone aboard might try something."

"Might try what?" Dan Peavy frowned.

Kruger took a deep drag on the cigarette. "That's . . . that's all he said. Just that he was afraid someone might try something."

"You got any idea who he mighta been talking about?" I asked.

Kruger shook his head. "I never . . . well, you couldn't question Elliot, if you see what I mean. He was . . ."

"The goose that laid the golden eggs?" I put in.

"Now, look here, Miller! I don't have to take that kind of talk!"

"That'll be enough, Pete," Dan said. "Mr. Kruger, how long had you been a friend of Jenner's?"

"Eight or ten years, I'd guess."

"What line of work are you in?" I asked him.

"Work?" he said, a look of distaste clouding his features. "I don't *work*, Miller. My position is that of Elliot's personal secretary, but I definitely do not physically *work!*"

Penny Liles made herself comfortable. "Yes, I was married to Elliot. If you want to go by number, I was number ten. We were married, let me see, twenty-eight months ago. I lived with Elliot for ten weeks."

"What happened?" Dan inquired.

"I was framed into a cozy little scene, and Elliot divorced me."

"Framed?"

She nodded. "I never was quite sure whether it was Elliot or that crony of his, Eric Kruger.

"I've been in and out of court ever since for some kind of settlement. I've given Elliot a run for his money!"

Dan frowned and ran a hand through his hair. "I ain't sure I understand this, Miss Liles. If you was one of Jenner's wives, and he's just got divorced again, and this Miss Mellon was set to marry him, and you was suin' him, then how come . . . What I mean is . . ."

"Why am I on this boat?" she said. She smiled and shook her head. "I'm not at all sure myself. Elliot phoned me about a week ago. He said he was about to sail for Florida and wanted me to come along. He said he had been feeling a little guilty about our divorce, and hinted that he might be persuaded to come up with a little financial settlement to get it off his conscience. The only trouble with that was that it didn't sound in character with Elliot Jenner. At least, not the way I knew him."

Dan's frown was deeper than before. After a moment he said, "Did he say anything more about that?"

She hesitated. "I—Elliot told me yesterday he had changed his mind. He . . . told me I'd never see a dime of his."

Dan scratched one ear. "I reckon that'll be all for now, Miss Liles."

When she was gone, I closed the wheelhouse door

and turned to Dan. "People have been killed for a lot less than that. Maybe she decided if she couldn't have his money, he couldn't either."

"I'm wondering how come she even *told* us that," Dan mused.

"It could be that somebody else knew she knew it," I said.

Dan cocked his head. "Could be, at that. Well, let's see what this Blakely has got to say."

From the look on his face, and the way his hand shook when he lit his cigarette, Irving Blakely was obviously a worried man.

"Sheriff . . ." he said. He ground the cigarette out after his first puff. "Sheriff, I can tell you right now I didn't have a thing to do with this, but I know it's not going to look good for me! It's some kind of attempt to frame me!" He shook out another cigarette, then narrowed his gaze at Dan Peavy. "Don't let 'em pull the wool over your eyes, *they're* not so damned innocent as they try to appear! You take that leech, Eric Kruger, lives off Elliot's money and all the time he's playing footsie with—" He cut off abruptly and attempted to light the cigarette.

"Playin' footsie with who, Blakely?" Dan said.

"I can't prove it, so why make the accusation?"

"We'll just keep in mind that you can't prove it. Now who was it?"

"Currently, that blonde who calls herself Honey du Mellon. She's not the first, however. I wouldn't be surprised if Elliott hadn't planned to toss the both of them out on their ears!"

"What's this about somebody trying to frame you?" I asked him.

Blakely seemed to be having trouble breathing. He took a couple of deep breaths and said, "I was handling some of Elliott's affairs, a real-estate development deal in Florida. Elliot isn't, rather, *wasn't*, much for doing his own work. Recently he called me to New York, and when I got there, he said it had come to his attention I was . . . was falsifying certain records. He said he wanted to hear my side of it."

"What was your side?" Dan said.

Blakely shrugged. "I *had* made a . . . a small loan from the company. I took a setback in the stock market and was having some difficulty repaying the money. But it was *good!* Good as gold!"

"Did Jenner know about this loan when you borrowed the money?"

Blakely stared out the window at the darkness, his face drained of all expression. After a few seconds he shook his head.

"Why were you on the boat?" Dan said.

"He told me to come along, that maybe we could work it out on the way south."

"And did you?"

"No. No, but I think we *could* have if . . . if *this* hadn't happened."

As soon as the door closed behind Blakely, I turned toward Dan Peavy. "And maybe he and Jenner couldn't work it out and Blakely killed him," I said.

"There's something screwy here," Dan said, pulling on the end of his nose. "Instead of makin' alibis, all these people are darn near incriminatin' themselves."

"Maybe they have to admit what they have. If it got to us from some other source, it'd make 'em look worse."

Dan closed his eyes and slowly rubbed his forehead. After a while he looked up at me. "Go get that Mellon girl and let's see what she's got to say about all this."

I brightened. "Yeah, let's see!"

Since I last saw her, Honey du Mellon had changed clothes. She wore a form-fitting black dress which, if it had been a cut a quarter-inch lower, could have gotten her into legal trouble sitting there before two officers sworn to uphold the law.

"This was part of my trousseau," she said, smoothing the dress over her lap. "But it's the only black thing I've got, and I thought I ought to wear it now . . . now that Poopsy's gone, you know?"

Dan cleared his throat officiously. "You and Poopsy . . . you and *Jenner* were goin' to get married when you got to Miami, is that right?"

She hung her head and nodded demurely, silently acquiescing.

"Did anything happen since you all left New York?"

"I don't understand what you mean, Sheriff."

"Anything between you and Jenner," I said. "Anything that might have upset the wedding plans?"

She bit her bottom lip. Her eyes went from Dan to me and back to Dan again, as if trying to say it wasn't fair to ask that. "Well," she began, "I guess somebody else would tell you if I didn't. Yes, we *did* have an argument."

"What was it about?"

"Poopsy was so *jea*lous! Why, if another man even looked at me he was fit to be tied! He—well, Eric was kissing me goodnight, just a friendly kiss, you know? Poopsy saw us and got *fu*rious! I tried to explain, but he simply wouldn't listen."

"He say anything about callin' off the weddin'?" said Dan.

She shook her head. "No."

"Who else heard what happened? I mean, beside you and Kruger?" I asked her.

"That funny little man that helps run the boat, the one that stays about half-drunk all the time, you know?"

"Sewell?"

"Uh huh. I think that's his name. He came out of the cabin while Poopsy was calling me and Eric all sorts of horrible names. But Poopsy didn't really mean any of it. I could have made everything all right if . . . if *this* hadn't happened . . ."

Watching the tears gather in those big eyes, I knew she could have made everything all right. She could make mass murder all right, given the proper conditions, such as an all-male jury.

"Miss Mellon," Dan said slowly. "Is that your real name?"

The tears vanished and the eyes widened. "Why, *sure* it is! 'Course, it wasn't always. My folks called me Rose. Rose Hobson." She smiled seductively. "Now who'd ever come to see anybody named Rose Hobson dance?"

What's in a name, I thought. I let my eyes drift freely from the tousled blonde hair, down over the well-filled black mourning dress, to the neatly turned ankles. A rose is a rose is a Honey.

Dan Peavy cut quite a figure standing there at the mahogany wheel of the yacht, wrinkled khaki pants and shirt, unruly white hair, a face like a relief map of the Bad Lands. He stared at the moon that had just come up over the trees on the other side of the river, then he turned around toward me.

"This is a tough one, Pete."

I didn't want to say it, but I had to. "It could have been her, Dan. Her and Kruger together. If Jenner caught 'em necking he could have given the ax to both of 'em."

But what would they gain by that?"

"Well, that safe was unlocked and empty. Could have taken what was in it. Fifty to a hundred grand certainly ain't peanuts, plus the jewelry Paget said he carried in there."

"Maybe. Well, let's talk to Sewell and that cabin boy, Sammy, and then call it a night."

Neither of them added anything new. Sewell said he had witnessed the argument between Jenner, Kruger and Honey. Sammy told us he was positive nobody else ever had a key to Jenner's stateroom.

After we finished with them, Jerry came in and gave us the benefit of his views.

"You're too *trustin'*, Dan!" Jerry said, waving his hands. "Here's how I figure this thing! They're all in on it, every last one of 'em! They busted that door down before Jenner was shot, they blasted him there in the tub, throwed the gun overboard, then called you! It's plain as the nose on your face!"

Dan Peavy checked his nose absently. The cabin door opened and Doc Stebbins stepped in. "I drove out here to let you know there's a damn poor joke on *some*body," he said.

"Whatdya mean?"

"This fella, Jenner, he didn't have more'n three or four months to live. Had cancer."

We all stared at Doc. "Are you plumb *sure?*" Dan said.

Doc took the question for what it was, a simple statement of surprise, and just nodded his head.

"Dan," I said. "Maybe Jenner knew this. Maybe he wanted out and didn't have the nerve to do it himself. And maybe he had one of his friends do it for him—"

"Or *all* of 'em," Jerry put in.

"It don't make sense to me," Dan Peavy said. "For one thing, if it was like that, why did they pull in and anchor? How come they wouldn't have killed Jenner while they were at sea, and just dumped his body overboard. That way there wouldn't be a murder investigation goin' on."

Jerry scratched his head. "Yeah. I see what you mean. So somebody musta murdered him, not knowin' the guy was gonna die soon anyhow."

Dan lifted his arm and glanced at his watch. "I wanta check out a few more things in town. Pete, you and Jerry stay here on the boat tonight. Don't let anybody on or off till you hear from me."

There was a knock at the door. I opened it and Captain Paget came in.

"Cap'n," Dan said. "First thing in the morning I'd like you to run this boat back to where you was anchored in Kenston Sound. You think you can put her right where she was?"

"Yes sir," said Paget.

Dan nodded. "And I'd like the name of Jenner's doctor."

Dan instructed the passengers aboard the *Matilda J.* that they were to stay in their cabins for the rest of the night, except for the necessities. Each cabin had a button that would buzz the steward's quarters, and Sammy was told to check with me or Jerry before answering a call.

It was a fine night, warm and clear with hardly any breeze. Across the river in the woods I could hear crickets chirping and every now and then a fish would splash in the river. About eleven o'clock Jerry and I flipped a coin to see who would sleep first. I won.

"I'll be on that sofa back there on the fantail if you need me," I told him.

"Okay," Jerry agreed. "I'll take it till about three o'clock and you take it the rest of the night."

* * *

Dan Peavy arrived at the boat at seven o'clock and half an hour later the big yacht was headed south on the Intracoastal Waterway in the direction of Kenston Sound and Bird Island.

Dan took a cup of the black coffee Sammy brought to the saloon. "Me and Doc Stebbins got hold of Jenner's doctor in New York. He said he told Jenner about his condition a couple of months ago. Said Jenner took it as well as a man can, but he seemed to think that Jenner didn't tell anybody else about it. He gave us the name o' Jenner's lawyers, too, and we called one o' them. Seems Jenner drew up a new will about a month ago. The fella was home when we talked to him, but when we told him who was on the boat he said every one of 'em was in the will. Fifty thousand apiece for Miss Mellon, Kruger, Blakely, and Miss Liles. And there was pensions for Paget, Sewell, and that cabin boy, Sammy."

"It just don't make sense!" Jerry exploded. He stopped short and snapped his fingers. "I got it! One of 'em heard about the will, then had a fallin' out with Jenner and killed him before he could change the will! You told me he caught Miss Mellon and Kruger doin' a little neckin'. Well, maybe they done it!"

I looked at Dan Peavy. "You didn't tell us what we're going out to Kenston Sound this morning for."

"The scene o' the crime, Pete. A detective always takes a look at the scene o' the crime."

It was about eight-thirty when we reached the abandoned lighthouse at Bird Island on the south shore of Kenston Sound. Dan told Captain Paget to anchor as close as he could to the spot they were anchored the night Jenner was killed. Paget jockeyed the big boat around, lining up on the lighthouse, and when he was satisfied, down went the anchor.

"Now," said Dan, "I want everybody to go ashore and let's take this thing right from the time you all got here."

"Miss Mellon's still in bed, Sheriff," Sammy quickly voluntered.

"At this time o' day?"

The cabin boy smiled ruefully. "To her eight-thirty in the morning is just late at night."

The captain and the engineer-deckhand, Bud Sewell, lowered the motor launch, and, after Honey du Mellon had been wakened and had her coffee, everybody piled into the small boat and we went ashore.

Paget nosed the boat onto the beach and Sewell tossed the anchor out.

"We stopped right here, Sheriff," Blakely said. "The five of us came ashore here, took a swim in the surf a little further down, and Sammy charcoaled steaks for us right here on the beach in front of the lighthouse. There was a good bit of drinking after we ate, and then we went back to the boat and to bed."

The others agreed with his version.

"Did any of you go up there to the lighthouse, or anywhere except right here on the beach?" Dan inquired.

"Not to my knowledge," said Blakely.

"No," Kruger said. "I think Sammy ran the girls back to the yacht a couple of times, but that's the only time anybody left the beach."

Sammy corroborated the statement.

Dan Peavy walked to the high-water mark and began to pace slowly along, looking down intently at the sand. He had gone only about fifty feet when he stopped. Then he turned to his right and started walking up toward the dunes. "Come here, Pete," he called.

I joined him, the others following along.

"Somebody walked up this way. These footprints are fresh. Wasn't any wind yesterday or last night to cover 'em up."

We followed the single set of footprints through the dunes to a spot about a dozen yards from the base of the lighthouse. There they stopped, and the sandy soil looked as if it had been dug and then brushed over with something in an effort to hide the place.

"Well, now," said Dan. He looked around at the little knot of people standing behind him. "I wonder what happened here?"

"I'd say somebody dug a hole and buried something!" Jerry remarked. He got down on his knees and began pulling away the loosely packed sand. About twelve inches down he unearthed a plastic raincoat which was wrapped around something. He lifted it up and placed it on the ground beside the hole.

"What the devil is *that?*" exclaimed Captain Paget.

"My guess is it's the stuff outta Jenner's safe," said Dan Peavy. He squatted down and carefully untied the string holding it together. The raincoat fell open, revealing several packs of currency and about a dozen pieces of jewelry, including strings of pearls, diamond brooches, rings and a bracelet.

"Elliot must have put it here himself," Kruger said. "That's the only way it could have happened!"

"Ought to be some good fingerprints on that plastic," Dan drawled. "We can tell soon enough when we get it back to town." He looked around at the blank faces. " 'Course, we'll have to take you folks' prints—"

Kruger was standing about three feet to my right, and before I knew what happened he had taken a jump in my direction and whipped my revolver out of the holster. "He *told* me to do it! Elliot told me to bring that stuff up here last night and hide it! He said he was afraid of someone on board the yacht, and didn't want them to have the stuff!"

"If that's what happened, then how come you waited till now to tell us?" Dan said.

"I—when we found out he was dead, I figured nobody knew about this. I didn't see the harm of leaving it, and coming back here later and digging it up. I *swear* that's the truth!"

"Your only chance o' havin' anybody believe you is to give me that gun," Dan Peavy said.

Kruger's eyes narrowed. A muscle twitched in his lean jaw. "What chance would I have now? Nobody'd believe me!"

"You plan to shoot all of us? If you run off in the little boat where are you gonna go? Where can you hide?"

"I know what this looks like—" Kruger started. Dan had done what he set out to do—he had gotten Kruger's attention. I chopped my hand down hard on his wrist and the revolver dropped down into the sand.

I leaned quickly to scoop up the gun, but Kruger's left fist met me halfway, catching me squarely on the side of the head. I tried to keep from falling, but not a muscle in my body would heed the brain waves, and down I went, right on top of the revolver.

"Get him!" I heard somebody yell.

"Catch the blasted murderer!" Paget rasped.

"He killed Poopsy!" wailed Honey du Mellon.

I felt the muscles slowly reviving, and I pushed myself up just in time to see Jerry and the cabin boy, in a joint flying tackle, bring the fleeing Kruger to earth.

Vehemently protesting his innocence, Eric Kruger was taken back to the ship and locked in his cabin.

"We did it again!" Jerry announced proudly, "I figured it was him from the minute I laid eyes on him! Shifty-lookin'!"

"You were looking for what you found on shore?" I asked Dan.

"The cabin boy told us he thought he saw something or somebody swimmin' toward shore. The safe was open and you didn't find anything when you searched the boat. It was the only thing that made sense."

Jerry rocked back on his heels. "I figure it this way. Kruger was down in the cabin arguing with Jenner. The safe was open. He seen his chance, shot Jenner, grabbed the loot, swam ashore, buried it, and come back and went to bed."

"How'd he shoot him without anybody hearin' the shot?" I asked.

"How'd he . . ." Jerry rocked forward. "Gun had a silencer! Simple!"

"If that's the case, Dan," I said. "then the thing must have been premeditated! Kruger would have had to bring a gun with a silencer along with him from the start of the trip!"

Dan ran one hand through his thick white hair. "I don't believe this Kruger done it. I think he was tellin' the truth back there at the lighthouse."

"Didn't *do* it!" Jerry squealed. "It's the open and shuttest case we ever had! Whadya mean he didn't *do* it?"

"Pete," Dan said quietly, ignoring the outburst. "Get on that radio phone and call a couple of them boys in that skindivin' club back in town. Tell 'em to get out here as soon as they can. We'll put 'em on the county payroll for the rest o' the day."

"Dan," Jerry pleaded. "Dan, just you let me in there with Kruger by myself for fifteen minutes! I'll get a confession outta him!"

Dan Peavy chuckled. "We put you in there with Kruger by yourself, Jerry, and we'd sure enough have a murder case against him!"

It was almost noon when we saw the outboard cutting across the sound in our direction. It eased alongside the yacht. In it were two boys and half a dozen scuba cylinders. They came aboard and asked Dan what was up.

"It ain't up," he said wryly. "It's down. At least I think it is. I want you boys to search the bottom all around this boat. I'm lookin' for a pistol, and maybe something else."

"Water's clear today," one of them said. "Ought to be pretty good visibility. Sand bottom, too. If it's down there, Sheriff Peavy, we'll get it for you."

As we watched the bubbles coming up a few minutes later, Jerry said, "Dan, the killer, even if it ain't Kruger, might not of tossed the gun overboard here. The thing could be anywhere between here and Swensen's dock, and a million of them frogmen couldn't find it!"

"If my figurin' is right, Jerry, then the gun's right here," Dan said, his eyes intent on the bubbles that moved in a search pattern across the water.

It was some time later when the two divers popped to the surface. One of them took hold of the ladder, removed the aqualung mouthpiece from between his teeth, and looked up at the group lining the yacht's rail. He shook his head. "Ain't no gun within a hundred yards in any direction of this boat, Sheriff. We could have found a pin down there. Wasn't nothing there."

Dan scratched his head for several seconds. "You boys *real* sure of that? I mean, you couldn't of missed it?"

"No sir, Sheriff Peavy," said the other boy. "We use a search pattern. It overlaps, and with the visibility good as it is, and a clean sand bottom, well, we just couldn'ta missed a pistol. 'Course, the tide could of covered it over, but that ain't likely."

Dan shook his head slowly, then suddenly he straightened up, a broad grin spreading over the weathered face. "The dang *tide!*"

"You think it's covered up?" I asked.

He look around at Captain Paget. "What time was it when you folks dropped anchor here the other day?"

"Made a notation in the log. It was exactly 2031 hours—"

"Speak English, man!"

"That's about half past eight at night, Dan," I said.

"You got a tide table, Pete?"

I nodded and pulled out my billfold. I always carried a tide table in case I could get in a little fishing. I handed it to Dan.

He ran his finger down the columns of figures. "Let's see, high tide was one aught-three night before last. Low tide was six twenty-nine. If you dropped your anchor here at eight-thirty, the tide musta been comin' in."

"Just like it's doing now," Jerry said.

"Right." Dan raised his eyes. He was smiling. "Now—" he consulted the tide table again "—if Jenner was killed before the next low tide at seven thirty-two, then the tide was goin' *out*."

It hit me. "And the boat was swung around the other way!"

Dan Peavy nodded. "And Jenner's cabin is right in the rear end o' the boat—"

"Plus the length of the anchor line—"

"—would put the thing a pretty good ways to the east o' where we been lookin'," Dan finished.

Less than an hour later the two divers stood on the fantail of the *Matilda J.* and handed Dan what they had found. There was a revolver, with a silencer on the end of the barrel. The gun was wrapped in a towel, with only the trigger and the end of the barrel showing, and the towel was tied tightly with twine. About twenty feet of light manila rope ran from the trigger guard to the other thing they had brought up, an iron sash weight.

"What in the devil is all *that?*" Irving Blakely said.

"It's the gun that killed Jenner," Dan Peavy said.

Honey du Mellon parted ruby lips. "But . . . how . . . ?"

Dan Peavy hefted the padded revolver. "Mr. Jenner shot himself."

Penny Liles shook her head. "I don't see *how!*"

"Let's all go down to Jenner's cabin," Dan drawled. "And, Jerry, let Kruger out."

Everybody, including the two scuba divers, trooped inside the yacht and down the corridor. Dan Peavy went to the porthole we had found open. He put the weight through and let it hang outside. Keeping the rope tight, he went into the bathroom and stepped into the tub. When he sat down in the spot where we had found Jenner, the line reached exactly. Dan held the gun in front of him, with the barrel aimed at his own forehead.

"I figure Jenner did this. Holding the gun just tight enough so's it wouldn't slip away from him, he pushed the trigger with his thumb, and when the bullet hit him, the gun dropped—"

He turned the thing loose. It went like a blue darter across the bathroom, hit the jamb of the door, changed direction, picked up speed across the carpet in the stateroom, leaped up the wall and vanished out the porthole with hardly a sound except for a little splash outside.

"Well, I'll be *damned* . . ." murmured Deputy Sealey.

Honey du Mellon began to sniffle. "Then . . . Poopsy shot himself so he wouldn't have to marry me? Is that it?"

"I don't think that was it," Dan assured her. "We found out Jenner only had a few months to live, and it's my guess that he was playing a right serious little game with a few people he thought had been out to take advantage of him. Oh, he was fair about it. You either paid, or you got paid."

"What's that mean?" said Penny Liles.

"You'll find out when his will's read," I told her enigmatically.

Kruger passed a hand slowly back and forth over his throat. "But . . . but it could have been the other way, couldn't it . . . ?"

Dan Peavy nodded. "Somebody could have had a murder charge tacked on 'em, with a pretty good chance of bein' found guilty." He turned to the two scuba divers. "You boys mind goin' down there again for that gun? We'll need it to wind up the case."

One of the boys grinned and shook his head admiringly. "This one's on us, Sheriff!"

There was little conversation as everyone traipsed out of the stateroom and headed topside. I followed along behind Honey du Mellon, watching that action that is universally admired by males from twelve to a hundred and twelve. The moon would be fine again that night, and maybe I'd be doing her a disservice if I didn't tell her about that little beach I knew where the moonlight is like no other place I ever saw. Of course, she couldn't find it by herself. I'd have to show her how to get there . . .

 **Bestsellers**

- [ ] CRY FOR THE STRANGERS by John Saul $2.50 (11869-7)
- [ ] WHISTLE by James Jones $2.75 (19262-5)
- [ ] A STRANGER IS WATCHING by Mary Higgins Clark $2.50 (18125-9)
- [ ] MORTAL FRIENDS by James Carroll $2.75 (15789-7)
- [ ] CLAUDE: THE ROUNDTREE WOMEN BOOK II by Margaret Lewerth $2.50 (11255-9)
- [ ] GREEN ICE by Gerald A. Browne $2.50 (13224-X)
- [ ] BEYOND THE POSEIDON ADVENTURE by Paul Gallico $2.50 (10497-1)
- [ ] COME FAITH, COME FIRE by Vanessa Royall $2.50 (12173-6)
- [ ] THE TAMING by Aleen Malcolm $2.50 (18510-6)
- [ ] AFTER THE WIND by Eileen Lottman $2.50 (18138-0)
- [ ] THE ROUNDTREE WOMEN: BOOK I by Margaret Lewerth $2.50 (17594-1)
- [ ] DREAMSNAKE by Vonda N. McIntyre $2.25 (11729-1)
- [ ] THE MEMORY OF EVA RYKER by Donald A. Stanwood $2.50 (15550-9)
- [ ] BLIZZARD by George Stone $2.25 (11080-7)
- [ ] THE BLACK MARBLE by Joseph Wambaugh $2.50 (10647-8)
- [ ] MY MOTHER/MY SELF by Nancy Friday $2.50 (15663-7)
- [ ] SEASON OF PASSION by Danielle Steel $2.50 (17703-0)
- [ ] THE DARK HORSEMAN by Marianne Harvey $2.50 (11758-5)
- [ ] BONFIRE by Charles Dennis $2.25 (10659-1)

At your local bookstore or use this handy coupon for ordering:

Dell DELL BOOKS
P.O. BOX 1000, PINEBROOK, N.J. 07058

Please send me the books I have checked above. I am enclosing $_____
(please add 35¢ per copy to cover postage and handling). Send check or money order—no cash or C.O.D.'s. Please allow up to 8 weeks for shipment.

Mr/Mrs/Miss_____

Address_____

City_____ State/Zip_____

☐ **The Black Marble**
Wambaugh's fifth bestseller and first love story—is "his best novel yet!" Five Months On The New York Times Bestseller List. $2.50 (10647-8)

☐ **The Choirboys**
"A noisy, wild, romping novel. Hell-raising, sex and booze. An unforgettable experience!" *Oakland Tribune*. Three million copies in print. $2.50 (11188-9)

☐ **The Blue Knight**
A hard-hitting, tough-talking realistic novel that provides a cop's eye view of police brutality. $2.50 (10607-9)

☐ **The Onion Field**
Wambaugh's frightening account of a cop-killing and its aftermath is especially horrifying because it's true! $2.50 (17350-7)

☐ **The New Centurions**
The big nationwide bestseller! "Do you like cops? Read *The New Centurions*. Do you hate cops? Read *The New Centurions*." *The New York Times*. $2.50 (16417-6)

Have You Read These Bestsellers by **JOSEPH WAMBAUGH**

At your local bookstore or use this handy coupon for ordering:

Dell | **DELL BOOKS**
P.O. BOX 1000, PINEBROOK, N.J. 07058

Please send me the books I have checked above. I am enclosing $_____
(please add 35¢ per copy to cover postage and handling). Send check or money order—no cash or C.O.D.'s. Please allow up to 8 weeks for shipment.

Mr/Mrs/Miss_____

Address_____

City_____ State/Zip_____

It's true... it's shattering... it's murder!

Blood and Money
Thomas Thompson

"The most gripping reading of the year!"
—*Los Angeles Times*

"A tale of guilt and gore, of passion and retribution classic in its tragic dimensions."
—*John Barkham Reviews*

"AN ABSOLUTE SPELLBINDER!"
—*Newsweek*

With exclusive new photos

The shattering true story of Joan Robinson Hill, society horsewoman of world rank, and her talented, ambitious plastic-surgeon husband. They are the larger-than-life Texans of myth —rich, attractive, reckless. Their story travels at breakneck speed from the moneyed elegance of one of America's most exclusive suburbs to the brutal and deadly underbelly of society. The most incredible thing about BLOOD AND MONEY is, it's true!

A Dell Book $2.50

At your local bookstore or use this handy coupon for ordering:

Dell | **DELL BOOKS** | Blood and Money $2.50 (10679-6)
| **P.O. BOX 1000, PINEBROOK, N.J. 07058** |

Please send me the above title. I am enclosing $_____
(please add 35¢ per copy to cover postage and handling). Send check or money order—no cash or C.O.D.'s. Please allow up to 8 weeks for shipment.

Mr/Mrs/Miss_____

Address_____

City_____ State/Zip_____